MW01222141

the
GEORGE
&HARVEY
series

- THE COMPLETE BOXSET -

THE SECRET
THE TRUTH
& THE FIGHT

Ashley John

Copyright © 2015 Ashley John

1st Edition: July 2014
2nd Edition and Print Edition: April 2015

All rights reserved. This book or any portion thereof may not be
reproduced or used in any manner whatsoever without the express
written permission of the author except for the use of brief
quotations in a book review.

All characters appearing in this work are fictitious. Any resemblance
to real persons, living or dead is purely coincidental.

For questions and comments about this book, please contact the
author at hi@ashleyjohn.co.uk.

ISBN: 1511796847
ISBN-13: 9781511796842

CONTENTS

Part One: The Secret - Page 1
Part Two: The Truth - Page 104
Part Three: The Fight - Page 207

GEORGE & HARVEY

- PART ONE -

THE SECRET

Ashley John

DEDICATION

This book is dedicated to my fiancé Reece for putting up with me through the process of writing this book and for acting as the best editor I could ask for (even if I don't always take your advice).

...and Jeremy, my cat

ABOUT THIS BOOK

George & Harvey: Part One
The Secret

Published: June 2014 (2nd Edition and print edition April 2015)
Words: 29,000

The Secret is the debut novella from Ashley John (**first published June 2014**), and the first part of **The George & Harvey Series**. This brand new edition has been completely refined and re-edited, with brand new content!

When 32-year-old married author, George Lewis, sees 19-year-old, Harvey Jasper, reading one of his books in the local bookstore, he can't help but be drawn to him. After giving Harvey his cellphone number, he soon receives a call from Harvey asking if he can intern under George. Reluctantly, George says yes, and agrees to let Harvey into his home for a whole month.

As they spend more and more time together, Harvey shares his heart-breaking story with George and his eyes are opened up to a whole new world, with whole new emotions. George soon discovers something he never thought he'd find in another man, but does he have the strength to tell his wife, or will he keep the secret?

ONE

"I'm off to check out the new releases," George whispered quietly to his wife as they wandered down the cookbook aisle.

He had formed a terrible habit of treating the bookstore like a library, which made him carry over the '*no talking*' policy.

It was George's Saturday routine to visit the local bookstore. He had been doing it since he was a child. There were many occasions where he wouldn't buy a single book, but there was just something about being around thousands of them that made him feel at ease. That was the born writer in him.

He'd spend most of his time devouring the back covers of the latest fiction books. He had no desire to read all of the books he would pick up, but as he scanned the few paragraphs that summed up the story, he'd be transported to another world for a few seconds.

It didn't matter to him that the world he imagined wasn't the same world that was in the book, because the thrill of his own imagination was enough for him.

When he married Paula, he dragged her into his routine, like a religious mother would drag her young children to church every Sunday. George didn't know how he managed to marry someone with so little imagination. Her reluctance to venture outside of the cookbook and travel sections told him this. Every week she'd buy a new cookbook to test at home, but he never had the heart to tell her she was a terrible cook.

The bookstore was George's playground, and he was happy to play in it alone. He loved walking down the aisles and spotting his own books out of the corner of his eye. He'd pretend not to notice, but the young boy inside him, who had always dreamed of being a best-selling author, would jump up and down with elated joy.

George was only 32, but he'd already had over a dozen books published, some of which had made it to the top end of the *New York Times* Best Seller list. Whenever his new book hit the shelves, the bookstore would always throw a huge launch party and the whole town would come out to get their copies signed.

Paula would call him a *'local celebrity'*, but celebrity status had never attracted George. It was the writing that he cared about.

As he wandered casually towards the latest releases stand, his eyes wandered delicately over the glossy covers of books that he hadn't read yet, willing one to catch his eye. When he wasn't writing his own books, he was reading other peoples. He liked to think of it as research, but he was really just taking a sly look at his competition.

He reached the end of the row, and the glossy red cover of his latest book, *The Crimson Letter*, caught his attention. This was mainly because he hated the cover and every time he saw it, it reminded him of the long and tedious arguments, via dozens of emails he'd had with his publisher about changing it.

Usually he would have moved on, but the book wasn't sitting with the new releases, it was clutched in the hands of a skinny teenager, sat cross legged on the floor.

George smiled to himself as he watched the kid getting lost

in his book. Watching people was another one of his passions. From looking at a person for a few seconds, he could fabricate a whole life for them, even if it was completely fictional.

"Good choice of book kid," George couldn't resist, "the ending is brilliant!"

The boy shot his head up, which caused his scruffy black hair to flop back. George could see his face clearly now. He had a pale but smooth complexion that was screaming out for sunlight. A light dusting of sandy colored freckles covered his nose and the cheeks under his eyes.

His crossed legs and arms looked too long for his slim frame, and on anyone else they would have looked strange, but he carried them well. He quizzically stared at George with his pale green eyes, trying to understand whether the stranger was trying to start a conversation, or if he was just making a passing comment.

"I love it. I've read all of his books," he smiled again at George, testing his reaction, "The name's Harvey."

His voice was deeper than George imagined it would be. He could tell he was teetering towards his early 20s, despite his boyish good looks.

George tried to stop the smirk that was trying to spread across his face. He didn't often bump into fans of his writing on Saturday afternoons. They were usually waiting at conventions with mountains of books for him to sign and full of questions about errors and inconsistencies they'd spotted after their fourth reading of a book that was published 7 years ago.

"Looks like you're getting to the good bit," George smirked when he noticed he was already past halfway.

Harvey closed the book and stood up. Next to George he was tall, but not taller than George. The beat-up leather jacket he was wearing didn't quite reach the end of his wrists.

Harvey quickly stuffed the book back onto the shelf, in the wrong place, a red flush filling his pale cheeks. George could sense that he was embarrassed, but he didn't understand why. He studied the boy, as he stood awkwardly in front of George, his hands in his pockets. When he noticed how short the sleeves on his jacket actually were, and how scruffy the rest of his clothes looked, things started to make a lot more sense. Could he be homeless?

Guilt swelled in George's chest when Harvey shot him a stern look from the corner of his eye, making George's face also turn hot and red. He wished he hadn't disturbed Harvey, and just made up his own story as to why he had been reading on the floor. He cursed his own vanity for not being able to resist praising his own book.

George teased his wallet out of the back pocket of his tight blue jeans, pulled out a crisp $20 and stuffed it in Harvey's pocket.

"Here kid. Get that book you were reading, I didn't mean to stop you," George whispered before turning to go and find his wife in the crowd.

"Hey Mr!" the boy called loudly after George when he'd reached the end of the aisle, "I don't need your charity."

George stopped when he noticed other people in the store turning around to see what was going on. He turned to Harvey, who was waving the $20 back at George. Had he read the situation wrong?

"Let's just say the author of that book you were reading would like it if you could enjoy the book at home and not on the floor of a bookstore," George whispered, pushing his hand away, "keep the cash."

"Oh yeah? What if the author loved reading on the floor of bookstores? What do you know?" the boy laughed, daring to challenge the stranger who had forced cash upon him.

The way he was holding the $20 made it look like tainted money. He looked uncomfortable with it in his hands which made George wonder if it was the first time he'd touched money in a long time.

Deciding that he liked Harvey's guts, he knew the only way to fix the situation would be to let Harvey know who he was.

"George Lewis," he smiled sheepishly with an outstretched hand.

The boy's eyes widened and his mouth fell open as if his jaw had just disconnected from the rest of his skull. With both of his hands he grabbed George's outstretched arm, carelessly dropping the $20 on the ground.

"You have got to be kidding me!" Harvey laughed shaking his head in amazement, "I'm like, your biggest fan. I want to be a writer like you one day."

George pulled his hand away from Harvey feeling that he had resolved the mix up and had his ego massaged in the process.

"Well, it was nice to meet you Harvey," George smiled politely, remembering that he'd left his wife wandering around the cookbooks and if he left her any longer she'd buy every book she could carry.

George still hadn't recovered from *The Great Curries of the East* from the week before, and neither had his bathroom.

"There's so much I want to ask you!" Harvey stepped forward.

"I need to find my wife, but you have a good day kid," George patted Harvey on the shoulder.

Part of him wanted to stay and chat with Harvey, but he was still feeling uneasy with how he'd misjudged him, so he wanted to get as far away from the situation as he could.

As he walked away, he glanced back over his shoulder and he saw Harvey bend down and hastily stuff the money in his pocket.

Paula had three huge books stuffed under her arm as she tried to flick through a fourth, which she was balancing expertly against one of the shelves. George prized the book out of her hands and dumped it back on the shelf. It was a guide, which pointed out the best tourist spots in Paris. George found this amusing because he knew his wife was terrified of flying and wouldn't step foot on a plane.

As the woman behind the counter bagged up Paula's books, George realized he hadn't looked at a single book himself. He considered running back to the fiction section to get something, anything, but the thought of bumping into Harvey again stopped him. He'd already embarrassed himself enough for one day.

It wasn't until they reached the sliding doors that George experienced an uncharacteristic urge to be spontaneous. He said *'fuck it!'* to himself and told Paula to wait outside before running to the large display case that held dozens of copies of his new book.

George smiled at the sign that read *'The Crimson Letter, the new novel by best-selling local author George Lewis'*. His agent would love that sort of free publicity.

He grabbed a copy of the heavy hardback book and ran back to the checkout where he pulled another crisp $20 out of his wallet and threw it on the counter. He borrowed a pen from the woman behind the counter and told her to keep the change.

Hastily, he scribbled on the inside cover of the book, wondering if he was doing the right thing after all.

Knowing that Paula would be getting impatient standing outside alone, he paced up and down the aisles in search of Harvey. When he was close to giving up, he found him cross legged on the floor, in the same spot he'd first found him in, reading the book, again. George quickly looked around the bookstore, realizing that Harvey had chosen the perfect spot to go undetected, so he could read in peace. It clearly wasn't his first time *'borrowing'* books.

"Here kid," George whispered as he handed Harvey the book.

Harvey narrowed his eyes on George before accepting the copy. Pushing it forwards, George tried his best to look humble and apologetic, because he knew he could easily be on his way to offending him again. After a long pause, Harvey cast the un-bought copy onto the ground and accepted the gift.

When he slowly opened it, a receipt fell out onto Harvey's lap to reveal George's phone number and signature on the inside cover. Harvey's mouth opened slightly, as his eyes wandered over the digits. He didn't know what had made him jot them down, but it felt like a suitable apology.

"If you ever have any questions about writing, give me a call sometime," George shrugged.

Feeling satisfied that he'd properly resolved the situation, he left Harvey on the floor and headed for the exit. He didn't think Harvey would ever call him, but he knew the gesture alone was enough.

"What about your cash?" Harvey cried, running after George with the new book clutched to his chest.

"Keep it," George spun around with a grin, "get yourself some lunch, on me."

As George stared into Harvey's grateful eyes, he knew that he'd done the right thing. He'd long since met all of his favorite authors at conventions and workshops, and they usually ended up being egotistical and rude. The least George could do was give Harvey a good memory to look back on.

That night after dinner, George retired to his study to work on his latest book. It was an epic tale of a mother who was searching to find her son after 30 years apart. Settling into his comfy chair behind his huge mahogany desk, his train of thought derailed when his cellphone vibrated against the wood.

He didn't recognize the number, so he just stared at the cellphone as it danced around. Unknown numbers made him feel uneasy. Reluctantly, he picked up the phone and pressed the green button.

"Hello?"

"George?" a smile spread across George's face when he instantly recognized the excited voice of Harvey.

"Harvey!"

He nervously apologized for disturbing George so late at night and started to ramble about how he needed to find an internship for a month, as part of a high school program. The fact that Harvey was in high school shocked George. He was seriously starting to doubt his people reading skills.

"I'm not sure I can help you there kid."

"Don't say no yet! I'll sit in the corner and make your coffee if you want me to. I really need to find somewhere or I'll fail the program and I won't be able to graduate. I wouldn't ask, but I'm desperate."

George rubbed his forehead and let out a quiet groan. He knew Harvey was clever, and he knew mentioning him not graduating would make George feel like he couldn't refuse. George really wanted to say a firm and final no before hanging up the phone so he could get back to his writing, but he found himself agreeing to it, more out of guilt than anything.

"You won't regret this Mr. Lewis! I'll be there first thing on Monday morning. Thank you so much," they discussed the finer details of the internship before George finally hung up.

His stomach sank as he tossed his cellphone back onto the desk, wondering if he'd just made a terrible mistake. The local high school had asked him numerous times to allow interns to shadow him, but he'd always kindly turned them away. He didn't think they could learn anything valuable about writing, watching George write.

Staring at the bright screen of his laptop, he wanted to call Harvey back to tell him he couldn't do it. Perhaps he could make up some excuse? He was trying to imagine up a complicated story as to why he couldn't let Harvey into his home, but he felt uncomfortable lying to him. He didn't want to undo the good deed he'd done earlier in the day.

Besides, there was something about Harvey that he couldn't quite figure out. Seeing him up close would give him a chance to work him out properly, seeing as he'd messed that up the first time. He told himself it was just character research for a future book and returned to his writing, trying to lose himself in the story. As he typed away into the night, Harvey's face would wander into his mind, and even though he tried to push it away to focus on his growing word count, he couldn't ignore the strange curiosity, which bubbled inside of him.

TWO

George nervously examined his reflection, chewing the inside of his lip. Wearing only a pair of tight, white briefs, he carefully adjusted his hair with his wax covered fingertips. He'd been obsessing over it for far too long, trying to force every strand to sit neatly where he wanted them to, but it didn't want to behave. In his younger days, his hair was a deep and glossy brown, but now there were a few strands of gray through the front and its natural shine had dulled down.

Paula had tried to make him dye it for years, but George quite liked his hair how it was. He certainly didn't look old in the face, so he told himself it added some mystery to his character.

Paula was the vain one in their relationship, but George wasn't the type to fuss over his image, even if he would describe himself as handsome. He had a strong, well-defined jaw, high and sharp cheekbones that sat just under his eyes and an almost perfectly straight button nose. His hair was swept off his face to one side, leaving his dark and defined brows to take center stage. His mother used to joke that he looked like a young George Clooney, and that was a compliment George had never been quick to deny.

He studied his abs, making a mental note to get back to training. He'd built a full home gym in one of the spare bedrooms, but every time he lost himself in his writing, he would neglect his body. He was still well built and toned, but George had an image in his head, which he was always striving for. He didn't do it out of vanity, but out of a promise he'd made to himself when he was a chubby kid in high school.

Over the weekend, he'd nervously been waiting for Monday morning to roll around. More than once he hovered over Harvey's number, to call and cancel. Each time, he'd throw his phone down, not able to bring himself to do it. The thought of Harvey's voice sounding disappointed made him feel uneasy, and he didn't want to admit it, but he was sort of looking forward to having somebody else around when Paula was at work.

It was so far out of his comfort zone that he thought the change might do him some good and he might be able to get some good stories out of it.

"There's still time to cancel," Paula called from the bathroom as George sat on the bed to pull on a pair of gray socks, "he could be crazy. He's just some idiot you met in a bookstore!"

George knew she could be right, but he had a feeling that Harvey wasn't the crazed, teenage fan Paula had spent the weekend trying to warn him against. He got the impression that he was sweet, and maybe a little feisty, but not crazy. A quick glance to the clock told him that he only had 15 minutes to get dressed.

"It'll be fine," George called back as he pulled on a pair of fitted, dark blue jeans.

The grumbling anticipation was starting to play tricks on his nerves, and he wasn't the type of guy who got nervous. He'd been on most daytime talk shows to promote various projects over the years, but none of them compared to how he was feeling.

"If you say so George. I need to get to work anyway," Paula sprayed her blue nurse's uniform with sweet scented perfume, "make sure you keep an eye on him. I don't want him stealing things!"

"I'll be a hawk," Paula gave him a quick kiss on the cheek, barely pressing her lips onto his skin.

He took one last look at the blazer and white shirt he'd carefully ironed the night before. The temptation to climb into his normal, casual writing clothes was strong, but he decided to leave that until tomorrow. He wanted to give off the impression that he was a professional writer, for the first day at least.

He stood in the mirror deciding how far up he should button the shirt. He settled on 3 buttons from the top, enough that he still looked comfortable and could show off his broad and smooth chest, but not too low down that he looked unprofessional.

The doorbell rang as he fastened the belt tightly around his waist. With a quick spritz of his musky cologne, he headed downstairs, taking the steps two at a time. Trying to look relaxed, he swung open the door with more vigor than he'd intended to.

He was expecting to see the awkward kid in scruffy clothes who he'd met in the bookstore, but instead he saw a handsome young man with jet black hair, neatly gelled back off his pale face. He was wearing a creased and ill-fitting suit, but George appreciated the effort all the same.

"Harvey! Come in, come in. You look very smart," George smiled as he shook Harvey's hand.

Suddenly, he didn't feel like the overdressed one.

"It's good to see you again, Mr. Lewis. I can't thank you enough for letting me do this," he sounded as though he was trying to steady the nerves in his voice.

"It's George. You can drop the Mr. Lewis thing," George laughed, slapping Harvey firmly on the back.

Harvey quickly looked taken aback by the huge entrance.

His eyes glazed over as they wandered from the grand white staircase in the middle of the hall to the gorgeous chandelier that hung from the second story ceiling. The stairs led to an open planned landing, which led off to the five bedrooms. George knew the house was far too big for him and Paula, but he had to spend his money on something.

"Wow. Nice place Mr. Le-, I-I mean, George," Harvey stuttered in awe.

As Harvey wiped away the sweat from his forehead, his obvious nerves seemed to ease George's.

"You can take off your jacket if you want?" George took off his own blazer and rolled up the stiff sleeves of his white shirt.

He undid another of the buttons, exposing more of his chest, feeling foolish for dressing in a way he never usually would. Harvey did the same, throwing his blazer and tie over a small, white leather chair. He followed George's lead and undid the top buttons of his shirt, exposing his pale chest. George didn't mean to stare, but Harvey was a lot more defined under the baggy clothes than he'd expected.

"It's starting to get hot out. April weather is always funny," Harvey laughed as he followed George into the kitchen.

"You've got that right. I heard it raining this morning when I was in the shower," George uncomfortably rearranged his underwear through the tight denim.

For a moment, he thought he caught Harvey's eyes gazing at his crotch, but he didn't think anything of it. He was sure if he saw a guy touching his junk, his eyes would wander there, out of curiosity. His recent discovery of skinny jeans had spiced up his lagging wardrobe, but they could be a little restricting around his cock.

"What do you drink?" George popped the cap off a chilled beer from the huge, double-fronted refrigerator.

"Water is good," Harvey smiled politely, hovering nervously in the doorway of the kitchen, with his hands behind his back.

"You can have a beer kid, I won't tell if you don't," George swigged the tangy and refreshing beer.

He could see Harvey thinking about it, looking increasingly more nervous. George was trying his best to make Harvey feel more comfortable, seeing as they were going to be spending a lot of time together. He passed Harvey a bottle of beer.

"How old are you kid? I was shocked when you said you were in high school," George slid onto a stool at the breakfast bar, motioning for Harvey to join him.

"19. I shouldn't be in high school, not really. I was supposed to graduate last year but I had to re-do one of my grades," Harvey focused on the cold bottle in his hands, avoiding George's eyes, before taking a careful sip from the glass neck.

George tried not to laugh when he noticed him wince. What 19 year old didn't like beer? George was in college when he was 19, drinking at frat parties every night.

"Re-do? Did you not get the grades you needed?" George had assumed Harvey was smart enough to pull the right grades.

"It's complicated," Harvey still looked nervous, "I had some family trouble so I missed a lot of school. When I went back, the Principal made me start the 9th grade again."

His nerves were starting to make George anxious. He tried to think what sort of family trouble would make Harvey miss enough school to warrant a re-do. He nearly asked, but he bit his tongue when he noticed how glazed over Harvey's eyes looked as he stared at the beer he wasn't drinking.

George had tried his best to treat Harvey like an equal, but maybe he'd approached it wrong?

"That sucks kid," George sucked the beer through his teeth.

They sat in silence for a couple of minutes before George jumped up, deciding to ditch the ill-judged beers, in favor of showing Harvey his study. He rarely let people in there and even Paula knew better than to go in when George was writing. With Harvey however, he felt like he'd appreciate the space, so he found himself excited to show it to him.

With a gentle touch, he eased open the door to the study, which was hidden at the end of the dining room. Harvey gasped, giving George the exact reaction he'd been hoping for.

He wandered into the study, leaving George's side. He spun on the spot, taking in the grand study, which looked more like a miniature library. Antique lamps sitting on little wooden tables next to elegant chairs, dimly lit the room. The center piece of the room was a huge, towering marble fireplace.

Hundreds and hundreds of colorful hardbacks lined the walls, from floor to ceiling. It was a collection George had been amassing since he was a child, so he loved having a special room for them to live. His writing desk sat at the bottom of the window-less study, cast in shadow.

"You like it?" George scratched the back of his head nervously.

"Like it? I love it! This place is like stepping into Narnia," Harvey ran straight over to the first set of books.

He quickly scanned the spines of the books, classic mixed in with modern. George knew that every book Harvey could ever want to read was in his study. Carefully, he ran his fingers over the spines, looking like he was resisting the urge to pull any of them out.

"I've spent years collecting this lot," George wandered over to Harvey.

He reached out and gently grabbed one of the huge leather bound books, brushing Harvey's shoulder as he did.

"This is a first edition *Charles Dickens* novel. This baby set me back a couple of hundred," he gently opened the cover to show Harvey the publication date.

He lifted his hand, but before his fingerprints touched the old paper, he stepped back and stuffed them into his pockets.

"I bet this book cost more than the apartment I live in," Harvey glanced down at the floor, looking away from the book.

Sensing the growing embarrassment, George pushed the book back onto the shelf. He didn't know for sure, but he didn't think Harvey had much. He hadn't intended to, but George felt like a fool for showing off.

"Do you live with your mom and dad?"

Harvey bowed his head and wandered across the study,

scanning the titles on the other side. George could sense how uncomfortable he was making him feel, with his prying questions.

"I live with my brother," he avoided the question.

George felt like he was holding something back, but he decided it was better not to push it. They'd have a whole month to get to know each other, so he didn't want to be too invasive on their first day.

For the rest of the day, George had Harvey sorting through his paperwork that had been stuffed in his desk, neglected for months. He wasn't sure how Harvey would react to being given such a boring task, but Harvey attacked it with an enthusiasm that reminded George of when he used to write for the local paper. He'd put all of his time and energy into tiny, 50 word stories, even though he knew they were merely to fill up the side columns. He'd treat them as serious as he would a 100,000 word epic novel and his editor, Theo, would laugh at him, but he could tell he admired his passion.

The hours sped by and when the front door slammed, George looked up from his laptop. His heart sank when he glanced at the clock and he noticed that Harvey was still on the floor, sorting through the paper.

It was 5:12pm, which meant that Paula was home.

Was he supposed to send Harvey home when school finished? If Harvey was itching to get home, he didn't show it. George peered over his laptop, watching Harvey flick through the paperwork, unaware that he was being watched. He looked content.

"It's past 5pm kid," George stood up, stretching his arms out, "I lost track of time!"

Harvey didn't drop the papers. Out of the corner of his eye, he looked over to George, and smiled nervously.

"I don't mind getting this finished," he shrugged.

"I can't keep you here all night," George laughed, folding his arms and leaning against the front of his desk, "c'mon, you can finish this stuff tomorrow."

Harvey didn't stop straight away, so George walked over

and pulled the paper from his hands. He seemed reluctant to let it go.

"Are you sure?" Harvey stood up, shaking his legs out.

"I'll make some dinner and then I'll drive you home," George patted Harvey on the shoulder, turning him in the direction of the door.

"No!" Harvey cried out, pulling away from George's hands, "I don't live too far away. I'll walk."

Harvey's eyelids twitched as he stared sternly at George. Had he hit another sore subject? Why did George suddenly have a habit of landing his foot in it?

"I'm insisting. I've been meaning to sort that pile out for months, so you've done me a huge favor. Paula always cooks for 5000, so there'll be more than enough for us all."

Harvey smiled sheepishly and nodded.

Following him out of the study, George's eyes wandered down to Harvey's backside, and he couldn't help but notice how his cheeks were moving under the loose pants. He didn't know why he was staring at them, but he didn't stop until they reached   the   kitchen.

THREE

Over dinner, Harvey laughed along to a story George told about his editor. He'd told the story so many times, but it never failed to raise a laugh with new people. They never usually ate at the dinner table, but Paula had insisted that they did, even if she didn't look happy that Harvey was still there. George was sure he caught her looking through the kitchen drawers, making sure all of their valuables were still present.

"This is really delicious Mrs. Lewis," Harvey mumbled, "I've never tasted anything like it."

George caught Harvey's eye and they both smirked at each other. The food wasn't good, in fact, it was pretty bad. It was spicy and sweet, all at once. Cumin overpowered everything and from the straining in Harvey's eyes, George could tell he was lying to be polite.

"Thanks," she said flatly, not looking up from her plate.

Whenever Harvey wasn't looking, Paula would stare at him out of the corner of her eye. George could tell she was judging him, and he didn't like it. He couldn't explain why, but he felt defensive over him, and he didn't want his wife making him feel uncomfortable. Harvey was a good kid, despite Paula's judgmental eye rolls.

After dinner, Harvey offered to help clean the dishes, but Paula practically snatched them out of his hand to toss them into the dishwasher. Deciding it was better to get out of there before she blew up, they headed out to the car. Harvey insisted that he was going to walk home, but it was getting dark and George refused to take no for an answer. He could be stubborn when he wanted to be.

"Get in the car, kid," George demanded, "I've kept you here all day and it's now past 8. I don't care what you say, just get in the car."

Harvey reluctantly jumped into the car and buckled up. With muffled directions, George drove slowly, turning when he was told. It didn't take him long to realize where they were heading. It was a part of town that usually hit the local news for all the wrong reasons. Crime and drugs were big there and George couldn't believe that Harvey would live somewhere like it. He hoped that they were just driving through it to get to Harvey's real house, but when he told him to stop outside of a 24/7 liquor store, his heart dropped.

George looked up above the store to a tiny, dirty window. Metal bars covered the outside, and through the dirty, closed drapes, he could see a soft light.

"This is your house?" George mumbled.

He tried not to sound judgmental, and he succeeded, because he sounded completely shocked.

"I told you not to drive me home," Harvey turned his face away.

A police car zoomed by Harvey's window and the siren echoed through the car, sending a shiver down George's spine.

"No, it's fine."

"I should go," Harvey mumbled, opening the door.

George reached over and grabbed Harvey's arm, his boney wrist feeling hot under his touch. He tugged, trying to get out of the car, but George wanted some answers.

"Where are your parents, kid?" George asked quietly, using his other hand to turn Harvey's face towards him.

He blinked slowly, like he was fighting back tears.

"They're dead."

George loosened his grip on Harvey's arm, sitting back in his chair. His parents were dead? Everything suddenly made sense. He resisted the urge to pull him into a hug. He'd probably already over stepped the boundaries between author and intern, but he couldn't let him get out the car without knowing the full story.

"What happened?" George asked tentatively, "you don't have to tell me."

Harvey gulped before talking, "Our house caught fire in the night, but I managed to get out through my bedroom window. I tried to save them, I tried to go back in, but there was so much smoke."

"And your brother?"

"He wasn't in," Harvey wiped the tears from his cheeks, "he didn't come home that night."

George's heart ached for his loss.

"Harvey, I'm sorry, I really am," George said, resting his hand on Harvey's knee, "I shouldn't have made you talk about it."

His hand felt heavy on Harvey's knee and even though he should have moved it, he didn't want to. He told himself it was the right thing to do. George wanted to lock the doors to drive back to his place. He didn't want to imagine the state the apartment would be in. Did Harvey even have a bed to sleep in?

George resisted the urge to hug him. He ran his finger gently over Harvey's knee, before pulling it away, realizing it was inappropriate. Harvey wiped away the final tears, switching off his sadness, before saying goodnight. Without looking back to George, he jumped out of the car and ran towards the liquor store, disappearing around the side.

Not wanting to drive away, not wanting to leave him, he

stayed and stared at the window. He saw a shadow behind the curtain and wondered if it was Harvey. Convincing himself it wasn't his place to interfere, he turned the key in the ignition and slowly headed home.

Turning up the radio, he attempted to lose himself in the pop music. He tried to stop imagining Harvey's pain, but he knew all too well what it was like to lose a parent.

***

"Where have you been?" Leo didn't look up from his beer bottle, "You're late."

"I told you Leo," Harvey sighed, "I'm doing an internship."

"No you didn't," Leo attempted to stand up, but he stumbled sideways, collapsing again into the chair.

How long had he been drinking for? When he'd left him in the morning, he was already on his second bottle. Harvey imagined that his douchebag friends had been around all day, drinking themselves into oblivion.

"I'm going to bed," Harvey didn't bother helping Leo up as he slouched down the side of the couch.

Settling into the small mattress on the floor, he pulled the old sheet over his shoulders, not bothering to change out of the suit he'd borrowed out of Leo's pile of clothes. He wasn't particularly tired, but being in the bedroom meant that there was a door, no matter how thin, between him and Leo.

Closing his eyes, he tried to imagine what George would be doing. He imagined him walking around his house, changing out of his shirt, ready for a shower before bed. He imagined the water running over his body, his hands massaging in the soap. He tried to shake the images from his head, but the warmth it brought him in his stomach was too nice.

He'd shared things with George that he'd never wanted to share with anybody, but he wasn't going to let that get in the way of the month they were going to have together.

FOUR

"**Y**ou should have seen it Paula. God, I wouldn't wish that place on anybody," George pulled the sheet over his naked body.

Paula switched her bedside lamp off and rolled away from George, so all he could see was her blonde hair. He'd lost count of how many months it had been since they'd last had sex, so seeing the back of her head wasn't an unusual sight. Where had the cuddling gone? The distance between them felt so much wider than the gap between them in the bed.

"He's 19, he's an adult," she muttered sleepily.

"But he's still in high school. He can't support himself," he said, "we need to help him."

"No, we don't," Paula fluffed her pillow heavily, "go to sleep and forget about him, he's not your problem. You didn't burn his house down."

George rolled away from his wife, letting his eyes adjust to the dark. He'd spent the night trying to work on his novel, but the image of Harvey crying kept creeping into his mind and he couldn't focus. Even an urgent email from his editor, reminding him of the tight deadline, couldn't force his fingers to type.

Every time he managed to get comfortable, he'd imagine where Harvey was sleeping, and his bed would suddenly feel lumpy. It took all of his strength not to jump out of bed, grab his keys and drive right over to bring him back. He didn't realize people actually lived like that, especially intelligent and sweet people, like Harvey.

At 3am, Paula's words were still echoing around his mind and he considered that she could be right. He didn't really know Harvey, and he had no real loyalty to him. In a month, things would go back to normal and he'd never have to see him again, but even as he told himself this, he felt a strange protective instinct rise inside of him. He didn't need to help, he wanted to, and that's what mattered to George.

After a restless couple of hours, his alarm clock pierced through his dream. Groaning loudly, he hit his head against the pillow, his heavy eyelids flickering, crying out for just a couple more minutes in bed. He let the sleep drift back in, but when Harvey's face appeared in his mind he jumped out of bed and straight into the shower.

Letting the hot water rush down his back, his body started to awaken. The morning shower always provided the perfect opportunity to jerk off, out of Paula's way. He started stroking his growing member, his free hand running up and down his stomach. He wanted to finish there and then, but he was far too tired to perform, so he dried off and got ready for Harvey's arrival.

When the doorbell buzzed, George was already waiting in the kitchen. He'd opted for his familiar dark jeans and a white polo shirt, which hugged his arms and broad chest nicely. He looked much more like himself. Opening the door, he greeted Harvey with a bright smile, forcing the sleep to the back of his mind and hoping that the dark circles under his eyes weren't too obvious.

Harvey looked shy and nervous again, but George knew it was for a different reason than yesterday. He was glad to see he was dressed more like the young man he'd met in the bookstore, instead of looking like an overly dressed business student.

"Have you eaten?" George asked, leading Harvey into the kitchen.

"I forgot," he mumbled, shrugging.

"Good! How does bacon and eggs sound?" George was already pulling the ingredients from the fridge.

As he fried the eggs and bacon, he'd glance over his shoulder to Harvey, and their eyes would catch each other. A small smile would flicker across Harvey's lips and George couldn't help but return the smile. They settled down into the breakfast bar with the food and coffee, and George wasn't sure if it was because he was an amazing cook, or if Harvey was just starving, but he wolfed the food down, barely stopping for air.

"Ready for round two?" he asked.

Harvey shook his head, "No thanks. That was really good though."

George didn't want Harvey to feel like he was patronizing him, but he couldn't help treating him differently. He wanted to look out for him, but he didn't know how to do that without it coming across as pushy.

He dumped the plates in the sink and opened up the double French doors at the bottom of the kitchen, which opened up onto their impressive pool and beautiful garden. The garden was George's pride and joy, and he'd tended to it for years, making it perfect in every way. When they'd first moved into the house, it was nothing more than a patch of grass, but now, well pruned roses lined the fences, with bright flowers in the beds below. George left Harvey standing by the pool as he disappeared into a tiny shed to grab his tools.

***

Harvey was as impressed with the garden as he was with the house. A huge blue pool sat on a white tiled patio, and the rest of the huge garden was filled with beautiful flowers and bushes. Neatly trimmed and tall trees lined the fences, completely boxing them in and even though Harvey knew there must have been neighbors on either side, it was like they were in their own secret paradise. At the bottom of the garden he could make out a BBQ and a hammock, just like the one they'd had at his parents' house. He tried not to imagine them, but as sadness swept over him, he couldn't help it. It had been so long since he'd spent time in a place like it, he'd almost forgotten how beautiful flowers could be.

"I thought we could do something different today," George emerged from the shed with a basket of tools under his arm, "how do you feel about gardening?"

Harvey grinned at George. He would have been happy spending another day sorting through his paperwork, just so he could be close to him, but he had to admit, gardening sounded more fun. He knew there was a reason he'd opted for a casual T-shirt and jeans instead of borrowing his brother's court suit again.

As they pulled weeds from the flowerbeds, George confessed to Harvey that when he wasn't writing, he loved to tend to his garden. Harvey had to admit, he'd done an amazing job on his own. It was like something out of *Home and Garden Magazine*. How George found the time out of his busy writing schedule, he didn't know.

As the sun hung high in the cloudless sky, sweat started to drip from Harvey's face into the soil and he could feel his gray T-shirt clinging to his back. He tugged at it, drawing George's gaze down to his body.

"Damn kid, you're sweating buckets," George laughed.

"You're not too dry yourself," Harvey dug his fingernails into the soil and tossed a handful in George's direction.

With a wink, George disappeared into the house and

reappeared carrying a tray with a tall jug of cloudy lemonade and two glasses filled to the rim with cubes of ice. Harvey was thirsty, but his eyes wandered right past the lemonade to George's torso. He'd taken his shirt off in the kitchen, and even though he didn't want to stare, his impressive body demanded attention. He marveled at the chiseled perfection, wondering when he had time to work out in all of the gardening and writing.

Stabbing the tiny trowel into the dirt, he shielded his eyes from the sun, using the cover to discreetly admire George's body through his lashes. Carrying the tray in front of him, his biceps bulging out, his eyes wandered down his washboard stomach to the perfect V shape, which ran into his tight jeans. Harvey knew his body was toned, but he would have killed to look as amazing as George.

He slid the tray onto a small, white, rusting iron table at the bottom of the garden, and dragged over two chairs. Before he sat down, he ran his fingers over his sweat covered abs, mixing it in with the dirt from his fingers. Harvey concentrated, trying to stay calm, but it was like something out of a *Diet Coke* commercial.

"This is good lemonade," Harvey sipped the sickly sweet drink.

"It's an old family recipe. I got it from my dad's cousin, Evelyn, over in California," he smiled as he leaned back in the chair, his body on perfect show, "if you're too hot, you can take your shirt off too."

Harvey examined George's perfect body as it shimmered with sweat in the bright sunlight. Despite feeling inferior, he could feel the drenched fabric sticking to every inch of his pale body, so he nervously sat forwards and pulled it over his head, discarding it on the lawn. Glancing down at his own body, he couldn't help but think the sun reflecting off the glistening sweat was making his own body look more impressive than it actually was.

As they sat drinking the lemonade in the afternoon sun,

chatting idly about the weather and George's books, Harvey started to notice George's eyes darting down his body every couple of seconds. At first, he thought he was imagining it, but he caught George's gaze when he was doing it, and he swore that he saw George blush through his tanned cheeks. He wanted him to look for different reasons, but he knew he'd only be looking because he was so skinny and small compared to George's Adonis torso.

It wasn't long before they were back in the flower beds, digging up the weeds and planting fresh bulbs deep into the dirt. As the afternoon wore on, their exposed chests were quickly caked in more layers of sweat and dirt and Harvey could feel the sun scorching down on his fair skin, something he'd likely pay for later.

His mind wandered to his high school. If he wasn't with George, he'd be sitting in a stuffy classroom, learning things that didn't matter to him. He'd always felt older and more mature than his other classmates, especially after the death of his parents and especially after being held back for an entire year. Facing something so traumatic had forced him to grow up quickly, and being with George, he felt more like his equal, rather than his '*pupil*'. He was no longer '*that kid whose parents died in a fire*', he was Harvey, somebody who actually meant something and could be valued.

They moved onto pruning the rose bushes and Harvey listened admiringly to George as he recited facts about gardening. He wouldn't have been interested in knowing things about gardening normally, but he loved listening to George talk. He was so caught up in listening to George recite his facts that he didn't notice the pruning scissors were heading right for his finger. A sharp, hot pain suddenly dragged him from his daydream when the blades met his flesh. He dropped the scissors and stared at the cut, but nothing happened. He thought he'd had a lucky escape, but blood suddenly started to pour from the wound, covering the white roses in scarlet paint.

"Jesus Christ kid!" George dropped his own scissors and threw his arm strongly around Harvey's shoulders as he felt himself sway on the spot.

His vision and mind blurred into one, no doubt from the shock. He stood up and let George drag him across the lawn, in the direction of the house, not noticing that their bodies were pressed up against each other as he used George as a support.

"This is my fault," George muttered, "you need gloves!"

He clenched his finger tightly, but blood seeped through his tight fist, dripping onto the neatly trimmed grass. He didn't want to look at how deep it had gone, so he focused on George's muscular arm, as it clenched tightly and securely around his shoulders. He could smell the musky, manly scent coming from George's underarm, and the feeling that stirred inside him was a comforting distraction.

In the downstairs bathroom, George washed Harvey's cut until the blood flow stopped. A nice, deep cut ran down the side of Harvey's left index finger, but it didn't look too serious without the gushing blood. The visions of losing his finger quickly faded from his mind. Sitting on the edge of the free standing bath, Harvey held his hand out and let George wrap a bandage tightly around his finger, not looking away from his eyes as they concentrated hard.

Harvey felt safe and looked after, and that was a bizarre feeling for him. It was something he could get used to. If he cut himself at home, he'd be lucky if his brother looked up from his drink to grunt, or hurl an insult.

"Don't scare me like that again, okay?" George rested his hand on Harvey's shoulder, "I saw all that blood and my heart stopped."

"It looked a lot worse than it felt," Harvey lied as he tried to ignore the stinging in his buried finger.

Softly, they stared at each other with relieved smiles. Harvey could have looked into George's swirling hazel eyes all day, but he pulled away, telling Harvey that he was going for a shower upstairs, leaving Harvey to bathe in the bath. After dropping off fresh towels, he disappeared, leaving Harvey to run the bath alone.

Once the hot bath was drawn, Harvey clumsily unbuckled the belt around his jeans with one hand. When he'd managed to pull the belt out, he fiddled with the buttons and slipped out of his jeans and tight white briefs. When he bent over to take his white socks off, he could feel the sunburn on his back stretching and stinging. Slowly lowering himself into the hot water, he felt it burning his sun-kissed skin. When he'd bravely lowered himself up to his knees, he glanced in the direction of the door, and through the crack he thought he saw somebody.

Not sure if he was imagining things, he quickly dropped himself into the water, ignoring the burning on his back. His eyes darted straight for the crack again, but whatever he'd thought he'd seen had vanished. Had the steam played a trick on his eyes, or had he seen George lingering by the door, watching him lower himself slowly into the bath?

Using the expensive looking soap and shampoo on the side of the bath, he washed himself the best he could with one hand, feeling relief as the mud and water mixed together, leaving his skin fresh and clean. The water started to cool, so he jumped out, wrapping one of the towels under his hips, letting the dark tuft of hair poke out over the white towel.

Not wanting to get back into his dirty jeans and sweaty T-shirt, he tiptoed out of the bathroom and to venture up the grand staircase, in search of George. At the top of the stairs, he was met with more doors than he knew what to do with. He couldn't believe how big the place was, especially compared to his tiny apartment. What could Paula and George want to do with so many rooms?

The faint sound of gushing water directed Harvey to a door at the very end of the hall. He slowly crept into a bedroom, and the sound of running water grew louder. The clothes that George had been wearing were scattered across the floor, along with a tiny white jockstrap and the thought of George wearing the jockstrap all day caused a stirring under the towel and blood started to rush to Harvey's shaft. As he felt his member grow, he couldn't deny how deeply attracted he was to George.

He knew it wasn't right, but there was something about him that was starting to drive him wild.

He was about to reach out, to brush his fingers along the jockstrap, when the sound of running water suddenly stopped and he heard wet footprints walking heavily across tiles. In a panic, he turned back to the door and he almost darted out in the hall but he was sure that George would catch him before he even reached the stairs. The growing erection under his towel was causing it to tent up awkwardly, and the more he tried to stop it, the more it seemed to grow. When George emerged from the bathroom with an identical towel wrapped around his waist Harvey instinctively dropped his hands to his crotch.

"G-George," he stuttered, "I-I-I was just looking for some clean clothes?"

George smiled, and his eyes darted down to whatever Harvey was trying to cover. He either didn't notice the solid wood being pushed down into the towel, or he was too polite to say anything. Not saying anything, he flung open the doors to his impressive closet and produced a gray pair of sweat pants and a white T-Shirt.

"Here kid, these should fit," he tossed the clothes in Harvey's direction, making Harvey jump forward to catch them.

He felt his cock spring forwards, launching the towel with it. Doubling over, he managed to catch it before it dropped to the floor. Cheeks burning red with embarrassment, he didn't dare look at George. With the clothes and towel clutched to his chest, just about covering his modesty, he tiptoed out of the room, not wanting to expose his bare buttocks. He didn't take his eyes off of the cream, fluffy carpet until he was safely in the hallway.

In George's clothes, Harvey felt even more narrow than usual. The T-shirt hung loosely over his slim frame and he had to pull the drawstring in the sweatpants so tight it created a big knot in the front. He lingered at the bottom of the staircase, waiting for George, not sure if he'd be able to look him in the eye, even if his awkward boner had vanished. When George descended the stairs wearing similar clothes to Harvey, he looked masculine and model like, because they fit him so perfectly. They hugged every part of his muscular body, and the bulge in the front of the sweatpants let Harvey know he was wearing another jockstrap.

He tried not to imagine how the strap would look framing his cheeks, or how tightly it would be hugging his junk. Shaking his head of such thoughts, he breathed deeply, not wanting to excite himself too much.

"Now, I was thinking about how we could spend the rest of the afternoon," George stroked his stubbly chin playfully, "I have more paperwork for you to sort…or, we could just say *'fuck it'* and watch a movie?"

Involuntarily, Harvey bit his lip, feeling his skin blush. He knew he was supposed to be on an internship, learning all about the world of writing, but as he stared at George, smiling down at him, he couldn't think of anything else he'd rather be doing.

"Movie?" Harvey shrugged.

"I hoped you'd say that," George winked as he pulled a DVD case out of the back of his sweatpants.

Harvey smiled and held his breath as he followed George into the living room, wishing that he could have reached in and grabbed the box himself.

FIVE

"**H**ave you seen this before?" George bent over and slotted the disc into the DVD player.

Harvey stopped turning the case over in his hands to steal a glance at George's backside, but as soon as George straightened up, Harvey darted his eyes back down to the case. The words '*The Woman In The Attic*' were scrawled across the top of the case and he was sure he recognized the title, but he didn't think he'd ever seen the movie.

"I don't think so," he shrugged, tossing the case onto the floor.

"It's a Direct-to-DVD movie adaptation of one of my books from a few years ago" George smirked as he sat down dangerously close to Harvey on the sofa, "and it's really, really shit."

George hit play and it wasn't long before Harvey realized what George was talking about. Harvey remembered reading the book years ago, but he didn't recognize any of George's brilliance in the tacky movie. The sets were cheap, the acting was terrible and the script was lacking any sparkle.

"Oh god," Harvey laughed, "this really is shit!"

"Tell me about it. This was the first and last time I sold the film rights to any of my books. It's too painful to watch."

George pushed his face into a cushion as he listened to the wooden actors failing to convey any of the passion George had woven into his manuscript.

"It's like they didn't even read the book," he said.

"I don't think they did," George turned to face him.

They laughed softly, their eyes lingering for a little too long.

As the credits started to roll, Harvey started to wonder what he'd have to do to have a life like George one day. The movie may have been bad, but it was still a big deal. If he remembered correctly, the book had been a best seller when it had been released, and he wanted that.

"How old were you when your first book was published?"

"21," he nodded, "and that was already too late. I must have had 12 novels rejected before that."

"12?"

"Yep! My agent was starting to hate me. It was a long, hard struggle to get people to take me seriously."

Harvey couldn't imagine anyone crushing George's ideas. He was one of the best writers Harvey had ever read. His ability to capture characters had always left Harvey in awe, and it was something he always tried to convey whenever he tried to write, but he didn't know if he had the strength to break into the industry. Could he handle 12 books being rejected? Could he even write 12 books?

Later that evening, Paula called to let George know she was doing overtime, and even though Harvey tried to resist, George ordered him to sit at the breakfast bar as he cooked dinner for them both. He didn't like feeling like he was hanging around where he wasn't wanted, especially if George was doing it out of pity. Even though that's what he thought, it didn't feel like that's what was happening. Was he imagining it, or did it feel like George liked having him around?

After they'd finished eating, it was almost 9pm when George drove Harvey home. Harvey didn't try to put up a fight. Instead, he enjoyed the drive home with George.

"I'll see you tomorrow?" George rolled his window down and called to Harvey as he walked down the sidewalk.

"Tomorrow," Harvey smiled, waving his bandaged hand at George.

As he headed up to his tiny apartment, he was already starting to miss George.

***

As the night wore on, George buried himself in his book. He'd had a strongly worded email from his editor letting him know that he was behind on his word count targets for the edits for his new book, and the release was around the corner. He'd been given a couple of weeks to polish things up before the book went to print, and he'd intended to do those edits during the day, but it had been more fun hanging out with Harvey. He couldn't put his finger on why, but he felt himself drawn to him.

When he heard a soft knock on his office door, he blinked away from his laptop screen and glanced sleepily at the clock.

1am.

Where had the night gone?

"Come in," he rubbed at his tired eyes.

Paula slowly opened the door and ducked into the office, fully dressed, wearing her jacket and shoes. Her long blonde hair was tied tightly off her face, in a huge messy bun and she was clutching her phone and her car keys. Even through the darkness, George could tell that her eyes were red and puffy.

"What's happened?" George towards her, grabbing her face in his hands.

"Don't," she pushed him away, glancing down to the ground.

Why did she always sound so detached?

"Paula?"

"It's my mom," she scratched her cheek with her car key, "my dad called and he said she's in the hospital."

"Is she okay?" George tried to look her in the eyes, but she wouldn't return his gaze.

"I need to drive back home," she said.

"Okay," he nodded, "let me just go and pack a bag and we'll set off."

"No," she held her hand up, looking into his eyes for the first time, "I've packed my stuff. I'm setting off now."

"Oh," George stepped back, "okay."

They stood in awkward silence, before she spoke again.

"I don't know how long I'll be away for," she dove in and kissed him lightly on the cheek, but she didn't linger, "you need to stay here and work."

He followed her to the door, but she didn't look at him as she ducked into her car, her bags already in the backseat. As he watched her pull out of the driveway, he waved, but she didn't acknowledge him. He tried to tell himself that she was acting weird because she'd just found out her mom was sick, but it was no different to how she'd been acting for months. As he watched her car disappear, he couldn't help but feel relieved that they were having some time apart. Maybe that's what their marriage needed?

Later that night, he rolled over in an empty bed, feeling lonely, but not for the first time. Even though it was the first time Paula hadn't been next to him, it didn't feel that different. Her body may have been there, but any connection had gone. He could try pretending everything was fine, but he knew it wasn't.

Softly closing his eyes, his thoughts wandered to Harvey, and more importantly, Harvey lowering himself into the bathtub. He hadn't meant to stand and stare, but he couldn't help himself. When his eyes had wandered down Harvey's body, he'd felt something that he'd never felt.

It was a stirring, which he was feeling again, and he tried to vividly remember what he'd seen. He rolled back over, and his hands disappeared below the sheets.

SIX

The next week flew by and George didn't hear much from Paula. Aside from a couple of hurried phone calls, he had no idea what was going on, and she didn't seem in a hurry to share. From the start of every phone call, she'd had an excuse to get off the phone as quickly as possible. From what she had said, he'd managed to figure out that her mother was really sick, but she wouldn't go into details.

Even though George felt guilty for not being by her side, he was glad he wasn't. Paula's family had never liked him, so things would have only been awkward. He was starting to think that Paula was starting to share their views.

Harvey kept him distracted from thinking about Paula, but with each day, it felt less and less like work and more like old friends hanging out. They watched movies, read books, worked on the garden and George even tried to teach Harvey how to cook without having to blindly follow a cookbook. George was getting so used to Harvey being around, when he didn't see him at the weekends, he surprised himself with how disappointed he was. He was used to being in the house alone during the day, but he felt like he was wandering around, looking for something to do. He knew Harvey only had to show up on weekdays, but it didn't stop him wanting to see Harvey on his doorstep at 9am on Saturday morning.

He didn't want to, but he felt like Harvey was suddenly all he had, and spending time with him was all he looked forward to. He liked making him smile and he liked giving him his time, and even though he told himself it didn't mean anything, he couldn't stop the stirring in his stomach. He couldn't put his finger on the feelings, but they excited him.

"Come in, come in," George beamed when Harvey knocked on the door on Monday morning.

"Busy weekend?" Harvey kicked his shoes off and tossed his jacket over a chair, just like he did every morning.

"Not really, kid. I just worked on my book and I didn't leave the house," George passed Harvey a coffee, already pouring the pancake mix into a hot frying pan.

Eating breakfast together had become part of their daily routine, and it was something George always looked forward to. He wasn't sure if he was imagining it, but Harvey looked like he was finally getting some meat on his skinny frame.

"How was your weekend?" George asked.

Harvey's eyes instantly darted down to the ground, and he squirmed in his chair, letting George know something wasn't right.

"Boring," he shrugged vaguely.

George was going to ask more questions, but Harvey's cheeks burned, just like they always did when he was uncomfortable. They ate their pancakes in silence.

"How does a trip to the library sound?" George asked as he cleared up the plates.

He was running out of fun things for them to do to distract Harvey from the fact he was getting no real work experience.

If Harvey had noticed that he was learning nothing about writing, he wasn't complaining about it. He seemed happy, and that was good enough for George.

When they got down to the library, they wandered around the aisles, side by side, reading the spines and backs of books. With their books in arms, they dumped them in the trunk of George's car.

"I don't know about you, but I'm hungry!" George rubbed his washboard abs over his shirt.

"I don't have any money," he sounded embarrassed.

"My treat," George winked, locking up the car, "my favorite Italian is around the corner."

***

Harvey had to admit that he was starting to feel hungry, but he hated the thought of not being able to pay for his own food. He hadn't even bothered to take his wallet with him to George's, because it had been empty for so long. They headed towards *Sloppy Joe's Italian Place*, and Harvey didn't notice the drunk stumbling down the street in their direction, but when he did, he instantly recognized who it was.

It was his brother, Leo.

"Shit."

"Do you know that guy?" George looked to where Harvey was looking.

Shaking his head, he tried to duck into the restaurant unseen, but Leo's blurry gaze locked on him.

"Bro! What you doing here?" Leo shouted, propping himself up against the menu board.

The smell of beer and sweat radiated from him, and it was clear it had been more than a couple of days since he'd showered.

"Get out of here Leo," he mumbled.

"I thought you were meant to be with that douchebag writer?" he stumbled sideways, knocking the menu over, but catching himself against the door.

"Go home. You're drunk," Harvey tried to sound stern, but he could hear the wobbling in his own voice.

Leo straightened up, focusing his eyes on Harvey. He instantly saw the change.

"Don't talk to me like that, you fag," he took a step towards Harvey, "I asked you a fucking question."

"I'm George. I'm the douchebag writer," George stepped in between Harvey and Leo, holding his hand out.

George was there to protect him, and he felt a little relieved that he'd stepped in between them, because George towered over Leo. Sneering, Leo looked George up and down, stumbling backwards.

"You look like a faggot too," he slurred, trying to point at George, but his finger missed.

"Let's leave him" Harvey wished the ground would swallow him up.

He had never felt so embarrassed in his life. It was bad enough that George knew where Harvey lived and the truth about his parents, but he never thought George would meet his alcoholic brother, and he never wanted him to. Leo was the part of his life he tried to ignore.

"Hiding behind your lover, you little fag?" Leo tried to push George out of the way, but George didn't budge.

George didn't retaliate to being pushed by Leo, instead, he just kept his ground, crossing his arms so that Leo couldn't pass.

"Get yourself home," George sounded calm, "for your own sake."

They hovered for a second, but George didn't stick around to listen to Leo's reply. Tucking his arm around Harvey's shoulder, he pulled him inside of the restaurant. Leo's venomous screams burst through the door, but the attendant stopped him from entering, kicking him to the sidewalk. People were straining their necks trying to see what the noise was, but Harvey didn't dare look back. He let George take him to a booth at the back of the restaurant, only noticing how tightly he'd been holding him, when he let go.

Fighting back the tears, Harvey scanned the menu blankly, not really reading the words, as they blurred together. He pursed his lips together, breathing out slowly, but his breath trembled out of control.

"Do you want to talk about it?"

He dropped the menu, his hands shaking. He clasped them together to stop the shaking, and with a glance up to the light, which dangled over their table, he forced the tears back, not wanting to show how much his brother scared him.

"Where do I even start?" he tried to laugh, but it only made his lips tremble, "That's Leo, my brother. He's a drunk and a mess, but he's all I have. He'd rather spend his money on alcohol and drugs, so the cupboards are always empty and the apartment is a mess."

"You deserve better," George clenched his jaw.

"Do I?"

"Listen to me," George reached out his hands, stopping before they touched Harvey's, "you're something, kid. You've got a sparkle, and when you were around your brother, it was dimmed. You don't need that in your life."

George didn't sound judgmental, he sounded concerned and honest.

"He was my legal guardian when my parents first died. At first, he wasn't too bad. He tried his best, but eventually he turned to drink to numb the pain and then he started taking drugs and things got worse. You know, this last week is the most food I've eaten, in such a long time?"

He didn't want to make George feel sorry for him, nor did he want to make him feel guilty for showing him a different way of life. He'd never realized how bad things were, until he was welcomed into George's world. It all seemed so normal compared to how he'd been expected to live.

"What's he like to live with?"

"He goes out a lot, leaving me in the apartment alone. There's no TV so I just sit and read library books, and the books I can't get in the library, I read in the bookstore. You know, that book you bought me is the first book I've owned since the fire."

Harvey choked, and even though he tried to stop the tears, they tumbled softly down his cheeks. He didn't want to cry, to show George his weakness, but he knew everything about him. Quickly wiping his tears away, he tried to stop them, but they wouldn't stop. Nobody had showed they cared like George, and he was sure that's why he was crying. It had been a long time since he'd been able to cry for his parents, or Leo.

"You're staying with me tonight, kid," it wasn't a question, it was a demand.

Could Harvey really accept that offer? He didn't want to say no, but he didn't want to intrude on George's life any more than he had done. He'd been happier with George than he had been in so long, and every night, he had to go back to his apartment, that happiness would fade.

"You don't have to do -,"

"No," George interrupted, "I do. You'll stay with me until we can figure something out. I've got that entire house to myself until Paula gets back, and she's probably going to be gone for a couple more weeks."

Harvey's stomach twisted at the mention of Paula's name. It was a mixture of jealousy and surprise, because he'd forgotten all about her. He wanted to throw his arms around George's neck because he didn't have the words to thank him for what he was doing. He was about to try, but when the waiter placed a pizza in the middle of the table, all he could think about was food. Harvey didn't hesitate to grab a slice, his stomach rumbling.

"This is good pizza," Harvey laughed through the last of his tears.

"Told you," George smirked.

In that moment they had a mutual understanding of each other. There was no need for thanks or apologies. George wasn't being kind to him out of pity, it seemed like he really did care about him, and Harvey had to admit, he was suddenly excited about staying with George full time.

After the pizza, they had ice cream, which Harvey attacked as hungrily as he had done the pizza.

"Brain freeze!" George winced, squeezing his eyes tightly shut.

Harvey erupted into a fit of laughter, spraying ice cream everywhere.

"It's not funny!" George swiped out at Harvey, bursting into laughter himself.

They laughed long after the brain freeze had vanished. Harvey laughed until his sides burned and his jaw ached. A tear of happiness escaped the corner of his eye. To his surprise, George reached out and wiped away that tear with his thumb. George lingered on his cheek, so he closed his eyes and held his breath, wanting the moment to last for as long as it could.

When he pulled his hand away, a soft smile covered George's lips, and Harvey let himself smile back. He let himself relax into his chair, still feeling George's lingering touch on his skin.

SEVEN

George paid for the food and they left the safety of the restaurant, venturing back out into the afternoon sun. Nervously, Harvey glanced up and down the busy streets, scanning the faces in the crowd, expecting to see his brother staggering around looking for him. As they walked down the street, he felt himself tense up every time he saw a tall, thin guy with dark hair, but none of them were his brother. If he was lucky, he'd be asleep in a gutter somewhere.

"Wait here, I'm just going into this store," they stopped outside of a shop.

Harvey marveled at the shop window. It seemed to be an expensive gift shop, and it wasn't long before George emerged with a small white bag. Harvey was about to ask what was in the bag, but the way George was clutching it tightly, he stopped himself. Whatever it was, it was probably secret, and he didn't want to look like he was being nosey.

On the way back to George's house, they stopped off at Leo's apartment to grab some of his clothes. He nervously unlocked the door, the smell of dirt and cigarettes hitting him in the face. Not stopping to look around at the trash, which covered the apartment, he headed to the one bedroom, and when he didn't see Leo, he started gathering up his things, stuffing them in his school bag.

When Harvey emerged from the tiny bedroom with a bag slung over his shoulder, he saw George walking around the apartment, looking at the hundreds of beer bottles that covered the place. It was filthy, and Harvey should have been embarrassed inviting George inside, but it wasn't his home, and it never had been

"Let's get out of here," he said, not wanting to spend another second longer in the place than he had to.

Before he could reach the door, George walked over to him, and to his surprise, he wrapped his hands around his shoulder, pulling him into a tight embrace. Harvey didn't resist, resting his cheek on George's shoulder, as George's lips pressed against the top of his hair, sending a warm shiver running down his spine.

"I'm sorry this happened to you," he whispered, "I'm sorry you've had to live like this."

"It's not your fault."

George pulled away from the hug, but Harvey didn't want to let go. He let the smell of George's cologne linger in his nostrils.

"You'll never have to come back here, okay?"

Harvey nodded. George had no way of knowing that, and he wanted to believe that he wouldn't have to, even though he didn't know what the future would hold.

As the car pulled into the driveway of George's house, Harvey focused on the huge white building which was to become his home. The memories of his apartment were already slipping away.

For the first time in a long time, he felt like he was going home.

The guest room's bed had already been perfectly made up to resemble something out of an expensive hotel. Harvey felt like he was stepping into a dream when he saw the en-suite bathroom.

He'd traded the slums for *The Ritz*.

"Thank you so much for all of this," Harvey started to hang his few clothes in the huge closet, "I don't know how I'll ever repay you George."

Shaking his head, George held his hands up, "You know I don't want repaying."

Harvey glanced over at the white plastic bag George had dumped on the edge of the bed, and it seemed that George noticed Harvey's eyes trying to figure out what was inside, because he pounced on the bag and handed it over to Harvey. He had the biggest grin Harvey had ever seen.

"I got you a little something. I hope you don't mind," George scratched the back of his head.

Carefully, Harvey reached into the bag and he felt his hands close around something cold. Was it leather? Slowly, he pulled an expensive looking, leather-bound journal out of the bag. A metal latch twinkled in the light of the late afternoon sun. It was stunning.

"Put all your thoughts and ideas in here. Don't edit, just write. You never know when you're going to need to use them one day."

Harvey unlatched the metal clasp and flicked through the thick blank pages. It was more than just a *'small gift'*. The smell of the leather and how heavy it felt in his hand told him this.

"George," Harvey started, "this is too much. You've already done so much for me."

"Just tell me you'll use it," he smiled warmly, "I get most of my novel ideas from journals I wrote when I was your age."

If that was how George did it, that's how Harvey was going to do it. He was, technically still on his internship, so maybe he would learn something after all.

"I promise," he nodded, clutching it to his chest, "I love it."

With a rather awkward lingering smile, George bowed out of the room, telling Harvey that he was going to give him some time to get used to his new surroundings. The second he'd closed the door, he wasted no time searching for a pen. He found a beautiful fountain pen in the nightstand, and instantly dropped himself onto the huge, plush bed to scribble down his thoughts.

He wrote about how embarrassed and ashamed he was of his drunken brother, he wrote about how he had found a new home that he never wanted to leave, and he wrote about how he was starting to feel things for George, and he didn't know if he could control them.

EIGHT

George's eyes burst open as the sun poured into his bedroom, through the tiny gap in the curtains. He rolled over looking for Paula, forgetting that she hadn't been there all week. Groggily rubbing the sleep from his eyes, he remembered that Harvey was in the guest bedroom next door and with a smile, he jumped out of bed and pulled on his dressing gown. Slowly, he crept down the hallway, pushing open the already open door to see if Harvey was awake.

The door creaked open and George let out a small gasp when he saw Harvey's bruised body on the bed, face down. He was less concerned about the cover falling off in the night to expose his slender body, and more concerned with the deep purple bruises that covered every inch of his back. Only a few small patches of pale skin were left untouched.

Standing in Harvey's doorway, he tried to think back to when he'd seen him when they were gardening. He couldn't remember any bruises, but then he remembered the weekend he hadn't seen Harvey, and he immediately started to piece things together.

When Harvey rolled over, he jumped back into the hallway,

heading straight to the kitchen to prepare breakfast, but he had more than food on his mind.

"Do I smell bacon?" George spun around and saw Harvey walk into the kitchen wearing a dressing gown that was tied tight up to his chin.

His short black hair stuck up in every direction, his eyes still half shut with sleep.

"Hungry?" George smiled weakly, trying to hide his anger as he slid the huge plate of bacon on the counter.

George watched Harvey tucking into the bacon and he felt satisfied that he'd done the right thing bringing him home. How could he start asking Harvey questions about the bruises without letting Harvey know that he'd seen him naked on top of his bed. He hadn't meant to stare, but his eyes had wandered down his body, even if he tried to stop them.

"I came into your room this morning to see if you were awake," George started.

"Oh?"

"I saw the bruises on your back Harvey."

Harvey swallowed the piece of bacon he'd been chewing and tossed the leftover onto the plate.

"It's nothing," he folded his arms, staring at the bacon.

"He did this to you, didn't he?" George asked, sounding angrier than he intended to.

He emphasized *'he'*, not wanting to say Leo's name.

"I said it's nothing," Harvey mumbled, "just forget you saw it. I've already forgotten about it."

George couldn't believe he was still trying to protect his brother after everything he'd done. He wanted to drive straight to his apartment and do the same to him. George wasn't a violent person, but there was something about Leo that made him want to be.

"It's not fine! Your back is black and blue," his voice was getting louder with every word, "please, let me see it properly. What if something's broken?"

"He didn't break anything."

That was as good a confession as George needed, and it

only made him hate Leo even more.

Leaving George at the breakfast bar with the quickly cooling bacon, he slid off the stool and walked over to the sink, filling a tall glass with water. George could tell he was trying his best to avoid him, but George wasn't going to let it drop so easily.

"Please Harvey," he walked over to Harvey.

He sipped the water slowly, but tossed the rest back into the sink, sending it splashing all over the counter. Hands shaking, he dropped the glass onto the side, and spun around, pulling his dressing gown tightly together.

"C'mon George, just leave it?" his voice was trembling.

"I can't just leave it," George reached out, grabbing at the tie around the dressing gown.

He hadn't meant to, but he ripped open the dressing gown. Yellow and purple bruises covered every part of his upper body. George's eyes followed the dark trail of hair down Harvey's flat stomach. He'd been expecting him to be wearing underwear. It was only for a couple of seconds, but his eyes lingered, taking in the sight of Harvey's flaccid penis.

Ripping his eyes back up to his bruised chest, the anger bubbled away in his own chest.

"Look what he's done to you!" George whispered softly, as he reached out, stroking his fingertips across the tender bruises.

In a flash, Harvey yanked the dressing gown together with trembling hands. Not looking George in the eye, he knotted the tie, and folded his arms across his chest, as if to tell George not to do it again.

"It's not as bad as it looks," he mumbled quietly.

"How can you say that?" he yelled, not meaning to sound so angry, "I could have stopped this happening. I should never have let you get out of my car the first time I dropped you off."

"I don't need you to save me!"

With that, he pushed past George, making sure to hit their

shoulders together. Clinging onto his dressing gown, he ran out of the kitchen, and George heard his footsteps head back up his stairs.

Not wanting to make the situation any worse, George slid onto one of the breakfast stools, planting his face heavily in his hands. He instantly regretted pushing Harvey, and even though he felt like he needed to apologize straight away, he stopped himself, knowing it would be better to give him some space. He ran his hands through his hair and down his face. Every time he thought about Harvey's bruised body, his mind wandered down the dark treasure trail, below his waist.

An hour and three cups of strong coffee later, George plucked up the courage to confront Harvey. He crept up the staircase and knocked gently on the guest bedroom door, not wanting to startle Harvey. He waited a few seconds for an answer, but when he didn't get one, he gently pushed the door open.

George's heart dropped to the ground when he didn't see Harvey in the room. He ran over to Harvey's closet expecting to see it emptied, but all of his clothes were still hanging where they'd put them the night before.

There was only one other place Harvey could be.

"Is everything okay in there?" he knocked softly on the bathroom door.

"Everything's fine. I'm just in the bath," he didn't sound fine.

George hesitated at the door. He didn't want to make things worse, but he had an overwhelming urge to properly explain himself. He shakily put his hand on the knob, twisted, and entered the bathroom.

Harvey's eyes widened. He was sitting in the middle of the bathtub and the sight of George entering made him pull his knees close to his body. George stepped over the dressing gown and sitting on the floor next to the bath, not trying to avert his eyes. Leaning his head against the cold porcelain, he looked into Harvey's bright green eyes, making sure to look as sorry as he could.

"I'm so sorry I did that," George didn't look away, "I should have controlled my anger better, I just -,"

"You just?"

"I feel so protective over you, and I don't know why. I shouldn't, but I do, and seeing you like that, I wanted to hurt Leo so bad."

Leo's name tasted dirty on his tongue.

Harvey broke the eye contact and gently rested his chin on his knees, small drops of water running from his wet hair and down his face.

"It happened at the weekend," he started, "I was going to come here on Saturday afternoon, but he came home. I told him that I was coming to see you and he just flipped. He started calling me all these names and he called me a waste of space and he started to hit me. I fell to the ground to cover my face, but he started kicking me instead. You probably didn't even want me here. It was the weekend and -"

"I waited for you to come," George interrupted, "I really hoped you would."

George wanted to reach out and stroke Harvey's wet hair out of his eyes, but he resisted. He'd already over stepped the mark once.

"He was screaming at me '*You should have died in that fire with them you little faggot*', and I got to thinking, that maybe he was right?"

A small drop of water ran down Harvey's cheek and splashed gently into the water. George couldn't figure out if it was a tear or not.

"Listen to me Harvey, you've got so much to live for. You're going to be an amazing writer one day very soon. You can't die until you have your book made into a better movie than mine."

Harvey laughed softly.

"I doubt that will happen."

"I'm not going to let anything happen to you now. You've got my promise. I'm here for you as long as you need me, and you are staying here as long as you need to."

"What about Paula?"

George hadn't even considered Paula. He felt guilty that he'd barely even noticed she wasn't there anymore. He knew the second she returned home, she would flip about Harvey being there, but he'd cross that bridge when he came to it.

"I'll deal with Paula. Right now, it's just you and me."

He liked the sound of those words out loud.

'It's just you and me.'

"I feel like there's something connecting us, ever since I met you in the bookstore. You remind me so much of myself when I was your age."

He couldn't explain why, but he felt like there was an invisible rope drawing him to Harvey, and every minute they spent together, the rope was shrinking, dragging them closer together.

"I didn't mean what I said," Harvey said, "when I said you didn't need to save me. I kind of like you saving me."

Harvey closed his eyes and rested his cheek on his knees, and he smiled softly with his eyes. George didn't know what compelled him, but it was like he couldn't stop himself. Slowly, he leaned in, brushing his lips tenderly against Harvey's. It tingled, and excited him, as Harvey leaned into the kiss, his body relaxing in the water. Opening his mouth to Harvey, he let their tongues brush together softly. Harvey's breath was shaking, reflecting his own.

Cupping Harvey's cheek in his hands, he felt the soft stubble against the palm. He stroked even harder, kissing him deeper, the stubble grating against his skin. That's when he remembered he was kissing a guy, that's when he remembered he was kissing Harvey.

"You're just a kid," George muttered, almost to himself.

"I'm 19!" Harvey protested.

George tried not to look at Harvey, his kiss still fresh on his lips. When he did look, Harvey was begging him to kiss him again.

"I'm sorry," George mumbled as he clumsily stood up,

knocking a potted plant off a small table, causing it to fall to the ground and smash.

Soil and terracotta pot scattered across the bathroom floor.

"George?" Harvey whispered.

"I'm sorry," he said again, "I shouldn't have-,"

***

George ran out of the door, leaving Harvey hugging his knees tightly against his chest. Any warmth he'd felt had quickly left his body as quickly as it had entered. He felt as though he was sat in a bath of ice cold water.

NINE

Weeks passed and the kiss wasn't mentioned. George seemed like he was trying to pretend it never happened, and Harvey was trying to find the right moment to bring it up.

The end of April signaled the end of Harvey's internship and he was soon at high school once again, but Harvey was surprised when George didn't ask him to leave on the last day. They never talked about it, but when he came back from his first day back at school to find his clothes still in the closet and his journal still on the night stand, he knew that George was going to keep up his promise to keep him safe.

Kiss, or no kiss.

Harvey quickly learned all about George's *Annual Writer's Barbecue*. Every year, George invited hundreds of his fellow writers, publishers, editors and agents from all over America for a huge get together in his garden, and he'd promised Harvey that it was the social event in the writing world's calendar. For one night, they'd pretend they weren't in cutthroat competition with each other and they'd drink all of George's wine, eat all of his food and mock each other's books with dry smirks on their faces.

"Can you grab me the burgers from the trunk kid?" George chopped onions, "people should be arriving soon."

They'd been to the grocery store early that morning to get every possible supply they could need. When George collected his special order of 300 burgers and 300 sausages, Harvey knew he wasn't joking when he'd said *'hundreds of writers'*. He was even more shocked when he saw the bill.

The last barbecue Harvey had attended was one his father had hosted. It made him yearn for his parents to be there. As he grabbed the boxes from the trunk, he pushed the thought of his parents to the back of his mind, not wanting to ruin what was promised to be a fun day.

"Let's get changed," George nervously glanced at the clock, "we don't have long."

Pulling a pair of torn jeans and a stained shirt from the closet, he knew nothing would be right for the party. He wanted to impress the people George was inviting, not just because they were part of the world he wanted to be part of. He wanted them to like him, by George's side.

With a soft knock on George's bedroom door, he pushed open the door, not waiting for a response. It's what they both did, neither of them seeming to care about the other one walking in. Stepping onto the soft, cream carpet, his heart stopped when he saw George, standing in front of the floor length mirror, in nothing more than a pair of tight, white briefs. Harvey admired him for a second, George seemed to be unaware that he was standing there. He'd seen him shirtless before, but he'd never seen the legs to match. The backs of his thighs were strong and defined, lightly covered in hair, running up to meet with his perfectly plumb backside.

Clearing his throat, Harvey stepped forwards.

"George, I have no idea what to wear. I don't think I have anything nice enough."

George's head turned in the mirror to look at Harvey, but he didn't try to cover himself up. He smiled, tilting his head to the side.

"Who you trying to impress, kid?" he smiled through the reflection.

George ducked into the closet to dig through his clothes, so Harvey walked over, hovering by the entrance, watching as George reached up, the muscles in his shoulder stretching out.

"This might fit you," George pulled a blue shirt with a white collar from the closet, "It hasn't fit me for years."

Harvey thought about going back to his bedroom to try it on when he realized George had already seen him naked. He pulled his T-Shirt over his messy hair and glanced at his bruised body in the mirror. The bruises were starting to fade slightly, but his chest and shoulders were still covered in yellow and pink blotches.

In the mirror, he caught a glimpse of George's bulge in the tight underwear. He held his breath for a moment and stared, but when George's eyes flicked in the mirror, he looked away and stuffed his arms into the crisp shirt.

"What do you think?" Harvey buttoned up the shirt.

He could never have imagined George being as slim as him, so he was surprised that it fit him so well. George turned around to look at Harvey as he buttoned up his own shirt.

"You look perfect," he grinned.

Harvey stood for a moment and admired him, somehow feeling like they were a real couple. Borrowing each other's clothes and getting dressed in front of each other was something he thought only people in love did. They were so relaxed around each other, it made Harvey yearn for so much more. He tried to push the images of sleeping with George to the back of his mind when George spritzed them both with his usual manly scent. Harvey inhaled deeply. Every time he breathed in, butterflies bounced around his stomach.

Within the hour, just as promised, hundreds of guests started to arrive, filling George's house and garden.

"I met most of this group at writer's conventions," he

introduced Harvey to a group of stylish writers, "they're a strange bunch aren't they?"

"Oh shut it Georgey boy," one of the women with glasses laughed, "Come back to me when someone makes a *successful* adaptation of one of your books."

Her emphasis on '*successful*' made everyone laugh including George. He was the first to admit how terrible his movie was, Harvey knew that.

"Have you seen the *Terminal* movie series?" he whispered as they walked towards another tiny group of writers besides the pool.

Harvey nodded. He loved those movies.

"Well you just met the writer of the books. She's a snooty little bitch, but that's why we love her."

Suddenly aware that he was probably surrounded by bestselling authors, he glanced around the garden, wondering how many of their books he read sat on the bookstore floor.

"Greg, I want you to meet Harvey," George introduced Harvey to a man with white hair who he'd had earlier pointed out as his publisher, "Harvey is an up and coming author and he's rather talented. He puts me to shame."

The little man, looked Harvey up and down curiously and shook his hand.

"Harvey, eh? Have I read any of your work?" he raised a white eyebrow.

Harvey didn't know what to say. He hadn't written anything for him to read, apart from in the journal George had bought him. He'd written in that every night since he'd given it to him, but he wasn't ever going to show those words to anyone.

"Not yet Greg, my old friend, but the minute he finishes his manuscript, we'll make sure to give you first refusal."

Greg gave them an amused smile as he headed off to talk to another group of people.

"Why did you tell him that I was an amazing writer with a half-finished book?" Harvey was dumbfounded

"Because he's the best in the business and I just got your

57

foot in the door," George winked at him out of the corner of his eye, "you can thank me later."

He left Harvey chatting with another group of authors, to fire up the barbecue. They were all fascinated with George's new prodigy and probed him all about his book. Out of nowhere, Harvey started telling them all the story of a boy who lost his parents and was left, to be raised by his alcoholic brother until the love of his life came along and saved him.

Harvey couldn't believe it when they all started lapping it up with enthusiasm and the more times he told it, the more he convinced himself he had already written the book. He was sure he'd even seen one woman tear up.

Harvey couldn't believe his luck. He was at a party with authors and publishers telling them about his work, which he had yet to write. He knew that whenever he came to release something, these people would be eagerly waiting and claiming to have known him before he made it big. He couldn't imagine ever having a priceless experience like it, if he'd never met George in that bookstore.

The afternoon turned to evening and the party roared on. People got steadily drunk as the hundreds of dollars' worth of alcohol dwindled down. Even Harvey let himself have a few glasses of wine.

Midnight approached and the party started to thin down. After George managed to politely push the last few hardcore partiers into taxis, he collapsed into a chair on the patio, next to the pool. Harvey was walking around the pool collecting cans and plates of food, stuffing them into a trash bag.

"Oh, just leave that kid," George laughed, "we'll deal with it tomorrow. Come sit."

Harvey walked over to George, his head was lulled to one side. He'd seen George drinking considerably more than he had, and the few glasses of wine he'd had were already wearing off.

"Thank you for tonight," George grinned.

"What did I do?" Harvey collapsed in the chair next to him.

"Whatever you were telling those people, you made them

freaking love you. They all think I've discovered the next big thing in writing."

Harvey wanted to tell him about his book idea, but he was nervous about how he'd take the ending.

"I haven't written anything yet," Harvey gazed sleepily at the twinkling lanterns in the trees, as they reflected in the calm blue surface of the pool.

"No, but you will when the time is right. And when you do, these vultures will be waiting."

Harvey knew he was right. He knew the pressure should scare him, but he quite liked the thought of people wanting to hear what he had to say for a change.

"It's such a beautiful night," George turned his head lazily to the sky, "so many stars out."

Harvey chuckled. This was the first time he'd seen George drunk and he was enjoying the cuteness of it.

"Let's go swimming!" George shouted, stumbling up and pulling his shoes off.

Harvey ran over and grabbed George before he fell into the pool fully clothed. For a moment, George struggled, but he relaxed and stared down into Harvey's eyes. His hot alcohol breath hit Harvey's face.

A wicked look spread across George's face as he grabbed Harvey's arms in a tight grip. He picked Harvey up like he weighed no more than a bag of sugar and launched him into the deep end of the pool, cannonballing straight in after him.

The water hit Harvey like a cold slap to the face. After a few seconds under the water, he resurfaced, gasping and rubbing the chemicals from his eyes. He was surprised it was so cold considering how hot it was outside, even at midnight. He shuddered as the sensation swept over his body, his clothes clinging awkwardly to his skin. George's hysterical laughter broke through his shivering.

"You think you're so funny don't you?" Harvey said through chattered teeth as he kicked his legs to try and stay above the water.

He wasn't the strongest swimmer.

He splashed George in the face then gave in and joined in the laughing. George swam over to him and they started wrestling, fully clothed in the water. Through the laughter and splashing, Harvey could see how much fun George was having, and it warmed him inside.

"What are you thinking?" George asked through heavy breaths.

"That I'm happy."

The small smile on George's lips made Harvey's heart warm, despite being in the cold water.

"Me too," George whispered.

As they got out of the pool, Harvey tried to hide the bulge in the front of his jeans, and he was sure that he noticed George trying to do the same.

***

After peeling the wet clothes off his muscular body, George jumped into the downstairs shower. He was still rock solid so he took his shaft in his hand, gently massaging it.

The alcohol washed over him and images of Harvey raced through his mind. He thought about him getting in the bath, he thought about him naked on the bed, he thought about his robe hanging open and he didn't try to push the images from his head. Instead, he let them in.

He knew it was wrong, but he wanted it.

Closing his eyes, he let the hot water run over his body, thinking about the kiss. He pumped and pumped, imagining what it would be like to kiss him again.

TEN

George stared sleepily into the mug of coffee. Hugging it close to his body, he tried to remember what happened the night before. Choruses of laughter and endless glasses of wine raced through his mind. He tossed the aspirin into his mouth and forced it down with a mouthful of the boiling, black coffee.

The door opened, and Harvey walked in, fully clothed. Pulling his dressing gown tightly across his chest, he leaned forwards and put his coffee on the table.

"Did we have plans?" he asked, surprised by the new croaky quality to his voice.

As he stared at Harvey, he suddenly felt water rushing over his body. Had they gone swimming?

"It's Leo. He wants to meet me," Harvey didn't make eye contact.

"No way," George suddenly felt a lot more sober, "not a chance!"

He jumped up and pulled his dressing gown together as the

tie started to wriggle lose. There was no way he was going to let Leo get anywhere near Harvey.

"He called me this morning, asking where I've been. I told him I've been at a friend's."

"It took him long enough," George was bitter.

Whenever Leo was mentioned, his blood started to boil in a way that made George feel uncomfortable. He quickly ran upstairs, ripping his dressing gown off as he did. He emerged minutes later fully dressed, pulling on a leather jacket as he ran down the stairs.

"If you're going, I'm coming with you."

Harvey looked like he was about to protest but he didn't. He pursed his lips slightly, and smiled, nodding in agreement. George knew that Harvey would never ask, but he could see it in his eyes that he didn't really want to face Leo alone.

As they drove in silence to the café where Leo was waiting, George looked nervously at Harvey more than once. He didn't think this was a good idea, but he didn't want to say that. If Harvey wanted to do it, he'd stand next to him, but all the bruises on Harvey's body wouldn't leave his mind, making him tighten his knuckles on the steering wheel. For Harvey's sake, he was going to stay cool, even if he had the urge to do something else.

***

Outside of the small café, Harvey could see Leo through the window, already waiting for him. He tried to reassure himself that everything was going to be okay, especially with George by his side, but it wasn't that simple. Nodding to George, they headed into the café, the small bell above the door ringing out.

"What's he doing here?" Leo jumped out of his seat, looking ready to attack.

"I asked him to come."

Harvey didn't mince his words. He wasn't in the mood to pander to Leo's pathetic games. He wanted to know what he had to say, and then he wanted to get out of there and get back to his life without him.

"I wanted to talk to you. *Alone*," he whispered, leaning into the table.

Harvey settled into one of the seats, and George sat next to him, so that he was directly across from Leo.

"Too bad," George's voice was flat, "I don't trust you, or your fists."

His face quickly turned a deep shade of red, his fists clenching on the table. He shot Harvey a look that said *'why would you tell him?'*, but he couldn't hold his gaze.

Glancing up to him again, he was sure that Leo's eyes were focusing a lot more than usual. Was he sober, or was he just waiting for his next drink?

"What do you want?" Harvey asked bluntly.

Leo shrugged, and leaned back in the plastic chair, looking down at his hands, as they fumbled together.

"I wanted to know where you've been bro, I was worried about you," he muttered.

Leo was worried about him? Harvey wanted to laugh. He hadn't been worried about him for years.

"He's been gone for weeks, and now you're worried?" George jumped in, the anger rising in his voice, "Have you lost your punching bag?"

Harvey stamped on George's foot under the table, cutting him off before he said anymore. George's shoulders dropped, and he relaxed back into the chair. Luckily for both of them, Leo didn't take the bait, he didn't even look in George's direction.

"When are you coming home?"

"I don't know," Harvey stared at the menu, which was taped messily to the table in front of him, "I might not be coming home."

Leo breathed in slowly, turning his head to stare out of the window at the sunny sky. Squinting his eyes, he looked calm and casual, but it wasn't long before he shot his head in George's direction, his eyes turning to slits. That was the Leo

Harvey knew.

"This is your fault," he hissed, "we were fine until you showed up with your books. You make me sick."

This was the ammunition George had been waiting for. Standing up, he knocked the plastic chair over with a crash, towering over Leo, his shoulders and chest inflating as the veins in his neck bulged out. Harvey could do nothing but sit and watch.

"I'm sick?" he cried, "I've seen your apartment and I know what you've been doing to your brother. You're the disgrace here, not me."

Leo stood up and squared up to him over the table, their foreheads almost touching. Harvey knew that Leo wouldn't be scared of George, despite his slight frame.

Harvey watched, frozen, as they looked ready to rip each other's throats out. Feeling the eyes of everybody in the small café on them, he knew he was the only one who could stop them.

"Stop it, please!" he said, "Both of you, just sit down."

They hovered, still staring at each other, but George was the first to back down, picking up the chair and sitting next to Harvey. Leo copied, and they sat in silence, Leo and George still staring each other out.

"I'm not coming home Leo. I'm staying with George until I figure out what to do next."

Leo's lips snarled into a dry smirk.

"You know he's a little queer, don't you? Caught him with a guy once," Leo's eyes darted to Harvey, "didn't you know?"

Leo's words cut through Harvey like a knife, his cheeks burning red. He could feel himself starting to shake, but he didn't dare move. George didn't move, he just continued his death stare.

"I bet you're a queer as well. I bet you and my faggot brother have been fucking every chance you get. You're a sick pervert," Leo whispered darkly.

"I'd shut up if I was you," George stayed calm.

Harvey darted from Leo to George, knowing whatever

happened next, he couldn't stop it.

"What you gonna do? Kiss me?" Leo stood up again.

George followed, towering over Leo. They dared each other to make the first move, edging further across the table, as if they were actually going to kiss. As if in slow motion, Harvey watched Leo launch his arm back, before striking George in the side of the mouth. He looked like he tried to duck out of the way, but he wasn't fast enough.

Everyone in the café suddenly sprung out of their chairs, backing away to the edges of the room. A woman gasped loudly, as George wiped away the blood from the corner of his mouth. Harvey wasn't sure what was going to happen next, so he stood, watching, like everyone else.

With a swift punch under the chin, George sent Leo crashing backwards, into one of the plastic chairs, the legs snapping under his weight. Plates of half-eaten food slid off the upturned table, the smashing crockery echoing around the silent café.

"George!" Harvey found his voice, "Let's just get out of here!"

George seemed reluctant to look away from Leo, as he scrambled up from the ground. Glancing around the café, his eyes and face softened, and the George who Harvey knew returned.

He opened his wallet and threw a fist full of bills on the counter, apologizing to the thin, old woman who owned the place. He opened the door for Harvey and the small bell above it rang throughout the silent café. He glanced again at Leo, wanting to feel regret, but all he felt was pity.

Leaving Leo to deal with the mess in the café, they headed back to George's house, in silence. It wasn't until they were back in George's house that he spoke.

"I'm sorry."

"It's fine," Harvey shook his head, kicking off his shoes, "I've wanted to do that for years."

George gave him a small smile, dropping his car keys on

the side table.

"Is it true what your brother said?"

Harvey's stomach dropped. He knew exactly what he was talking about, but pretended not to.

"What are you talking about?"

"Are you gay, Harvey?"

Harvey reached in and dabbed at the fresh blood with his sleeve.

"Does it matter?"

He'd never told anyone before.

"Of course it doesn't," George said softly.

He reached out, and pressed Harvey's hand into his cheek, gently wrapping his fingers around Harvey's. Harvey wanted nothing more than to lean in and kiss George, but he stopped himself. The kiss in the bathtub had been a mistake, he knew that. It was obvious George had regretted it, because he never mentioned it again.

Pulling his hand away, he turned around and faced the front door, unsure of what to say. Was there any point hiding anymore? He'd never kept it a secret from George, he'd just not told him. If George had known from the start, would he have acted differently with Harvey?

"Yes. I am. I'm gay."

When he turned around George was directly behind him, so that they were now chest to chest. Staring down at the cut on George's lip, he reached in again, touching it with his fingers, unable to stop himself.

"Why didn't you just tell me?" he whispered softly, "It's not a big deal."

"I didn't want you to hate me," Harvey shrugged, not taking his eyes away from the cut.

George slid his fingers around Harvey's shoulder, pulling him in tightly. Harvey let him, wrapping his arms around George's middle. Resting his head on his shoulder, he inhaled George's cologne.

"I could never hate you, kid," George's voice tickled Harvey's ear.

Harvey smiled wildly, burying his face even further into George's shoulder. They were so close, closer than he'd been to anyone in a long time. Softly, George's fingers stroked his shoulder blades, his lips practically touching his ear.

He didn't know what made him want to say it, but he suddenly couldn't stop himself. It was on the tip of his tongue, and he let it fall out.

"I love you," Harvey whispered.

ELEVEN

"**W**hat do you mean, you can't do anything?" George shouted across the desk at the principal.

"I'm sorry Mr. Lewis," Principal Jenkins stayed calm, "Unless Harvey comes to us personally to ask for help about his situation, we can't do anything."

"But I'm telling you about his situation!" George cried.

The little man sat behind his desk and didn't flinch. He looked just like the principal from George's high school, so he instantly disliked him. The few strands of hair left on his head were combed messily over the huge bald patch in the center of his shiny scalp. He was a short dumpy man in a creased suit with a thick gray mustache covering his top lip, which moved when he spoke.

"We appreciate your assistance with Harvey's internship, but your duty to Harvey has already ended. Thank you," and with that he looked down at his paperwork over his glasses, letting George know it was time for him to leave.

Back in his car, George was trying to calm himself, but he was furious. He'd gone to the high school to tell the principal about Harvey's brother beating him and being an alcoholic in hopes they could help Harvey, missing out that Harvey was currently living with him.

The last few days had been tricky for him. He didn't know what to do or what he was feeling. He felt like he was getting in too deep. Ever since Harvey's admission, he'd felt weird. Not because it sounded like the confession of a silly lovesick teenager, but because it sounded very adult and very real, and he didn't know how it made him feel. He couldn't deny that he'd felt something rumble inside of him when he heard the words, but he'd quickly pulled away from the hug.

He didn't know what to say to Harvey any more, nor did he know how to act around him.

He hit his hands down on the steering wheel, causing his horn to let out a long and loud honk, making a group of teenagers jump and curse violently at him.

Later that day, when Harvey arrived home from school, he slammed the door, causing the front part of the house to shake. George felt it from the kitchen and decided the best thing to do was to confront Harvey in the hall.

"Why were you at my school today?" Harvey dumped his bag, planting his hands on his hips.

Had he seen him? Had the principal told him? He hadn't wanted Harvey to find out.

"I went to talk to your principal," George confessed, "to try and get you some help."

Quickly blinking, Harvey furrowed his brow in confusion.

"I thought I had help? I thought you were my help?" his voice started to rise, "You told me you wouldn't let anything happen to me."

George didn't know what to say.

"Things have got complicated," George ran his hands through his hair.

"Complicated? More complicated than you moving me in? More complicated than you watching me in the bath and kissing me? More complicated than you touching me every chance you get? More complicated than me telling you that I love you and you saying nothing back?"

Harvey looked hysterical, but George didn't know what to say. Hearing everything fired back at him like that, it was all too much. Harvey was right about everything. He'd been pushing him further and further, seeing how far he could go, without even meaning to.

George couldn't say anything. He didn't have the words to defend himself, because there were no words. Instead, he grabbed Harvey's shoulders and pulled him in. Staring down at him, he closed his eyes and quickly pressed their lips together. He didn't know what he was expecting, but he liked it, even more than the time he'd kissed Harvey in the bath. He didn't stop himself, instead, he pulled Harvey in again, kissing him even harder. Their lips smacked together, George's tongue pressing against Harvey's lips, trying to force its way in. It felt so right, even though he knew it was wrong. He wasn't thinking about Paula, or that Harvey was a guy, because somehow, it felt right.

"See what I mean," Harvey pushed him away, his lips red, "You're messed in the head. I feel like your toy."

George didn't' know what to say, he just wanted to kiss Harvey again, and he didn't want to stop. He wanted to go further than he should have, wanting to feel one with Harvey. He wanted to give him everything, to protect him from the world, to keep him close.

When he felt the urge to scream out, he didn't stop himself.

"I think I love you too, okay?" he screamed.

"What?" was all Harvey could say, "You think you love me?"

George didn't think it anymore. He knew it. He didn't understand it, but he knew that's where his protectiveness came from. It was fresh and exciting, and it was something he'd never felt before.

"You've brought me back to life and you're the reason I wake up in the morning. You're so fucking amazing Harvey and you don't even know it. I got scared. I have a wife, and this situation is a mess -"

Harvey silenced George with a kiss. He led George up the grand staircase, not breaking away from his lips. They tore each other's clothes off and collapsed onto George's bed.

TWELVE

"I'm so sorry for your loss," George whispered sleepily into the cellphone, to Paula's brother.

George assumed that Paula was too distraught to call him herself to let him know that her mother had died. Harry, her brother, let George know she would be staying for a couple more weeks to help arrange the funeral.

Hanging up the phone, he threw it onto his nightstand in the dark and it bounced off and landed with a soft thud on the carpet. The red LED display of his alarm clock let him know that it was 4am. Rolling over in the bed, his body brushed against Harvey's, and for the first time in a long time, he didn't feel lonely anymore.

None of it had been a dream.

Smiling he leaned into Harvey and started kissing his neck. Harvey rolled over and smiled out of his sleep grabbing George and returning the kiss.

As they rolled over holding each other closely, George should have felt sorry for Paula, but he surprised himself by feeling nothing. It was then that he knew their marriage had been dead for a long time, neither of them wanting to admit it.

***

Light poured into the bedroom and Harvey groggily opened his eyes. He looked over to George's naked body on the bed next to him and smiled wildly to himself. He couldn't believe what had happened but he wasn't going to question it. Before jumping out of bed he leaned over and kissed George gently on the lips before heading down to the kitchen.

"Don't move," George's voice startled Harvey as he was pouring the coffee.

He almost splashed it on his naked body.

Harvey wanted to turn around to see George, but he stood still as he was told.

"Perfect," George sighed, "just perfect. I could stand here staring at that gorgeous butt all day."

Harvey laughed and turned around to see George also completely naked. He placed the two cups of coffee on the counter. He pinched himself, expecting to wake up any moment. It felt like a weight had lifted, and they were doing what they'd wanted to do for weeks.

"You did, several times last night," he said as he draped his arms around George, kissing his neck over and over.

"I'm so happy right now," Harvey whispered softly into George's ear, "I want you to know that."

"So am I," he leaned in and kissed Harvey softly on the lips, "and Paula's mother died last night so she won't be coming back for at least another month."

Harvey examined George's face and for a second he couldn't believe that George was happy about the death of his mother-in-law, but it meant they had weeks more of uninterrupted happiness.

"I'm sorry," Harvey mumbled.

"She'll be fine," he shrugged, "she has her family. I don't even think she wants me with her. She hasn't called me in weeks."

ASHLEY JOHN

The question about what happened when Paula did eventually come back, burned loudly in Harvey's mind. He knew the weeks would fly by, and it couldn't continue like it had been when she was home. Would she even let him live there?

"How do you feel about getting out of town for the weekend?" George asked as he drank his coffee and flicked through the morning mail.

Harvey smiled and sat next to George at the breakfast bar.

"What do you mean?" Harvey laughed.

"I have a little cabin up in the woods. It's gorgeous and there's a lake, and it's completely secluded."

"It sounds perfect," Harvey said, leaning in to kiss George.

"Good! Go pack a bag, we're going now," George jumped up and headed for the door, motioning for Harvey to follow him, "or are you just going to sit there all day and stare at my dick?"

"Can't I do both?" Harvey laughed.

"You did that several times last night," George winked, echoing what Harvey had said earlier, and ran up to the bedroom.

As they sped down the freeway, Harvey couldn't believe how fast things had moved. Overnight, George had told him that he loved him, and now they were heading to a romantic cabin for a lovers getaway. He looked over to George in his sunglasses, as the wind from the rolled down window ruffled his hair. He wished he had a camera in that moment because he wanted to capture all of George's beauty.

"Stop staring at me," George smiled, not taking his eyes away from the road, "it's weird."

Harvey laughed and looked ahead, "Sorry, I can't help it, you're just too damn gorgeous."

George took his eyes off the road for a moment and threw Harvey a cheeky smile.

"No," George said, "you're the gorgeous one."

As George drove down the tiny, bending dirt roads through the forest, the trees blurred as they whizzed past the window.

He drove like he knew the roads like the back of his hand, twisting and turning without hesitation.

Harvey nearly didn't spot the cabin, it's wooden exterior almost blending in beautifully with the trees. It was a small log cabin, raised off the ground on small stilts. Up a small flight of stairs, there was a little porch deck with two wooden chairs. Directly across from the cabin was a clear and calm lake, which went on for as far as the eye could see.

It was perfect.

Harvey tried to see another cabin along the tree line, but he couldn't. He wondered if they were all as well hidden as the cabin in front of him, or if they really were truly alone.

"My Dad built this. He was a carpenter," George started to unload the car, "they bought this plot of land when I was just a kid. I spent so many summers here."

"It's amazing."

It was like something out of a fairytale. Harvey's heart started to swell in his chest. He felt like he was in a fairytale, and George was his prince charming.

When George opened the door and they stepped into the dark, musty cabin, Harvey felt like they were stepping into their first home together.

"I haven't been up here for a long time. I used to come up here to write a lot in the beginning," George headed out back to fire up the generator.

As Harvey pulled the dustsheets off all of the furniture, the lights suddenly sprang into action, revealing a beautifully decorated cabin. A wood burning, stone fireplace was embedded into the wooden wall, and the rest of the walls were lined with family photos and deer heads.

Harvey examined the photos closer and he saw photos of a man and a woman smiling at the camera with a small boy in between them with scruffy brown hair. Harvey's skin tingled seeing George as a little boy. He couldn't believe how cute he looked.

"I see you've met the family," George returned with fresh

firewood.

He dumped the logs on the ground and joined Harvey, who was admiring a picture on the fireplace. It was of a small boy stood next to a lake holding a huge fish proudly in his hands. Harvey recognized it as the lake outside. A pretty woman with peroxide blonde hair stood next to him, beaming down at her son.

"Your mother is beautiful," Harvey said placing a hand on George's shoulder, "you looked like a really happy family."

"Yeah. We were back then," George said as he started to toss the logs in the fireplace, "It's crazy how things can change so quickly."

The fire sprung into life and the flames gently roared in the fireplace, the amber lights licking wood, making him think back to his own mother and father. He'd always wondered if they'd woken up and tried to escape, or if the smoke had taken them in their sleep.

His mind wandered to his brother. He imagined him sat alone in his apartment, drinking. Maybe he had his scumbag friends around, or maybe he was slouched in a gutter somewhere, begging for money? Harvey tried not to feel sorry for him, but he couldn't help it.

"Wine?" George pulled two glasses out of the cupboard.

George's smile had a strange effect on Harvey. It made him weak at the knees and made him forget everything else. As they sat at the wooden table drinking a vintage bottle of red wine, Harvey found himself enjoying alcohol for the first time. He never wanted to drink because of his brother, but he was starting to like the feeling as the warm fuzziness spread over him.

"I can't believe we're here right now," Harvey laughed, taking another sip of the dark liquid, "this is insane."

"Tell me about it," George smiled as he reached out and grabbed Harvey's hand, "I'm not questioning it though. I just feel so happy."

"What about Paula?" Harvey said.

He regretted the words the moment they'd left his lips, but

he was dying to know where he stood in relation to the wife. They had been married for nearly ten years. Harvey didn't know if George still had feelings for her, but he knew he must have once.

George nervously pulled his hand away from Harvey's and topped up his glass.

"We'll cross that bridge when we come to it," George smiled weakly.

Harvey's stomach knotted at the realization that George might not leave his wife for him. He wanted to push the matter, feeling confused, but he didn't want to ruin what was supposed to be a romantic trip.

Harvey tried to make eye contact with George, but George was avoiding his gaze.

"What are we going to eat?" Harvey asked, realizing they hadn't packed any food in their hurry to get on the freeway before the mid-afternoon rush.

He glanced over to the cupboards, but he assumed they were empty.

"There's a store about a mile east. It's a tiny place, but it'll have what we need for a few days. Either that, or we could go hunting?"

Harvey laughed, but as George nodded towards the many deer heads mounted lifelessly on the walls, the thought crossed his mind that he might not be joking.

"You're kidding, right?" Harvey gave the nearest deer a nervous sideways glance.

George jumped up, a wicked smile spreading across his lips.

"When you said a romantic break, this isn't what I had in mind," Harvey said as he stepped over a tree branch into a huge muddy patch of dirt.

It seemed that George's family had been keen hunters, as they had all of the hunting gear and guns locked away in the cabin. As Harvey stepped into the muddy bog in his borrowed boots, he secretly thanked George's father for having the same size feet as him.

"This is fun!" George laughed, grabbing Harvey's hand and pulling him further into the forest.

"Is this even legal?" Harvey shouted as he rushed ahead, with his gun slung over his back.

"Who cares? Who's gonna hear anything out here?" George laughed, "Come on, the tracks go this way."

Harvey started to think that this place was less like a fairytale and more like a horror movie. He was sure he'd heard stories of people being taken out into the woods and shot where nobody could hear them. Harvey tried to convince himself that George wasn't a crazy person, as he stared nervously at the huge riffle bouncing against George's back.

He had to admit that George looked handsome in his leather boots, brown jacket and hunter's hat. His broad shoulders made him look grand and powerful.

George stopped walking and put his arm out, stopping Harvey. He put a finger to his lips and slowly pulled the gun from behind his back. Harvey squinted to where George was looking, and he saw a deer grazing on a patch of grass, totally unaware he had company.

George pulled the gun up to his shoulder and his finger softly started squeezing on the trigger.

"Please don't kill it," Harvey whispered, holding his breath.

Harvey was hardly an animal rights activist, but there was something about George killing a helpless deer. He didn't want to see George kill anything. He didn't want to see George shoot a gun.

He also suddenly remembered Bambi and how it almost ruined his childhood.

"Shhh," George purred softly.

Harvey reached out and put his hand on the top of the gun and slowly pushed it down.

"Think about its family," Harvey said, almost jokingly, "we don't need to eat deer tonight."

George glanced at Harvey out of the corner of his eye. He was doing his best puppy dog eyes, and the urge to kill disappeared from George's eyes.

Dropping the gun on the floor, he pushed Harvey up against the rough bark of a tree, grabbed his soft face and he kissed him passionately. Harvey heard the deer scarper off into the forest.

"This is why you're so special," George said as he pulled away from the kiss.

Harvey bit his lips and stared into George's deep, hazel eyes. Any trace of the hunter that scared Harvey was gone, and he'd never looked more attractive to him than he did then. Harvey grabbed George's face and they kissed wildly as George's hands fumbled with the awkward buttons on Harvey's jeans.

He ripped them down to Harvey's knees, and pulled down the tight blue underwear Harvey was wearing. Kissing Harvey's neck, he turned him around and pushed him up against the tree as he undid the belt on his own jeans.

THIRTEEN

H arvey smiled to George down the aisle as he examined an all-day breakfast in a can. He could see George's eyes staring in amusement as he tried to figure out how they fit a full breakfast into a tiny tin.

Shopping in the small supermarket reminded Harvey of when they first met in the bookstore. It felt so long ago, and so much had changed since then. Here they were, shopping in a tiny store in the middle of nowhere, further away from his brother than he'd ever been, but he'd never felt more at home.

George was his new home. Wherever George was, that's where Harvey wanted to be.

"This tiny can has a sausage, egg, tomatoes, toast and bacon," George whispered as he held the can up to Harvey.

The old man behind the counter gave George a look that read '*stupid tourists*', making George hastily put the can back down on the shelf.

The place was so small and there were only five aisles. Harvey didn't know how a place like this could even call itself a grocery store. It was more of a shack that happened to sell food.

When they walked to the counter with their small cart, the tiny, frail, white haired man gave George and Harvey a skeptical look.

"We don't get many of your kind round these parts," he said in a deep accent that Harvey didn't recognize.

"What kind is that?" George started to pack the groceries as the man scanned them.

"Y'know. Fruits," the man said, without a hint of irony.

For a second, Harvey nervously watched George. He wasn't sure if George knew how to handle it.

"Two men alone in the woods. That's not natural is it?" he said as he scanned the last of the items.

Harvey could see the anger bubbling up in George's face, but he didn't react.

"It's unchristian. I blame that Obama for supporting you lot," the man grumbled, almost to himself.

George slammed down the bag on the counter, making Harvey jump back. At first he thought he was going to reach over the counter and pull the tiny man over, to throw him up and down the aisles with his fist. Instead what he did, took Harvey by total surprise.

He grabbed Harvey's arms and locked his lips in the most passionate kiss Harvey had ever experienced. For a second, he almost forgot where they were and wanted George to take him there and then.

George pulled away from Harvey and pulled out his wallet.

"Now, are you going to take my queer money, or not, because I don't have a problem driving 30 miles to the next store."

Harvey suppressed a laugh when he saw the man's eyes open wide and his mouth gape. The man muttered the total and took George's money without another word.

George suppressed a smile as he shoved his wallet in his back pocket and bundled the paper bags in his arms, "Have a nice day."

George calmly walked out of the store. The little bell rang and Harvey ran after him. He threw the bags into the back seat and smiled gingerly at Harvey.

"I can't believe you just did that," Harvey ran over to the car, "You're insane."

"I am insane," he said as he pulled Harvey close by the waist, "and I'm not going to let anybody treat you like dirt ever again."

George kissed Harvey on the forehead before they got into the car and headed west, back to the log cabin as the sun started to set. When they pulled up outside the cabin, it was dark and the fire was still roaring inside. It was a warm night and the stars shone brightly in the sky, reflecting in the lake.

After they unpacked the shopping, Harvey hoped they could stay there forever. It was Saturday, and he didn't know how long they were staying for. He was back in school on Monday, but he didn't care if he never went back again. He'd only decided to finish high school over a vague promise he'd made to his parents at their funeral.

"Can we stay here?" Harvey asked as they sat down to eat a delicious meal of garlic chicken and steamed vegetables.

"If that's what you want, then we'll stay here forever," George laughed.

Harvey knew that George was joking, but he did know that George would do almost anything for him. As they ate their dinner by the twinkling candlelight, a question raced around Harvey's mind.

Would he ever leave Paula for him?

FOURTEEN

The weekend went by quickly by, and by Sunday night they were driving back to George's house. They'd spent Sunday swimming, having sex and sharing stories. George talked about the many summers he'd spent there with a warm smile on his face.

When it came to packing the car, Harvey begged George to let them stay, just a few more days, but he insisted they go back in time for Monday morning for Harvey's school. Harvey's graduation was around the corner and soon he'd be free. George promised to bring him back for a longer stay when high school was behind him and he had his diploma.

The hundreds of cars in the other lanes blurred past Harvey's eyes and he felt a sorrow that he couldn't shake off. He knew once they were back in town, their love would go back to being a dirty little secret. There'd be no kissing in stores, or holding hands on long romantic walks, it would be confined to the walls of George's home.

The car pulled slowly into George's driveway, and Harvey's stomach dropped as he saw a body slumped against the front door under the soft glow from the porch light.

"Shit," Harvey muttered.

Harvey got out of the car and slammed the door, making the body jump slightly.

"Leo, what the hell are you doing here?" Harvey marched over to his drunken brother.

Leo shakily rose to his feet and leaned messily against the door. It looked like he'd been on one of his long drinking sessions.

"It's nice to see you too bro," he slurred.

Harvey didn't understand why he was here, and how he'd found where George lived.

"How long have you been here?" Harvey demanded, with George beside him.

"About an hour, maybe two? What does it matter? I knew you and lover boy would have to come home eventually," he laughed.

"What do you want?" George demanded.

"Don't talk to me, faggot," Leo spat at George's feet as he took a staggered step off the porch towards George and Harvey, "you're the one that took my brother away."

"Why can't you just leave me alone?" Harvey roared, running his hands shakily through his hair, "Why do you hate the thought of me being slightly happy? You always want to drag me down in the gutter with you."

"So you admit there's something going on between you two," Leo laughed, wagging his finger from Harvey to George, "what a cute couple you make."

Harvey felt sick.

"There's nothing going on. I'm just looking out for Harvey seeing as he has nobody else to do that. He's sleeping in my guest bedroom until we can sort something more permanent out for him," George said sternly.

Harvey resisted the urge to correct George. He wanted to

blurt out how in love he was with him. George's denial of their relationship hurt Harvey, but he knew why he was doing it. He was doing it to try and prevent another freak out from Leo.

"Just leave Leo," Harvey sighed, "please, just go."

For a moment, he thought Leo was going to try and attack George, but instead he sniggered and pushed through them both, heading off into the night. Harvey knew he was that drunk that he probably wouldn't find his way home in the dark, but he didn't feel guilty about the thought of him sleeping in the streets.

"I'll get my brother back," Leo shouted as he staggered down the road, "you're not going to take him away from me Georgey Boy,"

George pushed Harvey into the house, with Leo's words echoing around the street. George locked and bolted the door, and he noticed his hands shaking as he did it. The minute they were safely inside of the dark house, Harvey banged his head against the wall and slid to the ground as the tears started to roll down his cheeks.

"He's never going to let me go," Harvey tried to wipe the tears away, "I'm never going to be free."

Harvey was surprised when George didn't immediately comfort him. George just looked at Harvey as he crumbled into a pile on the floor. Had Leo's words shaken George up that much?

***

As he stared at Harvey, he started to consider that what he was doing was totally wrong. He was having an affair with someone who looked up to him and trusted him. Had he abused his authority position over Harvey?

George's heart felt heavy. He dropped to his knees and wrapped his strong arms tightly around Harvey, gently caressing his hair as he rocked back and forth. As Harvey calmed down, he knew that it was too late to doubt anything about how he felt. He was in too deep and he'd fallen too hard for Harvey to stop things.

Harvey's breathing slowed and his body turned limp as he started to gently snore.

George scooped his arms under Harvey's slender body, and carried him up the grand white staircase and laid him gently on his bed. He pulled the covers over him and kissed him gently on the cheek. He nearly climbed into bed next to him, but instead he went down to his study and buried himself in his work.

George was jolted from his laptop when he heard what sounded like smashing glass. He blinked heavily and glanced at the clock.

It was nearly 4am.

George shook his head and convinced himself he'd imagined it, but when he heard the sound of a metal tray hitting the wooden floor, he jumped out of his chair and ran into the living room. He was met by a dark figure riffling through a drawer next to the fireplace. He pulled the drawer out and emptied it onto the floor. George flicked the light on, and the figure spun around clumsily.

He had a hood pulled over the top half of his face, but George would recognize that smirk anywhere.

It was Leo.

George instinctively ran towards Leo, but he pulled a knife from inside his jacket. George raised his hands and backed off, giving Leo space. Leo slowly headed towards the door of the living room and George heard him run across the marble floor of the hall and out of the front door.

George ran into the hall, but he was already gone into the night.

What had just happened?

He glanced to the floor, and the glass from the window next to the door littered the marble. He knew Leo was looking for something, and he didn't know what it was, but he could take a good guess.

Money.

"What's all the noise?" George turned around to see Harvey at the top of the stairs rubbing his eyes, still wearing the clothes he'd fallen asleep in.

"Nothing," George held his hand out, "go back to bed Harvey."

FIFTEEN

"**P**lease, don't call the police," Harvey reached the bottom of the staircase.

George's cellphone was in his hand and he was already hovering over the keypad.

"How can you be serious?" George gasped, "He broke in here and if I wasn't in the study, he would have taken whatever he could have got his hands on."

Harvey knew he was right, but he didn't want his brother to be locked up in a cell. He hated him, but he was still his brother. He was the only family he had, and he felt so conflicted. Harvey slumped down on the bottom step and rested his head against the bannister, staring at the broken glass.

"He's not been himself for years," Harvey sighed, "but he's the only family I have left!"

George stared at Harvey, his mouth gaping open. Harvey knew exactly what he was thinking, and he was right. He shouldn't still be defending him, but it felt like an instinct.

"You have me," George sat on the step next to Harvey, "and I'm not going anywhere."

He grabbed Harvey's shaking hand and squeezed it reassuringly.

"What about when your wife gets back? It shouldn't be too long now," Harvey said, in a nastier voice than he originally intended it to sound.

George pulled his hand away from Harvey, resting it on his knee.

"I told you, we'll cross that bridge when it comes to it," George sounded irritated.

Harvey wasn't in the mood for anymore bullshit. He knew George didn't have a plan for when Paula got back, and he knew that there was a possibility George would completely change the minute her little car pulled up in the driveway.

"He had a knife Harvey," George sighed heavily.

George's words sank in and he couldn't believe his brother had carried a knife. The thought of him stabbing anyone seemed so impossible. He might be an alcoholic and a drug user, but Harvey didn't think for a second he'd be capable of murder. This was the first time he'd seen George so vulnerable. Up until that point, George had been the strong one, but cracks were starting to appear in his armor.

"He wouldn't have stabbed you," Harvey said instantly.

"He might not have," George said, "but it's only a matter of time before he stabs somebody. He's carrying a knife around with him. That's enough convincing for me that he's going to use it one day."

Harvey blinked back the tears. He knew he was right, but he didn't want to believe it. Leo was the last piece of his family that he had left and even though George said he was there for him, he didn't know what the future with George would hold and that terrified him.

"I won't call the police if you really don't want me to," he said, "but if I see him anywhere near this house again, I won't hesitate to hand over the video surveillance to the police."

"Deal," Harvey leaned his head on George's shoulder.

Harvey couldn't go back to sleep, scared that Leo would return. After George nailed a piece of scrap wood to the broken window, they went out into the garden and lay next to the pool, staring at the last fragments of night in the fuzzy sky.

Holding hands, they watched the stars fade as the pink and orange haze was replaced with a bright blue sky. Harvey watched the sun slowly lift, and he knew it only meant one thing for him. It was one day closer to Paula returning and ruining everything.

"You better go shower before school," George said, pulling Harvey from his daydreaming.

He'd forgotten all about school and couldn't believe George was bringing it up. School was the last thing he was thinking about.

Reluctantly, he jumped in the shower in George's bedroom and tried to wash away the heavy sleep that lingered on his mind. He pulled on the first clothes he could find, and spritzed himself with George's aftershave, heavily breathing in the familiar and musky scent.

George kissed him goodbye and he didn't want to leave him alone. He wanted to stay home all day and be as close to him as possible.

"Are you sure you'll be okay?" Harvey asked for the third time as he stepped over the broken glass.

"Yes! Now get to school so you can hurry up and graduate," he said, giving Harvey another kiss.

As Harvey walked to school in the hot sun, he imagined Leo hiding in the bushes, waiting for him to leave so he could go back in and finish what he started. A knife gleamed in his mind as he imagined it sinking into George's skin.

He shook the images from his head as he walked through the gates of his high school. He wanted to go back to George more, but he knew he had a lot of work to finish if he wanted to walk with the rest of class at graduation.

It wasn't because he liked his class. He didn't talk to any of them. He didn't have any friends and just kept to himself, and that's how he liked it. He read books on his breaks and study periods, and kept his head down.

He couldn't wait to graduate because it meant when he did, he'd be able to spend as much time as he wanted with George, and that thought got him through the long and boring day.

SIXTEEN

As Harvey walked up the path to the big green front door, he noticed that there was a new sheet of glass in the small window next to the door. Harvey relaxed. It meant there had been repairmen in the house, and if Leo was going to do something, he was less likely to do it with people hanging around.

When Harvey closed the door behind him, George appeared from the kitchen with a huge smile on his face and he ran over and picked Harvey up, spinning him around and locking him in a kiss.

"Jesus kid, I missed you," George whispered into his ear with a smile, "never leave me alone for hours again?"

"Deal," Harvey laughed as George put him on the ground.

They softly kissed before George led Harvey into his study.

"I bought you something while I was out today," George said with a huge smile across his face.

He handed over a black box, a red ribbon wrapped neatly around it.

"What is it?" Harvey laughed as he inspected the immaculate ribbon on top.

"Just open it" George urged.

Whatever it was, he was clearly excited for Harvey to see it. Harvey gently tugged on one of the loose ends of the ribbon, and it collapsed. The box didn't feel particularly heavy.

Harvey dropped the lid to the ground as he stared at the gift inside. Warmth flowed through his body as he gazed down at a beautifully framed picture. The picture was one they had taken of them at the cabin. Two pearly white smiles beamed up at him. He could see George's arm stretched out of the shot taking the picture. They'd taken the photo soon after they'd put their clothes back on in the woods.

Harvey blushed.

"Do you like it?" George looked nervous.

Harvey really did love it.

"It's perfect," Harvey lifted the gold frame out of the box.

He pulled it to his chest and hugged it gently, not wanting to break it, but wanting it close to him.

George grabbed an identical framed picture from his desk.

"I got two," George held the identical frame in his hands, "so whenever we look at them, we'll always feel close to each other, no matter where we are."

Harvey felt overwhelmed. It was one of the kindest, most thoughtful things anyone had ever done for him. As he hugged the photo, pushing the tears back, George's words lingered in his mind. Harvey was sure he didn't mean anything by it, but he couldn't imagine being far enough away from George to need to remember him.

"I'm going to keep mine on my desk, right in front of me," he said.

Harvey glanced at the desk. He wasn't sure if he was remembering rightly, but he was sure he'd seen a framed photo of George and Paula's wedding day sitting there at one point.

"It really is beautiful," Harvey said, looking at the photo once more, "thank you."

That evening, they ordered takeout and they sat cross-legged on the living room floor eating Chinese food out of paper cartons, watching a cheesy game show on TV. The normality of the situation made Harvey feel so comfortable.

It had been so long since he'd felt so at ease anywhere. It was never something he could do with his brother in his apartment. There was no TV, and they had no spare money to waste on takeout. He thought about his brother and wondered when the last time he'd eaten was, as he dipped his chopsticks messily into the noodles.

He looked at George trying to forget Leo. He told himself that George was all he needed, but the harder he tried, the more Leo's face popped into his mind.

Suddenly, he realized something. The face that was popping into his mind was of Leo soon after their parents had died, when he was still there for Harvey. It was the face that had cared for him, before the alcohol and drugs. It was the soft face with a kind smile which once looked out for Harvey.

He forced himself to think about Leo's current state. His sunken eyes, sharp cheekbones and stained and chipped teeth replaced the once handsome face.

George laughed at one of the answers on the game show, but Harvey didn't hear the television. He wanted so badly to get his old brother back. He wanted so badly to get his parents back. He wanted to help his brother get sober, but he knew it was an impossible task. Leo had gone too far down the rabbit hole.

George laughed again, and it pierced through Harvey's thoughts. He stared at George's face as he bit into a prawn cracker, smiling at the stupidity being displayed on the television. He thought about his parents again and if they would have liked George.

Would they have approved of the age gap? Would they have told Harvey to stay away? George's eyes met Harvey's and he smiled, not wanting George to know the pain he was feeling. He laughed along with George, not knowing what was being said on the television. All he could hear was noise.

He suddenly realized that if his parents were alive, he would never have met George, because he would have had his own money to buy his own books, and George would never have found him on the bookstore floor. He would never have saved him, but he would never have needed saving.

He wiped the tear away and tucked into the sweet and sour chicken, forcing himself to live in the moment, but the reality of it was so much harder.

After Chinese, they cuddled up on the sofa and watched more TV. Harvey hadn't watched so many hours of TV in a long time, but he had to admit he was enjoying it. They watched another game show where contestants were ejected from a chair when they answered a question wrong, which made George belly laugh against Harvey's back.

As the night drew on, the roaring fire in the fireplace started to die down, casting the room into darkness. A few embers glowed in the grate as Harvey felt George's hand on his stomach as he softly kissed his neck.

He smiled and leaned into George's kiss. He was exhausted and on the edge of sleep, but he couldn't resist George's touch.

A noise outside made Harvey's eyes snap open. He thought he'd heard a twig snapping. He stared through the open blinds out into the darkness. His eyes adapted, and they focused on a face through the dark.

His stomach tightened and his mouth was suddenly dry. He felt sick to his stomach.

Unaware that Leo was watching them through the window, George continued kissing Harvey's neck, as Harvey lay paralyzed, staring into his brother's sinister eyes.

A wicked smile spread across his face and he saw him mouth something that resembled "*Gotcha!*"

SEVENTEEN

"George, stop!"

"What's up?" George said, still kissing his neck.

"Just stop," he snapped.

Harvey could feel how aroused George was, just from the solid shaft digging into his back as George slowly bucked his hips. Harvey would have wanted it, but he couldn't shake his brother's eyes from his mind.

Had he imagined it? Did the dark play a trick on him?

"There's someone watching at the window," Harvey whispered.

He couldn't bring himself to say his brother's name. Without any warning, George jumped over the back of the sofa and ran down the hall to the front door. He took a few steps out in the dark to get a view of the living room bay window.

***

"Who's there?" George shouted in to the dark.

Leo emerged from the bushes with a satisfied look on his face.

"Well, well, well Georgey boy," Leo laughed, sounding more sober than George had ever heard him, "so much for the guest bedroom?"

George stared in disbelief at Leo as he walked up towards him on the porch. He took a step back.

"I don't know what sick game you're playing, but you have ten seconds to get the fuck off my property before I call the police," George growled.

"I don't think so," Leo said as he grabbed the cellphone out of George's hands and threw it into the bushes, "I think I have something you want to hear before you do that."

George's stomach dropped. What could he possibly want to tell George? He shoved him into his house and flicked the hall light on. Harvey was standing at the end of the hall, squinting his eyes as they adjusted to the bright light.

"Looks like I was right about you all along, my little queer brother," Leo laughed and he leaned against a side-table.

"Don't you ever talk to him like that," George said, squaring up to Leo.

Leo slid a knife out of his pocket, and Harvey screamed out. George backed off even further. Harvey ran and protectively stood in front of George, shielding him from the tiny, shining blade.

"Leo, you've lost your mind," Harvey screamed, "go on and stab me. That's what you'll have to do if you want to get to George."

Leo stood in silence. His eyes flickered down to the blade in his hand, and he put it back in his pocket.

"I didn't come here to stab anyone," Leo said, holding his hands up.

"You've got a funny way of showing it," George nervously laughed, pushing Harvey aside.

He knew that Leo was a live wire, and he could snap at any

moment. He didn't want Harvey to be in the way when that happened.

"Just insurance," Leo said, looking from George to Harvey.

"You've caught us out, are you happy now?" Harvey muttered under his breath as he sat on the bottom step on the staircase.

"Not really. I didn't really want a fag for a brother. I hoped I was wrong," Leo spat on the floor towards Harvey and Harvey gave George a warning glance that read '*ignore it*'.

***

"I'm gay Leo," Harvey said as he ran his hands through his black hair.

This was the wrong time to notice that he'd let his usual short style grow a little too long.

It felt so good to finally say it out loud to the only family he had.

"How do you think Dad would have felt? He'd be so ashamed," Leo said, almost pleading.

Harvey was surprised to hear Leo talk about their father. Leo had forbidden Harvey from ever mentioning their parents, imprisoning them in his thoughts.

"Harvey is an amazing person," George said as he stood next to Harvey, "and any father would be proud to call him a son."

Harvey stood up and George grabbed his hand tightly. He wanted to believe what George was saying, but he had to admit he had no idea how his dad would have reacted. Leo was always closer to him, and Harvey was closer to their mom. Maybe he was telling the truth. The thought of his father hating him from beyond the grave made Harvey feel sick to the stomach.

"And then there's you," Leo said, turning to George, "George Lewis! Don't think I haven't done my research on you. The school was very helpful, giving me your details."

Harvey cursed the useless principal under his breath. He

now knew how Leo had found his house.

"A quick internet search threw a few red flags up. One being, that you have a wife," Leo smiled.

George's heart dropped and he let go of Harvey's hand.

"What do you want, Leo?" Harvey wanted him gone.

"I'm getting to that. I'm not finished," Leo spat on the floor again, "I found out more about Georgey Boy here. Did you know your perfect lover was arrested on suspicion of *man slaughter*?"

Harvey's mouth dropped as he took a step away from George. Leo was lying, wasn't he?

"Oh yes my little brother. This perfect writer was arrested on suspicion of murder only 5 years ago. Not just any murder, but the murder of his mother."

"I was never charged of anything!" George screamed, making Harvey take another step further away from him, "her death was an accident!"

"George?" Harvey whispered.

George looked from Harvey to Leo with scared looking eyes. Sweat started to appear in droplets on his forehead.

"Why don't you tell us what happened George? We're dying to know," Leo smirked.

For a second George stood there, staring wide-eyed at Harvey. He opened his mouth to speak, but nothing came out. After what seemed like an eternity, words finally left George's mouth.

"It was 5 years ago," George started, visibly sweating now, "I was driving my mother home after taking her out for lunch. It was going to be her birthday that weekend but I was going away with Paula, so we decided to do something earlier. Over lunch I had a couple of glasses of wine, but I knew I was still fine to drive, honestly."

Harvey stared in disbelief at what George was saying. He'd been so vague about his parents, and he hadn't wanted to push the information out of him, but he couldn't believe he hadn't told him any of this. Why had he not told him his mom was dead too?

"I was coming onto the freeway when a truck hit us side on. She died on impact. The car flipped over and it was hit by another car in another lane. I was sure I was a goner, but somehow I survived."

"That's not the end though is it?" Leo sneered, "As soon as you were in the hospital, they tested your alcohol level in your blood and you were two times over the legal limit."

"I was found not guilty! The truck driver swerved off the road and would have hit us if I had that drink or not."

George collapsed onto the step as if telling the story had used every last piece of his energy.

"Don't you see Harvey," George pleaded, "this is why I get what you've gone through. This is why I wanted to help you. I get it."

Harvey wanted to run over and comfort him, but he was frozen to the spot at the shock of not being told this before.

"What has this got to do with what you want?" Harvey pushed.

Leo laughed, "Oh nothing. I just wanted you to know that your lover boy killed his mother."

It was nothing more than a sick game to him.

George jumped up from the step, suddenly full of energy and he headed towards Leo with anger in his eyes. Harvey grabbed George's arm and pulled him back.

"You've done enough talking," George screamed in a loud and deep voice that Harvey had never heard before, "*Get out of my house!*"

"I will, as soon as you give me what I want," Leo's eyes focused on George's.

"Leo, just stop this," Harvey pleaded to the brother he knew was inside the stranger.

"I want $10,000 in cash, tonight," Leo said.

Harvey couldn't believe what he was hearing. All of it was because of money? It had taken him a long time to realize, but the brother he knew and loved, left a long time ago.

"What do you even need that for?" Harvey shot back at

Leo, already aware of the answer.

"I owe some guys some money," Leo shrugged vaguely.

Harvey knew when he said *'some guys'* he meant drug dealers, or loan sharks.

"Impossible," George scoffed.

"Get out!" Harvey screamed, feeling his blood boil in his veins.

"Okay, I'll go. I'll go right this minute," Leo said as he pulled a cell phone from his pocket, "but I'll be straight on the phone to your lovely Paula. I'm sure she'd love to hear all about your seedy little affair. You really should tell your wife to set her contact details to private on the Internet. Oh, it was far too easy."

George clenched his fists.

"Get out now, before I call the police myself," Harvey screamed, pushing Leo roughly towards the door, "you're not getting a penny, and I never want to see your face again."

Leo laughed as he resisted Harvey's hard pushes. Harvey knew he had the knife in his pocket but he didn't care if he tried to stab him. He just wanted him out of his sight.

"Why don't you ask Georgey boy what he thinks?" Leo said as he had his hand on the door handle.

"Tell him George," Harvey said confidently back to George who was still at the foot of the stairs, "tell him he can tell Paula. You were going to tell her eventually anyway."

George stood in silence staring at Harvey. Harvey couldn't help but feel like George was apologizing with his eyes. Harvey got a sharp pain in his gut.

"Tell him George," Harvey screamed in a shaky voice, "Tell him that you love me and you're leaving your wife to be with me!"

Tears were uncontrollably streaming down Harvey's face. He wanted to hear George say it more for himself than Leo. He could feel Leo smirking behind his back as he stared at George, willing him to speak.

"*George! Just say something!*" Harvey screamed, throwing his arms out.

Every fiber in his body was screaming out for George's love.

***

"I'm sorry," escaped George's mouth in a quiet throaty whisper.

George ran up the stairs three at a time as he headed for the concealed safe at the back of his closet. When he reached the top of the staircase, he turned around to see Harvey crumble to a heap on the floor, and he was sure he heard the sound of Harvey's heart breaking...

GEORGE & HARVEY BOXSET

GEORGE & HARVEY

- PART TWO -

THE TRUTH

Ashley John

DEDICATION

This book is dedicated to my Mother for being my biggest fan and for constantly being on my case to get this book finished. She just couldn't wait to find out what happened next for George and Harvey, so here you go Mother...

ABOUT THIS BOOK

George & Harvey: Part Two
The Truth

Published: June 2014 (2nd Edition and print edition April 2015)
Words: 27,000

The Truth is the second novella from Ashley John (**first published June 2014**), and the second part of **The George & Harvey Series**. This brand new edition has been completely refined and re-edited, with brand new content!

After Harvey's heartbreaking confrontation with his brother, Leo, he tries to pick up the pieces of his life, but he can't decide where Leo and George fit in.

When George's wife returns after spending time away looking after her sick mother, George must decide between his wife and his young male lover, and Harvey must decide between a surprise proposal from his brother, and George. Will Harvey finally get the man he loves? Will he find the family he longs for? Will George do the right thing and follow his heart, or will he keep breaking Harvey's?

ONE

Harvey pulled himself up from the ground and staggered towards the grand staircase. Fresh waves of tears poured from his swollen eyes, obscuring his vision, as his legs shakily navigated each step. His whole body ached. He wanted the pain to stop, but it had consumed him. He reached George's bedroom and fell into the door, sending it into the wall with a thud.

"Don't do this, George," Harvey didn't recognize his own voice.

George ignored him, stuffing handfuls of cash into a backpack.

"George, look at me," Harvey whispered.

George zipped up the bag and with his eyes planted firmly on the ground, he pushed past Harvey, as if he didn't want to see the pain he'd created

"*Look at me!*" Harvey screamed.

Harvey's voice bellowed around the bedroom, stopping George dead in his tracks. Slowly, he turned around to face

Harvey, but he didn't look in to his eyes.

"Why?" he choked, "Why are you doing this?"

George swallowed, his fingers tightening around the bag. Harvey glanced down to it, as if it was a bomb, ready to explode.

"I need more time," George finally spoke, "I can't do this to Paula, not after everything she's been through with her mother's death."

Harvey tried his best not to laugh.

"Were you thinking about poor Paula when you were fucking me in the woods?" he sneered, "Did Paula cross your mind when we were having sex in her bed?"

George shifted uncomfortably on the spot, the guilt obvious.

"I want to be with you," George reached out, but Harvey pulled away, "but I can't tell Paula yet. Just give me more time. It's not easy!"

He could plead all he wanted to, because for Harvey, the damage was done. He turned and headed back down the stairs, where Leo was waiting for his money, a smug expression on his face.

George followed Harvey, and walked around him to throw the bag into Leo's chest.

"Here. You've got what you wanted. Get out of my house."

Leo ripped open the bag and his eyes lit up when he saw the rolls of green bills.

"Thanks Georgey boy," Leo winked, "see you around."

"If I ever see you again, I'll kill you," he spat at Leo's feet, "now leave."

Leo lingered for a moment before ripping away from George's hateful glare. He swaggered slowly towards the door and headed out into the night with the loaded rucksack slung casually over his back.

Not wanting to stick around for a second longer, Harvey pushed past George, their shoulders colliding. He felt a hand tighten around the top of his arm.

"Get your hands off me," Harvey winced at the hand on his

arm.

"Harvey, please!" he begged, "I did this for us!"

"No George, you did it for you," he pulled away from George's tight grip and headed into the night after Leo.

Squinting into the dark, he could see a hooded figure passing under the street lights. Sprinting faster than he thought his slender legs could carry him, he caught up with Leo, grabbing the back of his jacket.

"Wait!"

Leo slowly turned, but he didn't say a word. Instead he stared at Harvey with the same cold look he'd given George.

"I have nowhere else to go."

Leo sniggered and took a step back from Harvey.

"You should have thought about that before leaving me to be with that queer," he spat, "I'm not having a queer for a brother."

"Leo, please. I don't have anyone else," he tried to force back the tears, "you're the only family I have. You're my brother."

"No," Leo said, "my family died a long time ago."

He gave Harvey one last look up and down, before setting off hastily into the night. A drop of rain fell from the sky and hit Harvey on the end of his nose as he watched the darkness swallow his brother up. As Harvey's heart opened up to cry a whole new set of tears, the dark heavy clouds above him did the same. The tears flowed until they couldn't flow any more, but that didn't stop Harvey painfully wailing into the dark. Drapes twitched to see what the noise was, but as he leaned against one of the streetlights, he didn't care.

Glancing in the direction of George's house, he knew he couldn't go back. He squinted through the rain and could see the lights inside of the house. He yearned for the perfect life they had experienced, even if it was only for a fleeting moment.

As he set off aimlessly into the rain, he'd never felt more alone. He was given a glimpse of a life he'd always longed for, but it was ripped from his hands as quickly as it had been given to him.

He knew he'd never have that life.

He knew he didn't deserve happiness.

TWO

"Hello? Excuse me, are you okay?" Harvey peeled his eyes open, to a blinding light.

A sharp pain quickly spread throughout his back and neck as he rubbed the last remains of sleep from his eyes. A slender, elderly woman with kind eyes stood over him, wearing a big coat over a floral dress and apron. Her gray hair was pulled tightly off her face into a small bun at the back of her head.

He jumped up, embarrassment sweeping over him. He didn't remember what had happened. He didn't know how he'd come to be asleep outside of a café in the center of town. He was sure he'd seen the place before.

A knife sank deep into his heart when George's face flashed through his mind, as memories of the night before flooded back. For a few moments, it had all felt like a bad dream.

"Are you okay?"

"Yeah," Harvey muttered, his voice croaky, "I think."

He shivered, the damp clothes clinging to his pale skin. It

wasn't particularly cold, but everything looked gray and dull. Harvey wasn't sure if being in love had made every day look like the height of Summer. If it had, he was now in the middle of the coldest winter.

"You're shivering!" the woman pulled a big bundle of keys from her pocket, "come inside. I'll get you some coffee."

Harvey stepped aside to let the woman unlock the door. Her thin, bony hands were shaking as she tried to fit the key into the lock. Maybe it was cold after all, or maybe it was her age. If Harvey had to guess, she was at least in her late 60s.

"Come in, sit," she said softly, pulling a chair out for Harvey.

Harvey looked around the café and instantly recognized it as the setting for Leo and George's fight.

"I don't have any money," Harvey mumbled, embarrassed.

He had no idea what he was going to do for money. That was another thing he was going to have to sort out on his own. Could he drop out of high school, so close to his graduation? He didn't even know where he was going to live.

He tried to imagine home, but all he could see was darkness. He tried to remember what the front of his parent's house looked like, but all he could see was fire and smoke.

"Don't be silly," she cooed as she flicked on the lights and fired up the coffee machine, "coffee and breakfast on me. I'd like to think someone would help my sons out if they were in your situation."

Harvey didn't know what she thought his situation was, because even he didn't know how to explain it.

She set the coffee in front of Harvey, her smile friendly. Her razor sharp nose twitched, and out of nowhere she produced a tissue to dab it.

"Have I seen you before?" she asked, arching one of her fine eyebrows as she stuffed the tissue into her bra.

Harvey didn't know if he should reveal that he was involved in the fight that had happened right there only a few weeks earlier. She was sure to retract her kindness if she knew the truth.

"You were in here a couple weeks ago weren't you? With those men who started wrecking my place," she clapped her hands together, pleased that she'd figured it out on her own.

"Lady," Harvey said, already pulling his chair out from under the table, "I'm sorry about that. I'll just go."

"Oh, don't you worry about it one little bit," she smiled and put her hand comfortingly on Harvey's shoulder.

It nearly made him jump. He wasn't used to motherly affection.

The gray clouds outside started to clear, revealing a bright blue sky. As Harvey slowly sipped his coffee, he let the hot liquid run over his body. He promised himself that he'd create his own permanent summer. He tried to tell himself he didn't need any help, but George appeared in his mind, telling him that he needed him to survive. Harvey pushed the thought away, cursing his own imagination for torturing him.

"Here you go. my love," she placed a plate full of fried food in front of Harvey, "enjoy!"

The plate was piled high with bacon and eggs, and he finished every last scrap, not knowing when he'd eat next. When he finished, he took the plate and empty cup over to the counter, and slid them across to the woman. She was serving a man his morning coffee fix, but she winked out of the corner of her eye at him.

"That was amazing," Harvey smiled weakly at the woman.

He had no way to repay her, and he didn't like that feeling.

"There's no need for thanks! I believe things happen for a reason, and you were put on my doorstep for a reason. If I can't give you a good meal, then I'm not doing my duty."

Harvey beamed at the woman. He wasn't particularly spiritual and didn't believe that things happened like that, but his full stomach was glad that's how this woman thought.

She put her hand softly on Harvey's, to reveal a screwed up ten dollar bill.

"I can't take this!" Harvey protested, not wanting to take advantage of the woman's kindness, "You've done enough already."

"Don't you try to give me that money back! You need it more than I do right now. I don't know your story, but I couldn't sleep if I sent you out into the world with nothing."

Harvey felt a fuzzy warmth inside his chest.

"Thank you," Harvey mouthed as he took the money and shoved it into his damp pocket.

"Besides, last time you were in here, that handsome man threw a fist full of money at me. There was almost $100 there!"

That sounded like George. He didn't seem to understand the value of money. The way he handled his finances and paperwork told Harvey that long ago.

"If you ever need me, I'm here most days," the woman said softly, "If I'm not here ask for Ginger. That's what people call me. Most people around these parts know me, so I shouldn't be too hard to find."

Harvey looked at the woman's hair, which was scraped off her face into a neat, tight bun. Her hair was white with flecks of gray now, but he could imagine her hair being a fiery red color in her youth, and it only added to her warmth. Bidding Ginger goodbye, he left the safety of the café and headed back into the harsh daylight. He wandered slowly down the street, with no destination in mind. He patted the $10 in his pocket to make sure it was still there and vowed to pay Ginger back for her kindness one day.

Harvey turned the corner and the realization of where he was almost knocked him over. He could see '*Sloppy Joe's Italian Place*' just up ahead and his stomach churned. He thought back to Leo and George arguing outside of the restaurant. At the time, he'd felt so ashamed, but part of him longed to have two people fighting over him. At least people cared.

Now he had nobody.

He was torn from his daydream when he saw something big on the horizon. For a second he thought his eyes were deceiving him, but as George's familiar car sped down the road towards him, he suddenly felt like a mouse trapped in a cage.

"Get in, now!" George slammed his foot on the breaks and rolled down his window.

THREE

Harvey cowered into the wall behind him. The cold brick stung his damp back, but he didn't care. He pushed himself as far into the wall as he could, wishing it would swallow him up.

"Get in, kid," he demanded, "I'm not playing around."

He jumped out of the car, abandoning it in the center of the road. Horns sounded up and down the street as cars ground to a halt, but George didn't seem to care. Heavy purple bags hung under George's eyes and for the first time, Harvey thought he truly looked his age.

He tried to speak, but Harvey suddenly lost all control of his voice. Pressing his body further into the brick, he could feel the eyes of passersby upon him and George.

"Please," he stepped closer, reaching out his hand, "just come with me."

Harvey's heart burned when he saw George's bottom lip trembling and curling at the corners. He could see the tears collecting along his tired and raw eyelids. He violently pushed away the emotions that were bubbling up in his stomach, but they were too strong. A little voice in his head told him that he wanted George to hurt. He wanted George to be the one who was crying and hurting for a change.

Harvey knew he couldn't be that person. The love was too strong.

"I don't think I can," Harvey mumbled.

"I need you," George's voice was trembling as a tear trickled slowly down his cheek and through the fresh dark stubble on his jaw line.

Despite looking exhausted, Harvey still thought he was the most beautiful person he'd ever seen.

"You don't need me," Harvey mumbled, not feeling his own conviction, "you have Paula."

George smiled and shook his head. Another tear ran slowly down his cheek.

"Don't you get it? I don't have Paula. I haven't had Paula for a long time. It's you that I want and it's you that I need. I just can't break Paula's heart so soon, after what she's been through."

Guilt twisted and knotted Harvey's stomach, like a snake trying to free itself from a trap. In all of this, he'd failed to see past his own selfish needs, and his need for George. He'd not considered that other people might need him. He'd spent so long resenting her, he'd stopped seeing Paula as a human. Instead, he saw her as *'the problem'*.

"C'mon, I've been driving around looking for you all night," George pleaded, taking another step towards Harvey.

He was right in front of Harvey now, and he could see from George's bloodshot eyes that he was telling the truth. The ice melted from Harvey's heart, and the familiar warmth raced through his veins again.

He wanted to reach out and kiss George, but he stopped himself. He craved the touch of his lips, but he didn't want to seem weak. He didn't want George to think he could forgive him so easily.

"All night?" Harvey asked, dropping the coldness from his

voice.

"Yes," George sighed heavily with exhaustion, "five minutes after you'd left, I realized what a terrible mistake I'd made. I've been driving around, looking everywhere for you."

George's dedication warmed Harvey even more and the urge to kiss him was so strong. People were walking around them on the street, but it felt like they were completely alone.

"I can't believe you'd do that for me," Harvey's voice trembled as he took a small step towards George.

He breathed in deeply and he could smell George's scent lingering on his clothes from the night before.

"I'd do anything for you," George said, putting his hand firmly on Harvey's cheek.

Harvey leaned into his hand and closed his eyes. George's hand felt like hot coals on his face.

"Anything?" Harvey asked.

"Anything."

"Take me home."

He felt George's lips press softly against his, and any hatred he might have had left for George, disappeared completely.

George closed his eyes and let Harvey's touch wash over him. He'd been so sure that he'd lost him for good. He pulled away from the kiss, and the smile that he loved so much spread across Harvey's face, showing off his perfectly white teeth.

As they drove back to the house, George flicked the radio off and quizzed Harvey about where he'd been all night. Harvey nearly lied, but he realized that he had no alternative. He knew he didn't have any family or friends that he could have stayed with, and if he started telling George about ones he'd never mentioned, he'd know he was lying.

He told George all about Ginger and how she'd shown him kindness when he needed it most. He patted his jeans and remembered the $10 in his pocket. He almost asked George to drive back to the café so he could give her the money back, but he knew she wouldn't appreciate it. Ginger wanted to help him, and that was enough for her. She didn't ask for repayment, she just wanted to know that she'd done something good.

It reminded Harvey so much of his own mother. She was a kind and caring woman who devoted her life to her family. As they stepped into the house, Harvey vowed to himself that he would find a way to pay Ginger back, for his mother's sake.

As they walked into the house, Harvey started to think about his father, and Leo's words from the night before weighed heavy on his mind. He tried to imagine his father's reaction to finding out he was gay, but he couldn't imagine anything. He was a man's man. He loved sports and he ruled the house with a firm hold, but he wasn't an evil man.

Harvey wandered slowly down the hall. It was almost as if nothing had changed. He wondered if they could really get back to how they were after everything that had happened. With Paula's return on the horizon he didn't know how things would work out, but when he felt George's hands wrap around his waist, he promised himself that he would try to live in the moment.

George's tongue started to explore Harvey's neck, and as he nibbled and kissed his soft skin, the urge to rip his clothes off was overwhelming. He opened his eyes and glanced up to the bedroom, but as he undid his belt buckle, the thought of his bed was just too far away. George undid Harvey's jeans and pulled them down to his ankles. As he started to peel the damp T-shirt off Harvey's slim body, Harvey kicked his shoes and jeans off.

He pushed Harvey against the white wooden stairs. Starting at his neck he kissed down Harvey's body and when he reached Harvey's tight white briefs, he peeled them off with his teeth. As Harvey felt George's toned body against his own, he knew there was nowhere in the world that he belonged more.

George started to gently kiss his thighs, and he smiled quietly to himself as he tried to think about what the future would bring for him, but all he could see was George.

FOUR

"I'll tell him right away Greg," Harvey rolled over as George spoke on the phone, "see you soon. Take care."

George hung up the phone and threw it to the bottom of the bed. He rolled over and kissed Harvey as his eyes flickered open.

"Who was that?" Harvey yawned, stretching his arms out.

"It was Greg," George beamed at Harvey, "my publisher. You met him at the party?"

Harvey's mind flashed back to a small man with gray hair that had assessed him with curiosity at George's garden party. He remembered George telling Greg all about a book that Harvey hadn't even written.

"Oh, is he well?" Harvey asked, not really caring if Greg was well or not.

"He wants to see you," George smiled even wider, flashing all of his pearly whites, "he told a few of the guys at the publishing house about your book idea and they're really into it."

"What?" Harvey gasped, sitting bolt upright in bed, "I don't have a book!"

George laughed, "Don't worry kid, he only wants the first few chapters as a sample."

Panic quickly rose in Harvey's stomach. He didn't even have one chapter. He didn't even know if he could write a book. It'd been days since he'd last written in his journal. He wasn't even sure if he knew how to write fiction anymore.

"I can't do this," Harvey mumbled as he felt his body starting to shake, "I have nothing."

George leaned up and put his arms around Harvey's trembling shoulders, "You've got a few weeks left yet. I have faith in you."

Harvey was still shaking.

"Listen, kid," George said, turning Harvey around and looking into his worried eyes, "I have faith in you."

George repeating the words seemed to calm Harvey. He'd almost forgotten that George was one of the best authors in the business. He'd spent the last month falling in love with him, he'd nearly forgotten how he fell in love with his writing years ago. If George believed in him, Harvey knew it must be for a reason.

"First things first," George jumped out of bed.

Harvey admired his body as he bent down to pick up the nearest T-shirt.

"What's that?" Harvey asked.

"We need to get you a laptop," George smirked as he pulled on a pair of tight black briefs, "because I'm sure not sharing mine!"

He winked at Harvey as he pulled on his dark blue jeans.

"George, these are all too expensive," Harvey said as they walked down the aisle, filled with hundreds of laptops.

The last laptop Harvey owned was destroyed in the fire, and technology had moved on a lot since then. He couldn't believe how small and thin they had become.

"Shut up," George said as he gravitated towards the most expensive model, "it's an investment."

"Yes, but I don't have the money to invest," Harvey

protested as George started to play around with the display model.

"I'm investing in you," George said, distracted by the camera app that he'd opened, "just give me a nice dedication in your first best-selling book or something."

George pulled Harvey in close and took a grainy picture of them on the laptop and then moved on to look at another model. Harvey glanced back at the picture of them both smiling happily on the laptop screen. It warmed Harvey's heart to know that they'd left their mark on the world, outside of their own little bubble, even if it was just on a laptop in a store.

"This is the one!" George exclaimed as he typed away, "Buying a laptop is a lot like buying a dog. You don't pick it, it picks you."

George moved out of the way and grabbed Harvey and planted him on the seat in front of the display laptop.

"Write," he said, "just type anything."

As Harvey typed about a dog who went to the park without his owner, George started reciting off facts about why it was the best laptop to buy. Harvey wasn't bothered about RAM and hard-drives, but he knew that the laptop felt right under his fingertips. It was as if the keys were perfectly designed for him, and as he typed his nonsense story, he felt like he was writing something impressive and amazing.

George called over and exclaimed to the salesperson that they would take one in white. Harvey glanced at the price tag and his heart almost jumped out of his chest.

$2499.

"George!" Harvey gasped, stepping away from the laptop, like it was a radioactive bomb, "I'm not letting you spend this much money on me! There's a difference between buying me a journal and paying over two thousand dollars for a laptop!"

George put his hand on Harvey's shoulder and whispered, "But you're worth it."

Harvey argued all the way to the checkout, but George was buying the laptop despite his protests.

"Listen, my new book is coming out in two weeks, so my

royalties are about to get a little boost. It's all good."

As George slotted his card into the machine and punched his pin in, Harvey couldn't help but feel that George was trying to buy his affection.

Back at the house, George spent the rest of the morning setting up the laptop so it was ready to type. Harvey wasn't completely clueless when it came to technology, but he admired how George liked to take charge of these sorts of situations.

He was sure it made him feel important, and he adored that.

"Here kid, all set to go," George slid off the stool.

Harvey walked over to the breakfast bar and sat in front of his very own laptop. The bright screen displayed a picture of George and Harvey from their camping trip. It was the same picture George had framed and given to him as a gift. He smiled at the picture, and wished they could go back to the cabin again. George had decided that it would be a good idea if Harvey had a few days off school. Harvey suspected this was because George didn't want to let Harvey out of his sight.

As Harvey played with his new toy, George was on the counter flicking through a book he'd picked up from the bookstore after they'd left the computer shop.

A vibration in his pocket pulled George from his book. He threw it on the counter and slid the small cellphone from his pocket.

"Hello?" George sounded nervous.

He slid off the counter and walked across the kitchen towards the dining room. Harvey was about to follow him, but he closed the door.

Harvey had seen the look on George's face and he knew that only one person could make him look so worried. He knew it was Paula. He stopped typing and strained his ears, so he could hear what was being said, but George must have been talking in whispers, because he could hear nothing.

When the door finally opened, all of the color had drained from George's face.

"What?" Harvey whispered, "What is it?"

George walked back into the kitchen and threw his phone onto the counter. He collapsed into the chair and let out a deep and heavy sigh.

"She's coming back," George said quietly, "she's coming back in 3 days, Harvey."

FIVE

Harvey slammed the laptop shut and walked quickly through the open patio doors and stared into the deep blue pool. He wanted to jump in and let the water rush over him so he didn't need to think.

"It's going to be fine, kid," George said reassuringly as he followed Harvey out into the garden.

"Is it?" Harvey muttered under his breath, watching the tiny ripples in the water as flies danced on the calm surface, disturbing the peace.

George put his hand on Harvey's shoulder, but Harvey dipped out of the way and walked around the edge of the pool to the other side. He looked up from the water and stared at George. The sunlight was shining brightly in the water, making the ripples reflect on George's face. Harvey admired his strong features as blue reflections danced across his tanned skin.

"What now?" Harvey asked, feeling safer with the distance between them.

George thought for a second, before replying.

"Nothing changes," George said, "It's still you that I love."

Harvey turned around and looked out into the garden. He noticed that the grass was a little longer than he'd seen it before. They'd had a crazy few days, so he didn't blame George for neglecting his precious lawn.

"It will," Harvey whispered, "I'll go back to being a secret."

"It's only temporary," George joined Harvey by his side, "it's just for a few weeks. It's just until things settle down. I promise."

He squeezed Harvey's hand reassuringly, but Harvey wasn't so sure. He wanted to believe him more than anything, but he was finding it impossible.

In his mind, he could see Paula coming back and changing everything. With his wife home, he might not want to throw away his marriage, and that thought terrified Harvey to the core.

"I'll have to go back sleeping in the guest bedroom," Harvey sighed, dropping George's hand.

"It won't be forever," George said, following Harvey, "I promise."

Harvey walked quickly across the garden towards the hammock. The more distance he could put between him and George, the better he could think. Whenever George was close, the clearness vanished, and a fuzzy, warm haze washed over him, telling him everything would be okay.

Those feelings had lied to him before.

He knew they would do it again.

He reached the hammock and ran his hand across the coarse material. The urge to crawl into the hammock and sleep away his problems was all too strong.

"What if she doesn't want me here?" Harvey whispered when George caught up with him.

"I don't care. You're staying and that's that. You're staying, and in a few weeks, we'll come up with a plan and our real life will start."

Harvey leaned back against George's firm chest and rested his head into his shoulder. As George wrapped his arms firmly around Harvey's slim frame, he kissed him softly on the head. He felt safe.

Hearing George tell him that he wanted to start a life with him was all he needed to hear. It was all the comfort and reassurance he needed.

George let go of Harvey and jumped into the hammock, making it swing from side to side. Harvey jumped into the hammock and lay carefully next to George, not wanting it to tip over. George strongly took Harvey into his arms.

"I'm not going to let anything happen to you," George whispered into Harvey's ear as he stroked his hair, "I've told you this so many times. I love you, and I'm going to protect you."

"Tell me about our life when we're together," Harvey asked gently.

George smiled to himself and thought for a second.

"We'll be happy and safe and hopefully far away from this town," George started, "maybe we could rent an apartment in a big city. How amazing would that be?"

Harvey felt fuzzy inside.

"I like New York," Harvey smiled, "I don't know why."

"New York it is."

"Can we get a dog?" Harvey laughed.

"We can get two!" George said, kissing the top of Harvey's head.

They spent the rest of the afternoon planning out their future. They discussed wallpaper and dog breeds and everything in between. Harvey didn't care that most of it was just fantasy, he liked the fact that George was committing to their future. It made him feel secure.

After eating lunch Harvey tried to work on his book, but the words wouldn't flow from his brain to his fingertips. It felt so wrong writing about his upsetting past when he wanted to write all about his glittering future. He wanted to go into detail about the apartment they'd already planned out and what they were going to call their dogs.

"How do you cure writer's block?" Harvey asked, after

deleting everything for the fourth time.

"Sex always helps," George winked as he grabbed Harvey's hand and led him up to the bedroom.

The days flew by, and before Harvey knew it, it was the day before Paula was due to return. He'd gone back to school for the first time, but he couldn't focus for the entire day. He hated being somewhere where people didn't notice if he didn't show up for three days. He dreamt about his book, and becoming a best-selling author. He didn't care that he was letting his daydreams run away with him.

It was nice to dream about happiness.

Harvey had found himself thinking of the future a lot in the agonizing days up until Paula's return. He wanted to fast-forward to George's big reveal so they could start their new life together. It felt like someone had pressed the pause button on him, and he hated it.

"You should probably sleep back in the guest bedroom tonight," George said over dinner.

Harvey dumped his spoon in the bowl, splashing hot, homemade tomato soup all over his exposed knees. He cursed himself under his breath for choosing to walk around in just his briefs.

That was another thing that would have to change when Paula returned.

"Why?" Harvey snapped, "I thought we could have one last night together."

"It's not a last night," George smiled reassuringly, "these weeks are going to fly by, you watch."

"So why does it have to start now?" Harvey said as he slurped the hot soup.

"Paula rang me earlier," Harvey's stomach knotted at the mention of her name, "she said her flight gets in around 5am, so it's best that you're not in my room in case she's home before we wake up."

Harvey stared at the thick red liquid, feeling his pale skin turn a similar shade of red. Now that it was time to go back into hiding, he knew it was going to be a lot harder to give up the life he was now used to.

"And you should probably move all your stuff out as well," George said nervously as he slurped his own soup.

"Fine!" Harvey said, throwing the spoon down in the bowl, "I'll just go do that now, shall I?"

"Harvey, wait!" George called after Harvey, but he was already storming up the stairs, making sure to hit every step extra hard, so George could hear it from the dining room.

Harvey burst into George's room and started grabbing bundles of his things. With a huge ball of clothes in his arms Harvey paced down the hall towards the guest bedroom, when George appeared at the top of the stairs.

"Harvey, just calm down for a second, please?" George pleaded.

"No, it's fine," Harvey snapped, as he kicked open the guest bedroom door and flung the clothes messily inside.

"It doesn't have to be this difficult," George said, following Harvey back into the master bedroom.

"Not for you maybe," Harvey said as he started to pick up the underwear and socks that were hiding around the bedroom, "you get to go back to your cushy little life for a few weeks, but I'm shoved away in the guest bedroom like Anne Frank in the attic. There's a thought! Why don't you just lock the door and keep me hidden, then it'll be easier for everyone!"

"Harvey, that's not fair and you know it," George sighed, trying to calm Harvey.

Harvey hated himself for his constant over-reactions, but he couldn't help it. The love he felt for George was so strong, it had turned him into a live wire, and the slightest mention of someone coming in to ruin what they had, sent sparks flying from every part of his body.

Every time he heard Paula's name, he felt sick and tense, like a rabid dog who had just spotted a kitten.

"This is just hard for me," Harvey mumbled quietly, falling onto the edge of the bed, letting the clothes in his arms fall back to the floor, "I just don't want you to change your mind when she gets back."

"Is that what you think is going to happen?" George sighed as he flopped down on the bed next to Harvey, "we're going into this together, and we're coming out of this together."

They both stared silently at the ceiling for a moment. Harvey could hear exactly what George was saying, but a small nagging voice in the back of his head was telling him not to trust George and the voice sounded surprisingly like Leo's.

"Maybe I'm just being dramatic," Harvey sighed, turning to face George, "I just don't want to lose you."

"And you're not going to," George smiled.

He gently stroked his face and Harvey closed his eyes. He wanted to stay in this room forever. He hated the thought of sleeping in the guest bedroom without George. It would feel cold and empty. It was fine when he'd slept there before, but that was before he'd known the heat of George's love.

Harvey gathered the clothes up and spotted the framed picture of them on the nightstand. He walked over and picked it up with a sad smile.

"I suppose I better take this," Harvey sighed as he stared at the two faces beaming up at him.

It almost felt like looking through a window into happier times.

"I promise you, when all this is over and you've graduated, we'll go back there," George smiled.

He helped Harvey take the last of his things into the guest bedroom and they resumed dinner. When they'd finally returned, the chicken in the oven had burnt to a smoldering crisp and the vegetables had boiled over and turned to mush.

SIX

H arvey splashed his face with cold water and gasped. He could feel the sleep heavily on his eyelids and he wanted nothing more than to crawl back into bed.

It had been a difficult night sleeping alone. He'd got so used to being able to turn and cuddle George in the night, it felt so hard to turn over in an empty bed, especially when he knew George was only in the next room.

He'd once craved space, sleeping on a tiny, thin mattress, but now the space felt so cold.

Patting his face down, he stared at his reflection in the mirror. The freckles on his face were really starting to show after the hot weather they'd been having. Hours of gardening with George were starting to add a bit of color to his usually ghostly complexion, but it was only like painting a white wall in magnolia paint.

A door slammed and echoed throughout the house. Harvey stared sadly at his own reflection as he brushed his teeth slowly. He knew exactly who it was without needing to look.

Reluctantly, he spat the toothpaste into the sink and headed to his bedroom door.

"I can't believe you would do this!" Paula's screaming voice made Harvey take a step back from the door he was about to burst through in search of George.

He glanced back to the clock on the wall.

7am.

Paula must have only just got home from the airport.

"Is there anything else you've changed around here while I was putting my mother in the ground? Perhaps you've re-decorated the living room or remodeled the kitchen?" Paula screeched.

Her shrill voice sent shivers down Harvey's spine. He didn't know how George had stayed married to her for so long.

"He had nowhere else to go," George bellowed, "what else was I meant to do?"

"Not get involved?" Paula screamed back, "Just like I told you not to before I left."

Harvey held his breath and furrowed his brow deeply. George had never mentioned that he'd talked about him with Paula.

"He's staying, and that's final!" he shouted.

They were getting louder and louder.

"Oh? Is he?" Paula shouted back, even louder still, "We'll see about that!"

Harvey could hear her footsteps across the wooden floor of the landing and he took another step back, and braced himself for confrontation.

"Let me remind you whose house this is," George said, in a quieter, but just as angry voice.

The footsteps stopped, and Harvey held his breath again, as he waited for either of them to speak.

"I see where this is going," Paula sneered.

"It's my name on the deed, and I say he's staying," George growled, in a sinister voice Harvey had never heard before.

He couldn't believe how passionately George was fighting for him. He wanted to be out there fighting for himself, but he didn't trust himself not to tell Paula everything to speed the process up.

"You've got a few weeks," Paula sighed, "and then I want him out of our house. I don't care where he goes, he's just not staying here forever."

"Fine," George said.

Harvey almost laughed out loud. He knew exactly what George would be thinking.

Paula's heels clicked furiously down the stairs, and when Harvey heard them clacking along the marble of the hallway, he peeked his head around the edge of the door to see George leaning against the wall in between their two rooms.

"George?" Harvey whispered, not wanting to reignite George's fury.

There was something about the anger in his voice when he was talking to Paula that scared him, but he knew deep down he was only doing it to protect Harvey.

"Oh shit, Harvey," George sighed, "how much of that did you hear?"

"All of it."

George pulled Harvey into an embrace.

"It's not for long. I promise," George said.

Harvey breathed in George's scent for a second. He'd longed to touch him all night.

"Paula really doesn't like me, does she?" Harvey whispered, scared she might return at any moment.

"She doesn't like many people these days. I don't even think she likes me anymore," George sighed.

Harvey's chest tightened. He was sure he'd heard a sense of remorse in George's voice when he'd said that. Harvey stopped himself from over-reacting. Of course George was going to be sad. It was the end of a marriage.

"C'mon, let's get some breakfast," George smiled, leading Harvey downstairs by the hand.

"I'm sorry about your mother," Harvey said, trying to break the silence as they all sat around the breakfast bar eating the bacon and eggs that George had prepared.

Paula looked up and snarled coldly at Harvey. Harvey realized she wasn't going to make it any easier for him. She didn't care if she showed her dislike of him.

Harvey looked to George to try and ease the situation, but he didn't look at Paula or Harvey. Instead he focused on eating his food, like it was his last meal.

"I'm going to town," Paula said coldly, not directing it at anybody.

She grabbed her car keys from the bowl on the counter and stormed across the hall. The front door slammed and Harvey released a deep sigh of relief

"I'm not sure if I can keep this up for two weeks," Harvey sighed, "she's such a bitch."

George seemed disinterested with what Harvey had to say. He was still staring at his plate, even though it was now empty.

"What are we doing today?" Harvey asked, trying to force something out of George.

George looked up and stared blankly at Harvey. He hadn't heard what he'd said.

"I said, what are we doing today?" Harvey asked again.

"I feel like getting drunk kid," George said, "join me?"

With a quick wink, George snapped out of his daydream and dragged Harvey off to his study.

"Here, just try it," George said, pushing the small glass towards Harvey.

Harvey was suspicious of the brown liquid in the glass. It smelled strongly, and he'd only just got used to the taste of wine. George knocked his drink back and hit the glass on the mahogany desk.

"Ah, that's good shit," George said as he let the whiskey wash over his body.

Harvey looked around the study at all of the books. He loved the dimness of the room. The rest of the house was so bright and open planned, which only made the study feel even cozier and welcoming.

"C'mon kid. You're making me look bad," George poured another whiskey and knocked it back.

Harvey closed his eyes and threw the liquid to the back of his throat. It burned all the way down to his stomach and made his eyes water.

"Jesus Christ," Harvey gasped through the burning sensation, "is it meant to burn?"

George erupted laughing as he poured Harvey a second, and himself a third.

"That's the best bit," he winked at Harvey as he threw his third whiskey back.

Harvey drank the second, and it burned just as much as the first, but he had to admit he didn't dislike the taste as much as he'd expected to.

"So," Harvey said, wincing through the burning in his throat, "what's up?"

George furrowed his brow and stared at Harvey across the desk.

"What do you mean?" George asked.

"Well, we're drinking and it's not even 8am yet," Harvey laughed.

"Shit, what are we doing?" George laughed, pushing the glass bottle of whiskey away.

"I didn't say stop!" Harvey grabbed the bottle, pouring himself another, "I'm growing to like it."

Harvey tossed it back and started to look forward to the strange burning sensation travelling down to his stomach, which sent hot shivers throughout his entire body. He could already feel the alcohol clouding over his mind and mixing with the eggs and bacon in his gut.

"It's a real shit sandwich, isn't it?" he poured them another drink, "I just wish we could go away together."

"We could go," Harvey suggested, hoping that the alcohol was making George want to speed things up, "there's always the cabin?"

"It's bad timing kid. I mean, my new book is being released next week so I can't leave town."

That wasn't what Harvey was expecting to hear. So far, the only excuse he'd given him was that he didn't want to upset

Paula, so close to her mother dying, but now there was another excuse. He wondered if in 2 weeks when it came to telling Paula, there'd be something else.

Harvey grabbed the bottle and took a swig directly from the top, this time wanting the thoughts to stop racing around in his mind. He wanted to forget about Paula and book releases. He wanted to just be in the moment with George, but it was getting progressively harder to stay focused when there were so many distractions.

"Steady!" George said, grabbing the bottle from Harvey's tight grip, "Save me some."

He winked at Harvey across the desk as he snatched the bottle and started to swig it himself.

Harvey stood up and tried to walk around the study. He wanted to grab a book to read, but when he got up to his feet, he felt like his head was circling a drain.

"That stuff is strong," Harvey said.

His mouth and eyes were starting to water as the alcohol in his stomach started to settle.

George opened one of the stiff drawers under his desk, pushed past all of the papers and found a small digital radio. He switched it on and tuned it to a jazz station. A smooth big-band tune suddenly filled the study. To Harvey's surprise, George grabbed one of his hands and put one hand around Harvey's waist and they started to slowly dance, holding each other close.

"I love this type of music," George smiled, "It reminds me of my parents. Every Saturday when I was home from school, they'd play their records throughout the house, and we'd spend the day cleaning, listening to the classics."

"That sounds so nice," Harvey whispered into George's chest, "when we move to New York, we'll be closer to your father."

"I don't think he'll care," George sighed, "he blames me for what happened to my mother. I haven't spoken to him since the funeral."

Harvey closed his eyes heavily. He suddenly realized why

George understood his situation so much. He hadn't just lost one parent when his mother had died in the car crash, he'd lost two.

Big band music had never been to Harvey's taste, but as he danced messily with George, he was starting to find an appreciation for it. He wasn't sure if it was the alcohol or being so close to George, who was equally as intoxicating, but he was really enjoying listening to the instruments.

"When we get married, can we hire a big band? I'd love that," George said softly.

Harvey's heart felt like it was about to pop.

"Married?" Harvey almost choked on the word as it left his lips.

"Obviously I'd have to wait until the divorce finalized, and we'd have to do it in a state where it's legal," George started, "what do you think?"

Harvey paused for a moment and smiled into George's chest.

"I'd like that," Harvey whispered with a huge smile spread across his face, "we can do it in New York. It's legal there."

"Good," George smiled as they continued to dance.

Harvey felt something hard press against his stomach. He reached down and grabbed the growing bulge over George's tight jeans.

"I want you to fuck me against the desk," Harvey whispered softly into George's ear.

George pulled his head back and a wicked smile spread across his face. He picked Harvey up and let him wrap his legs around his waist as he carried him over to the desk. The eye contact was so intense, it was turning Harvey on without even being touched. George's presence was like ten shots of whiskey all at once.

Planting Harvey gently on the desk with a kiss, his fingers drunkenly fumbled with the buckle on his belt.

SEVEN

"**C**an we have white roses at our wedding?" Harvey asked, "From your garden?"

"That sounds like a perfect idea," George stroked Harvey's hair.

They'd been naked on George's study floor for hours discussing wedding plans. Harvey was wrapped around George's perfectly toned body with his head resting gently on George's well-defined chest. He could hear his heart beating gently as it rose and fell. He'd never felt so close to George as he did in that moment.

The sound of the door slamming made George jump up, sending Harvey crashing to the floor. They'd spent hours and hours drinking whiskey, having sex, drinking more whiskey and having more sex and now Paula was back to spoil things. George was scrambling around trying to pull his socks on at the same time he was pulling a T-shirt over his head.

"Quick, get dressed!"

It could have been the alcohol or a deep desire to get

caught, but he was in no rush to get his clothes back on. There'd be no way to explain why Harvey was naked on the ground, and it would make things so much easier.

George flung Harvey's clothes at him as he fastened the buttons on the top of his jeans and fastened the belt tightly, making the bulge in his pants stick out even further.

Reluctantly pulling his clothes on, Harvey heard footsteps across the dining room floor. He was sure he'd heard George say that Paula never came into his study.

As Harvey pulled his socks on and smoothed his hair back, the door to the office swung open. George was already behind the desk, furiously typing at the keyboard.

"Oh," Paula muttered when she saw Harvey awkwardly leaning against the desk.

She knew as well as Harvey did that George's study was a private place and he didn't like people being in there ever. Harvey shot Paula a look that said '*yes, he trusts me enough*'.

"George, can I talk to you in private please?" Paula said coldly ignoring Harvey.

Her emphasis on the word '*private*' made Harvey snicker, and he wanted to tell her what her husband was getting up to in his private time.

"Don't worry, I'm going," Harvey mumbled.

He walked past Paula, and he could feel her eyes burning into his skin every second he was still in the room. Instead of going to the kitchen or up to his room, he pressed his ear firmly against the door, to hear what Paula had to say.

"I've found these youth accommodations for homeless teens," Harvey heard her say.

He couldn't believe how intent Paula was at trying to get rid of him. He had to admire her determination.

"He's not homeless," George said calmly, "he lives here."

"Temporarily," Paula said coldly, "please just have a look at them."

"Okay, I'll have a look at them," George said.

Harvey darted out of the dining room and quickly ran up the stairs to the guest bedroom. When he was inside, he considered what George had said. Surely he was just saying he'd look at them just to try and get rid of Paula?

He suddenly remembered George visiting his principal behind his back and he felt uneasy. Shaking his head, he blamed it on the whiskey and collapsed onto his bed and instantly fell into a restless sleep.

***

The weeks passed and nothing much changed. Paula was just as frosty as the first time Harvey had met her, and George was avoiding her at every turn.

"How do I look, kid?" George asked Harvey as he walked into the guest bedroom.

Harvey was standing there in nothing but a pair of socks as he dug through his closet for something to wear to the release. Harvey admired George's muscled body in the tight white shirt. It looked like at any moment, the buttons would burst to reveal his bulging pecs.

"You look hot," Harvey laughed as he pulled on a pair of briefs, "you should wear a tie more often."

"Really?" George said, pulling the collar from his neck, "I feel like I'm being choked."

Harvey pulled on a white shirt of his own that George had bought him. He opted for a more casual look and left the top button undone. Before Harvey could pull his faded blue jeans on, George grabbed Harvey around the waist and they locked lips. Harvey could feel George's hands slowly reaching down the back of his underwear.

As George softly massaged Harvey's cheeks, his tongue explored Harvey's mouth, and he resisted the urge to pull George's new clothes off.

"You're going to crease your shirt," Harvey laughed through the kissing.

George stopped and grunted, he playfully slapped Harvey on the backside and gave Harvey one last kiss.

"We'd better set off or we're going to be late," he smiled,

"and I don't think they can have a book signing without the star."

When the car drove past the bookstore, Harvey couldn't believe how many people were queuing outside. Hundreds and hundreds of fans were waiting patiently to get a glimpse of their favorite author.

Harvey wanted to roll down the window and tell them all that he'd had more than a glimpse of the famous George Lewis.

"This is insane!" Harvey laughed as they drove around the back of the bookstore, "I can't believe how many people have come to see you."

"Hey, I'm the shit," George joked, "It's a good turn out this year. Greg has done a good job with the PR."

Harvey suspected it was less to do with PR and more to do with George being a big deal in the writing world. He was looking forward to reading the new book as much as the rest of the fans waiting in line to get their copy. George hadn't let Harvey read any of it.

He'd finished the book a few weeks before he had even met Harvey, but he'd been busily editing and perfecting the story, something George seemed to hate doing.

"George, good to see you!" Greg said as he warmly shook George's hand, "Lots of people! Lots to do! If this doesn't top the best sellers list then I don't know what will."

Greg flicked his eyes up to Harvey. He was a tiny man with a shot of thick gray hair sprouting messily from the top of his head.

"Harvey! It's nice to see you again," Greg smiled as he shook Harvey's hand, "I'm excited about our meeting next week!"

Harvey smiled weakly at the little man. He didn't want to let Greg know that he hadn't written a single word of the sample he'd asked for, and he was sure that was written all over his face.

"It's coming along great," George jumped in and saved him, "I've read a few pages and it really is brilliant stuff."

Harvey knew that George was only trying to help him out, but his constant reassurance that he was a brilliant writer only made Harvey feel even more uneasy, especially as he didn't seem to be able to string a sentence together. He'd tried nearly every night in his room to type up the sample, but the words would never come naturally. Whenever he'd read back what he'd written, he'd hit the delete button.

The only writing he was doing was in his journal. He'd nearly filled the thick leather-bound book with his deepest feelings, most of them about George.

"Are you ready, George?" Greg said, clasping his small hands together, "Your public awaits!"

Greg led George out to the front of the bookstore. There was a huge table set up for him. The minute the crowd saw him, they all cheered and whooped as they clutched tightly onto George's new book.

Harvey walked out into the store and the crowd of excited faces in front of him made his stomach do back flips. He couldn't believe how many people there were, just to see George. It made him all that more determined to write his own book. He knew it wouldn't happen overnight, but he hoped that one day he could walk out to this.

It would be nice to think that people wanted to hear what he had to say for a change.

Harvey hovered around the edge of the store, affectionately admiring George as he made small talk with his adoring fans before security moved them along. He was the perfect gentleman, but Harvey could tell that George was looking uncomfortable. Harvey knew he'd be the only one who'd notice that, and that made him smile. He was the only one who really knew George.

"Harvey?" Greg called, "Have you got a copy of the book yet?"

Harvey had to admire Greg's determination to sell books.

"I haven't yet," Harvey admitted.

"Here," he handed Harvey a copy of the book with a smile and walked off.

For a second, Harvey considered joining the line and getting it signed so he could experience it as the boy he'd been before he met George. He saw the line wasn't dying down, as more and more people were joining outside the bookstore. Instead, Harvey went over to his old spot by the new releases, and sat cross-legged on the floor. It had been so long since he'd been there, it felt strangely comforting.

He examined the cover of the book in his hands. '*The Missing Son*' was an epic tale of a woman who spent 20 years trying to look for the son she'd put up for adoption. George had a habit of pulling on the reader's heartstrings.

Opening the front cover, he pulled the book up to his face and inhaled the new book smell. It sent a shiver running down his spine.

He flicked through the pages and his eyes froze when he came to the dedication page. His heart stopped beating for a second, as he read the small sentence in italics.

'This book is for H, for bringing me back to life.'

EIGHT

"I thought I'd find you here," George smiled as he leaned over the shelf to find him on the floor.

"Old habits die hard," he laughed as he softly closed the book, folding the corner of the page.

He didn't know how long he'd been sat there, but he was already 1/4 of his way through.

"What do you think then?" George asked nervously, "It's not my best is it?"

"It's really good so far," Harvey said truthfully, "I especially liked the dedication page."

A warm smile spread across George's face as he sat on the floor next to Harvey. He kissed him softly on the cheek. Harvey looked around, but the people in the bookstore were still patiently lined up.

"I have half an hour for lunch," George whispered in Harvey's ear, "and I'm really hungry."

He jumped up and threw Harvey a seductive look. He started to walk to the back of the store and Harvey followed him. They walked past Greg with a friendly smile and George led Harvey into the bathroom. One of the security guards stood at the urinal. George walked over to the sink and started to wash his hands. Harvey joined him and they stared intensely at each other through the mirror. The security guard zipped up, nodded to them and left the bathroom without bothering to wash his hands.

The second the door slammed shut, he grabbed Harvey roughly around the waist and pushed him into the tiny cubical. He locked the door and unzipped the front of Harvey's jeans. The growing bulge in Harvey's underwear flopped out and George started to caress it while kissing Harvey wildly.

"What if someone walks in?" Harvey whispered as he felt every hair on his body stand up.

"I don't care," George mumbled through the kisses. He got down on his knees and pulled down the briefs to expose Harvey's growing shaft.

Harvey softly moaned and closed his eyes as he felt George's tongue exploring him. Every single one of his senses seemed to heighten at being in public. When he heard the door to the bathroom open, his ears pricked and he tapped George on the shoulder, but George didn't stop.

Harvey felt his entire body tense up and a warm feeling spread across him euphorically. George backed off with a smile and pulled Harvey's underwear back up and zipped the front of his jeans up.

"George?" Greg's voice called throughout the bathroom, "Is that you in there?"

"I'll be out with you in a minute Greg," George called, standing up and reaching around Harvey to flush the toilet.

He unlocked the door and opened it ever so slightly, slipping through the gap not wanting to expose his secret. Harvey quietly locked the door behind him and picked his feet up off the ground, balancing on the toilet seat.

***

"Everything okay in there? You looked like you were on your knees," Greg asked, raising his eyebrows at George in the

146

mirror.

"Uneasy stomach," George said, trying to fake a sick voice, "my lunch must have disagreed with me."

"Oh that's dreadful," Greg said, not really caring, "there's still hundreds of people out there waiting to get a book signed, and the line keeps growing."

George knew what he was hinting at so he agreed to cut his break short so he could get back to the crowd. He'd got exactly what he wanted anyway.

He asked the security to cut meet and greets down to 20 seconds so he could get through the rest of the people before the store closed. He didn't like making people feel rushed, but he didn't like the thought of leaving people out who had lined up for hours.

When the last few fans had signed books in their hands, the doors to the store were locked and Harvey retreated from his hiding place next to the new releases, already halfway through the book.

"What a long day," George sighed as they drove back to the house, "my hand is killing me."

George flexed his hand over the steering wheel, but it was no good.

"I'm going to start on my book tonight," Harvey decided.

"Good for you, kid!" George smiled at Harvey and glanced at him out of the corner of his eye.

"I want what you had today. I know it sounds dumb, but I want all those people wanting to know me," Harvey said quietly as he looked out of the window.

"That's not dumb," George laughed, "In fact, that's the best reason. Why else would you want to write other than to make people happy?"

"Well, if you put it like that," Harvey laughed, "that doesn't sound too bad."

"I like the signings, but I'd rather just have Greg tell me the opinion polls and send me the select reviews."

"That, and meeting guys on bookstore floors to get their opinions," Harvey said jokingly.

George chuckled softly as he remembered how they first met. It felt like a lifetime ago, but it hadn't even been two months. He glanced at Harvey again out of the corner of his eye, and his heart swelled up in his chest.

"Do you want to do something?" George asked as they drove through town, "I don't feel like going home yet."

"What did you have in mind?" he smiled staring into his lap.

"We could go see a movie?" George suggested.

He nodded and George drove them towards the movie theatre.

***

George led them to the back row of the movie theatre. Harvey followed the tiny lights on the edge of the stairs as he fumbled through the dark. The movie had already started and the few people that were already there eating their popcorn were throwing George and Harvey daggers as they interrupted things.

They'd bought tickets for a romantic comedy that neither George nor Harvey had any desire to watch, but it was the only one showing without sitting around waiting for an hour. They slouched in the corner of the dark theatre, and when George slid his fingers softly into Harvey's, his heart nearly stopped.

He was staring at the screen, but feeling George's hand gripping his softly in the darkness of a room with other people made him glad he was sitting down because he was sure he could feel his knees trying to buckle.

"I love you," Harvey whispered as he rested his head on George's broad shoulder.

"I love you too," George smiled back, unlinking his fingers and sliding them firmly around Harvey's shoulders.

Harvey was glad that they were watching a movie that didn't have much of a plot, because they'd already missed 15 minutes, but it was so aimless, it wasn't difficult to catch up. He laughed at the jokes and gags, and his heart was warmed

GEORGE & HARVEY BOXSET

when the guy got the girl in the end.

It made Harvey think about him and George and how their relationship so far was like something out of a movie. He'd heard of people meeting in bookstores and falling in love, but his story was already so complicated.

Even though he felt like he was living in his own romantic movie, he was terrified of what the ending would bring.

NINE

"**W**here have you been?" Paula cried from the dining room table when Harvey and George walked in.

A plate of half-eaten food was in front of her and a full plate was across from her. A candle separated the two plates but it had already burned halfway down. Harvey noticed there wasn't a place set for him.

"We went for a movie. No big deal," George said casually as he pulled his leather jacket off and threw it over one of the chairs.

"I told you this morning I was going to make dinner for just the two of us tonight," Paula sneered, shooting a sharp look in Harvey's direction.

Her emphasis on *'the two of us'* made Harvey feel funny. He didn't want to think of George having an *'us'* with anybody else besides him. He couldn't help but think that Paula was trying her hardest to win her husband back. Perhaps she could sense the divorce papers on the horizon.

"I'm sorry," George said, not sounding sorry at all, "the

signing ran over and we thought we'd just catch a movie."

"You didn't think to call?" Paula shouted as she pushed the plate away from her, sending it crashing into the candle.

The tall candle fell onto the cream tablecloth, splashing hot white wax everywhere.

"I forgot. You know what I'm like in the mornings," George grumbled, rolling his sleeves up, "let me clear these plates away."

As he walked over to the edge of the table where Paula was sitting, she jumped up and grabbed the plate full of food, launching it at the wall inches away from George's face. Cold drops of gravy bounced off the walls and onto George's crisp white shirt. Peas and carrots scattered messily across the room.

"What's your fucking problem?" George shouted, in a booming deep voice.

"My problem?" Paula laughed, "My problem is that my husband seems to be choosing a random teenage boy over his wife."

George took a step towards Paula, stepping over the small pile of food and broken plate.

"I don't care if you have a problem with Harvey. He's not going anywhere until I say," George shouted.

To Harvey's surprise, Paula didn't step down. Instead, she coldly slapped George across the face. Venom spread through Harvey's body like an infection. He clenched his fists as he tried to stop himself launching on Paula to rip out chunks of her perfect blonde hair.

A red handprint stung its way onto George's perfect skin. He raised his hand, and for a moment Harvey thought he was going to slap Paula back, but instead he softly touched his own face.

"Kid, just go wait upstairs," George muttered, without turning to look at Harvey.

His eyes were fixed on Paula. Harvey's feet didn't move. For a moment, he felt like he didn't belong with his body. Instead he was hovering over them all, watching the drama unfold. It took a second for him to realize that George was addressing him.

"I'm not leaving you here alone," Harvey cried painfully.

He didn't care if Paula could sense the love and anger in his voice. He was done with pretending he didn't love the bones of the man standing in front of him.

"Please, Harvey," George muttered quietly again.

Harvey resisted the urge to run over to grab George kicking and screaming. Reluctantly Harvey left the dining room, but instead of going upstairs, he hovered outside the door, which he left slightly open.

He could see Paula's arms flying around as she whispered angrily at George. Harvey strained his eyes to try to read her lips, but they were moving so fast he couldn't make out a word.

What George did next surprised Harvey. He grabbed Paula's arms and tried to pull her into a hug. She thrashed and beat against his chest trying to escape. He pulled her in again, harder this time, and she relaxed and embraced him.

A red haze clouded Harvey's mind when he heard the sound of Paula softly crying into her husband's shoulder. His heart twitched when he heard George clearly speak.

"It's okay," he whispered stroking her blonde hair, "It's gonna be okay."

Harvey's eyes brimmed with tears. He tried to blink them away as he scrambled for the stairs, but they wouldn't budge. He wanted to run back into the dining room to rip the leech off his love, but instead he staggered up to his room.

He ripped open his laptop and opened a blank document. For the first time in a long time, he knew exactly what he needed to write about. Without thinking he let the words pour from his heart onto the page. For hours he typed furiously, not letting himself stop until the pain eased. When the pain didn't stop, he typed faster and harder. He noticed the mistakes as he typed but he didn't care. He didn't want to change them, he just wanted to write.

Sleep started to creep into his mind. He tried to shake it away because the pain was still fresh in his heart. Heavy eyelids started to flicker over his sore eyes. They trembled, trying to focus on the white screen in the dark room. His fingers slowed down, and the sleep started to control his mind. He knew he was typing rubbish by that point, but he didn't want to let his fingers stop.

His face rested on the hot laptop and the sleep quickly washed over him, sending him into a land of restless and confusing dreams.

"Harvey? Harvey wake up!" Harvey shot bolt upright and stared at the laptop screen.

There were pages and pages of random letters. He knew from the indented feeling on his cheek that his face had been typing for him even when his fingers had stopped.

"You must have fallen asleep writing," George said softly.

He put his hand on Harvey's shoulder, but as he did, Harvey stood up and walked over to his bed. He glanced at the alarm clock.

3:42am.

"Won't Paula be wondering why you're not in bed?" Harvey asked in a flat voice.

"She's asleep, so I thought -"

"You thought you'd come and spend some time with me?" Harvey said coldly.

"Is that a problem?"

"I don't know, George," Harvey sighed as he leaned on the edge of the bed, "I don't know what the problem is anymore."

"What are you talking about?" George said as he tried to put his arm around Harvey's shoulders.

Shrugging him off, Harvey edged further down the bed.

"At first, I thought Paula was the problem," Harvey started, "but then I got to thinking that maybe you were the problem. Are you even going to leave her?"

"What's brought this on?"

"I saw you hug her and tell her that everything was going to be okay,"

Harvey felt George tighten up next to him.

"I-I-I don't -"

"You don't have to say anything," Harvey interrupted, "you should go back to your wife."

"It's you that I love," George mumbled desperately.

"Why do I sense a *'but'*?" Harvey sighed, shaking his head with exhaustion.

It felt like every time he made progress with George, he'd do something idiotic that would send the sky falling in. He wasn't just exhausted with the situation, he was exhausted with George.

"But she's my wife, and I can't just dump all of this on her out of the blue," George sighed, putting his head heavily in his hands, "I don't know how to handle this."

Harvey watched George rub his face roughly. He wanted to hold him, but he restrained himself.

"I know what I want," Harvey said quietly, "I just want you."

"I want you. That's all I want. You're the love of my life," George sighed, sounding even more desperate.

"So do something about it, because I can't carry on like this."

An awkward silence grew between them. Harvey could feel the heat radiating from George as he stared into the dark thinking about what he'd been writing. He wanted to show George. He wanted to show George his pain. Even though they were sitting only inches apart, he felt like there was an ocean between them.

"I'm sorry," George said, "I'll fix this. I just need more time."

"Time's running out, George," he said flatly, "make your move."

TEN

Over the next couple of days, Harvey made sure that his contact with George and Paula was minimal. He told George that he was working on his book in time for his interview, and even though he didn't seem to want to, George left him alone.

As he typed, the idea that George was choosing Paula kept creeping viciously into his mind. Every time it reared its ugly head, he'd try and forget the hurt it was causing. Instead of following his heart, he followed his head, working his fingers to the bone to get the sample of the book finished. He poured his heart and soul into the words because he knew that it was his real shot at being able to stand on his own two feet, and he wasn't going to let anything stand in his way.

"Are you ready?" George asked, popping his head around Harvey's bedroom door.

He'd borrowed George's printer and after many painful hours of editing, re-typing and molding the words into perfection, he was satisfied that he'd done the best job he could.

When the printer spat out the last page, a strange sense of

relief washed over Harvey. He was relieved that he'd managed to pull it off, on his own and without George's help. It was the first thing he'd done on his own, without needing to depend on somebody and it was a liberating experience.

"Do I get a preview?" George laughed, keeping his distance from Harvey as he neatly put the pages into a folder.

For a second, Harvey thought about letting George read the whole thing, but he knew that if he did, he probably wouldn't drive Harvey to see Greg and he knew he needed him for that at least.

"No previews," Harvey said, trying to sound polite, "you'll just have to wait for the book to come out."

George sighed. Harvey couldn't stand the distance that was growing between them. It was filled with polite smiles and awkward silences.

"I got you something," George said, pulling a chunky black box out of his pocket, "for luck."

Harvey's stomach twisted. He couldn't stand more gifts from George. There was a pattern emerging and it didn't take a genius to figure it out. Every time George used him like an emotional punch bag, he'd buy something expensive, and they seemed to be getting more and more expensive with each mistake. Could he have possibly topped the price tag of the laptop?

Reluctantly, he accepted the black box and snapped it open to reveal a glittering gold watch. A small gasp escaped Harvey's throat as he lifted the chunky watch from its red velvet bed. He wasn't a jewelry expert, but just feeling it in his hands, he knew it was expensive.

"George, you really shouldn't have," Harvey said, sounding more ungrateful than he'd intended, "this is really too much."

"For the man I love, nothing is too much," George smiled nervously, trying to gage his reaction.

Hearing George profess his love made Harvey look guiltily at the manuscript hidden in the folder lying on the edge of his bed. He wasn't sure if George would feel the same if he knew what his book was about.

George gently took the watch from Harvey and turned it over to reveal a tiny message etched in the back.

"I had it engraved," George said softly as he ran his fingers across the tiny gold letters.

Harvey's heart dropped to the ground when he read the tiny message. It felt like the biggest emotional slap he'd ever received.

'Harvey, with each passing day, I love you more than the last. Yours forever, George.'

He didn't know whether to laugh or cry. He wasn't sure if this was George just doing what he thought was the right thing, or if this was genuinely how he felt. The word *'forever'* burned painfully in Harvey's mind.

He wasn't sure if he had George right now, so he didn't know if George would be there forever. He tried to stop her, but Paula sprang into his mind. He couldn't help but feel like she had watches in a drawer somewhere with lovely inscriptions on the backs of them.

"It's really beautiful," Harvey said as George gently fastened the watch around Harvey's thin wrist.

The watch fit snugly on Harvey's wrist and he stared blankly at the white clock face, wanting to feel a definite emotion, but he was a swirling mash-up of intense love and bubbling anger.

"You don't like it do you?" George said glumly, taking a deflated step back.

"The watch really is beautiful," Harvey said truthfully.

He couldn't understand why George didn't get it. He didn't want expensive gifts, he just wanted George.

"What's the problem?" George's smile was shaking nervously.

Harvey wanted to tell him that it felt like another one of George's empty promises that never seemed to go anywhere, but he couldn't bring himself to do it. He knew deep down that he loved George with all of his heart, and seeing the look of confusion and disappointment, only made his heart hurt even more.

"No problem. I really love it," Harvey forced the most convincing smile he could, feeling the watch around his wrist like a ton weight.

"Good," George said as he put his arms around Harvey's neck.

He softly planted a kiss on Harvey's lips, but for the first time he didn't feel the fireworks in his stomach. He didn't even close his eyes, he just stared blankly at George's closed lids.

The watch felt like a big gold symbol of all of George's transparent promises. Harvey realized he knew so little about the man he'd fallen so madly in love with.

"We'd better set off," Harvey said as he pulled away from George, grabbing his manuscript and clutching it tightly to his chest, "I've got a book to sell!"

As they drove silently into town, Harvey could feel his wrist itching under the watch. He wanted to take it off because it was only acting as a distraction. He'd promised himself he was only going to focus on his book, but the watch was screaming at him. He wanted to wind the window down and smash it against the sidewalk.

Every time he caught George looking at him out of the corner of his eye, his stomach churned, getting tighter with each look. He was trying to summon the warm fuzzy feeling he loved so much about being in George's presence, but his body just felt empty.

Blaming it on the nerves, Harvey stared blankly at the manuscript on his knees. It was only five chapters of a book that might never get finished, but it felt like the whole of his future was resting on it.

It was only a few weeks ago that he'd looked into his future and all he could see was George, but now when he looked into his future, all he could see was darkness.

ELEVEN

"**H**arvey! This is brilliant stuff!" Greg laughed leaning back in his chair as he flicked through the pages.

Harvey shifted nervously in his chair as he watched Greg devour his soul in paper form. He was praying tightly that Greg didn't put two and two together and figure out who the story was about.

"I wasn't sure if you'd like it," Harvey mumbled nervously.

"It's so raw! It's so real! Who is this Benjamin character based on?" Greg asked, looking over the top of the pages.

"Completely fictional," Harvey lied, not wanting to say *'George'*.

George was sitting next to Harvey smiling politely, completely unaware what Greg was reading.

"And the wife, Becky? Fictional too?"

Harvey nodded. He could feel a dry lump rising in his throat. The plastic cup of water in his hand was shaking violently, spilling drops onto the white floor. He wanted to speak, but he could feel George's questioning eyes burning into his skin. He was convinced that Greg's little scraps of information were starting to put the pieces of the jigsaw together.

"I really like the Harry character," Greg said, slamming the manuscript on his desk, "he's so real and likeable. I'm already rooting for him. I think it's so clever how you've got Benjamin caught between his lover and his wife. You've really made Benjamin a confused man and it really works!"

George coughed as he took a sip of his own water. His face turned bright red, but Harvey couldn't look at him.

"I'm really glad you like it," Harvey smiled, still shaking.

He could feel George fidgeting uncomfortably in the chair next to him, but he still didn't turn to look.

"There's some things that need changing, and I'll need to see a treatment for the rest of the book, but I'm pretty positive this is something we'd be interested in," Greg smiled at Harvey.

He could almost see the dollar signs in Greg's eyes.

"Are you serious?" Harvey laughed, this time looking at George.

George didn't meet his eyes, he just smiled awkwardly to the ground.

"You've got raw talent, boy," Greg beamed as he stood up, "that's what I like. You can't teach what you do."

He walked over to a filing cabinet and pulled out a document. He slapped it on the desk and slid it across to Harvey.

"This is the kind of deal we'd offer you. You'd get a small advance, and it'd be a limited run at first, but with the right promotion, there'd be room to extend your contract," Greg smiled slyly as Harvey devoured the information on the white piece of paper.

Harvey couldn't believe he was staring at his dream right in front of him. It was all there in black and white. He wanted to sign on the dotted line before it vanished.

Greg pulled the paper away from Harvey and filed it back in the cabinet.

"Obviously, I'll need to discuss the best course of action with my team," Greg said, as he leaned back into his chair again, "but if I get the green light, I'll get a contract sent straight over to George's place."

"That's brilliant," George said.

Harvey couldn't decide if he sounded excited or bitter.

"You are still living with George, right?" Greg asked, raising an eyebrow.

"Yes," Harvey said coldly, "just until I'm on my feet."

"Well, your first advance would make a nice deposit on a little place," Greg said.

Harvey hadn't thought about it like that. He hadn't even considered getting a place on his own. Hearing someone tell him that he could stand on his own two feet without the help of George or Leo made him realize there was nothing stopping him. It seemed to all make sense, until he looked down at the watch glued to his wrist.

His heart started to pound in his chest to the rhythm of the watches loud ticking.

As Greg rose to show them out of his office, George grabbed the manuscript and thanked Greg.

Harvey stared at the manuscript clenched in George's fist. When they reached the fresh air of the car park, George flicked open the manuscript and started to read the opening. All of the color drained from his face.

"I don't understand why you'd do this?"

Harvey stared for a second and cursed George under his breath. He didn't know how he had the right to even be angry with him, after he'd spent weeks playing ping pong with his emotions.

"It's the truth," Harvey said sternly, "I just changed a few names."

"Well you can change the whole thing. This is never going to be printed!" George said loudly, as he threw the paper manuscript on the floor.

Harvey quickly scrambled to the ground and stuffed the manuscript in his jacket.

"I'm not changing anything," Harvey said as he started to walk away from George, leaving him standing outside of the office block.

"You can't just walk away," George shouted after him.

Harvey stopped in his tracks. He knew he didn't have anywhere to go but if he went back with George, it'd only blow up the minute they were inside the house.

"Just stop this, Harvey," George sighed as he caught up with him.

"Stop what?"

"This attitude!" George cried.

Harvey stared at him for a moment. He couldn't decide if George was just acting dumb, or if he actually didn't understand what was really going on.

"When are you going to leave your wife, George?" Harvey screamed in George's face.

George stared blankly at him, opening and closing his mouth slowly, but no sound came out.

"No, I didn't think you could answer that."

Part of him hoped that George would run after him, but he didn't. As he headed into town, he dumped the manuscript in a trashcan. He knew he had a copy on his laptop, but he knew George would never let it get published. He was probably already on the phone to Greg telling him that he was withdrawing Harvey's concept.

He wandered aimlessly into town. It felt like that night in the rain again, and almost instinctively, his legs headed in the direction of Ginger's small café. The tiny bell echoed throughout the empty café. When Ginger saw him from behind the counter, her face lit up with joy.

"I thought I'd be seeing you again!" she beamed as Harvey walked towards the counter.

Her kindness only made Harvey feel worse. Weeks of built up anger and confusion suddenly overwhelmed him and tears started to pour uncontrollably from his face.

Ginger's thin frame quickly ran around the counter and pulled Harvey close. Images of his mother flooded through his mind. He couldn't remember the last time he'd been hugged by someone who wasn't George.

She flipped the sign to '*Closed*' and locked the door, leading Harvey to a small private room behind the counter. It was a dim room with a small table. Trinkets and souvenirs lined the walls of the tiny, dark room. In a weird way, it reminded Harvey of George's study, which felt like a comfort and a torment at the same time.

Without hesitation, he poured his heart out to Ginger. He told her all about his parents, Leo and meeting George. She listened to the whole story as they sipped fresh coffee.

She nodded in the right places and gasped at the shocking parts, making Harvey feel like he was really being listened to and understood properly. He didn't care about telling Ginger that he was gay. He felt a strange connection to her that told him that she didn't have a judgmental bone in her body.

"You're in a right pickle of a situation, aren't you," she curled her thin lips into a warm smile as she reached her hand across the table and put it on Harvey's.

Her thumb gently stroked the back of Harvey's hand and he suddenly felt like a fool for burdening such a kind woman with all of his problems.

"I'm sorry," Harvey laughed as he wiped the tears from his cheeks, "I'm a mess."

"Now you listen here!" she said with a sternness that made Harvey sit up, "I told you I would be here if you ever needed me, and you clearly need me right now. Ginger is here to listen. You were put on that doorstep for a reason, remember?"

Harvey smiled and he felt fresh tears brim in his eyes, but he stopped them.

Her motherly instinct warmed Harvey through, more than George ever had. There were no conditions or problems to her kindness. She was just there to help people who needed it.

"You know what you need to do don't you, child?" she said as she wiped a fresh tear from Harvey's cheek, "You need to go over there and face him head on. You march over there and you tell him it's you or her and if he doesn't decide there and

ASHLEY JOHN

then, then he's not worth a dime."

She leaned back in her chair pleased with her own advice. Harvey let her words sink in and he knew she was wiser than he could ever be. He wondered what she'd been through to make her so strong.

"You know what, you're right," Harvey said, rubbing his eyes, "I'm just going to go over there and stop running away from the problem. Me or her."

A small smile spread across Ginger's face. She insisted on making Harvey a sandwich before he faced George because, as she explained, you should never make big decisions on an empty stomach.

When Ginger sent Harvey on his way, a small queue had gathered outside of Ginger's café waiting for her to open. He smiled as he thought of all these people that would wait around in the street for such a brilliant woman. He imagined she helped them all in some way, even if it was just with a smile as she poured them coffee.

As he walked through the streets heading back to the house, he felt a steel determination build up in his chest. He'd tried to squash any doubts or nerves he had, as he convinced himself that George was going to choose him.

He glanced at the watch.

'Forever Yours.'

When Harvey turned onto George's street, all of that determination melted away to nothing when he saw a little blue car in the driveway.

Paula was home.

TWELVE

When Harvey tried to open the door, his heart sank when the door didn't open. It was locked. He had images of George locking the door and never letting him in again.

Shakily, he knocked on the door, and as he heard footsteps walk quickly across the hallway he hoped and prayed that it was George.

His prayers were answered, when a relieved looking George flung the door open.

Without a word, George grabbed Harvey and pulled him into a tight embrace. Harvey pushed his face tightly into George's shoulder, not wanting the tears to start again. He breathed in George's aftershave, remembering all the times that he'd been close enough to smell it on him.

The question started burning in his mind.

Me or her.

Me or her.

Me or her.

Instead, he followed George into the house. He looked around for Paula but he couldn't see her.

Me or her.

Me or her.

George led him into the kitchen and pulled him into another tight hug.

"I'm so sorry, kid," George whispered, "I'm fucking this up."

Harvey appreciated that George was finally noticing his failings. The words he'd rehearsed the whole way home were on the tip of his tongue, but they vanished when he heard the sharp click of heels across the tiled floor.

"What's going on?"

George hastily pulled away from Harvey.

"Harvey's just had some bad news about a family member," George lied, "he's just a bit upset."

Paula raised an eyebrow and pushed past them both. She grabbed a salad box from the fridge and headed out into the garden.

"You're unbelievable," Harvey stuttered, "you could have just told her right there and then. You're such a coward."

George's eyes darted from Harvey to the floor and back again, and he could feel a few beads of sweat starting to appear above his eyebrows.

"I will tell her," George said feebly.

"When?" Harvey demanded, "I want a date."

"I was going to wait until after your graduation," George said quickly, "you don't want all of this drama when you're about to graduate from high school."

Harvey thought that George was making more excuses again, but when the words sank in, he found himself agreeing. He didn't want to admit it, but that was a better plan than blurting it out.

"You tell her the day I graduate," Harvey said in a cold voice, "or I'm gone."

"I promise," George whispered, stealing a quick kiss.

Harvey glanced to the garden, but Paula had her back to them. His graduation was only 4 days away. He'd waited so long already for the truth to be told, he told himself that he could wait 4 more days.

Just 4 more days.

Harvey chanted '*just 4 more days*' over and over as they ate their dinner. He gazed at George's face and let the warm fuzzy feeling wash over him again for the first time since he'd seen him hugging Paula in the dining room.

He wanted to rip George's clothes off right there, but he could suddenly hear Ginger's words screaming louder in his mind than anything else.

'*If he doesn't decide there and then, then he's not worth a dime.*'

He shook his head and told Ginger to shut up, as he felt George's hand gently rubbing his leg under the breakfast bar. He winked to Harvey and they headed off upstairs.

Paula's sweet and sickly perfume filled Harvey's nostrils as he followed George into the bedroom. A few weeks ago, he'd been living in there, but the briefs and socks had been replaced with bras and panties. It felt like the memories they'd made in the bed had been erased in the blink of an eye.

George grabbed Harvey's shoulders and pushed him down onto the bed forcefully. As they stripped down to their underwear, kissing the whole time, Harvey told himself that he was so happy, but Ginger's tiny voice was still echoing throughout his mind.

He wanted to hear George say '*I choose you*', but he reminded himself that he would be choosing him in 4 days.

As George started to slowly pull Harvey's underwear down, Harvey felt his heart jump out of his chest when he heard Paula's voice echo up the stairs.

"Fuck! Get in the shower," George panicked.

He pushed Harvey in the direction of the bathroom. Freezing cold water shot out and froze his skin when he jumped into the shower. He almost cried out, but he forced himself into a shivering silence.

Harvey could see George scrambling around the bedroom picking up the clothes. He threw them into the bathroom and slammed the door shut just in time for Paula to walk in.

"Oh, there you are," she said, "why are you naked?"

Harvey could hear the suspicion in her voice loud and clear, even over the sound of the water lashing onto the tiled floor.

"I'm just about to have a shower."

Positive they'd been caught in the act, Harvey held his breath and waited for Paula's hysterical reaction, but George was a better liar than Harvey wanted to admit.

"I'm going to have a nap," she said, "I can feel one of my headaches creeping in."

When she was on the bed, George slipped into the bathroom and peeled off his white briefs. The door lock clicked and he jumped into the shower to join Harvey, looking seductively into his eyes.

George seemed to be secretly enjoying the danger of the close encounter. He grabbed Harvey by the hips and pushed him roughly up against the wet tiles, locking him in a passionate kiss.

"She's going to catch me," Harvey whispered as he dried his ghostly white body.

"She falls asleep really quickly and we've been in that shower for at least an hour," George winked, slapping Harvey's exposed backside.

Harvey knew that from the crinkling of the skin on his fingers that George was right.

With his clothes on, he slowly opened the bathroom door to see Paula's chest rising slowly. Creeping across the bedroom, he left George to dry himself, but when he reached the foot of the bed he found himself cautiously pausing. He could see the door to safety out of the corner of his eye, but instead he chose to stand over Paula and watch her sleep. The buckling of a belt let Harvey know he only had a few moments.

As he watched her sleep, guilt filled him, but in 4 days he knew he'd be stealing her husband. He tried to remember how mean she was when she was awake, but as she lay asleep, on top of the bed, her blonde hair draped angelically over her shoulders, Harvey felt her power melt away.

She started to stir from her dream, making Harvey take a quick step back. For a second her lids flickered and he thought he'd been caught, but she rolled over onto her side, softly snoring.

Feeling daring, he tiptoed around the edge of the bed and crouched down to Paula's eye level. As he stared at her flickering eyelids, he reminded himself that she was the problem.

Paula was the reason George kept ruining their plans.

"He's going to be mine," Harvey whispered.

The second the words slipped out of his mouth, he wished he could take them back. Knowing he'd gone too far, he ran across the fluffy carpet. Before leaving, he turned back to check if she was still asleep, but she was still in the same position.

He wasn't sure if his mind was playing tricks on him, but he was sure her breathing wasn't as heavy as it had been.

THIRTEEN

"You look amazing, kid!" George opened the changing room door.

Harvey stood there in his graduation gown and cap, and he felt a sudden wash of relief. So much had happened in the last few months, his graduation felt like a long time coming.

"Are you sure it looks okay? It feels huge on me!" he turned around to look at the back of the gown in the cubicle mirror.

It drowned him, but it was the smallest size they had in stock. On a normal 19 year old, it probably would have been tight, but not everybody had Harvey's slight frame.

"It looks fine," he didn't sound convinced, "they're meant to be big, aren't they?"

As Harvey examined the black tent drowning out his figure, the realization that he was about to graduate high school hit him square in the chest. He felt like the gown was skin tight to his body and the cap was closing in around his skull. He started to think about his parents and how they wouldn't be there to see him graduate. Thinking back to being 14 and having his parents alive, he could never have imagined them not being there.

"Are you okay kid?" George asked, resting his hand on Harvey's shoulder.

"Get this off me."

George ripped off the hat and Harvey's messy black hair flopped forwards. With Harvey's help, he pulled the gown over his head and dropped it messily to the floor. George grabbed Harvey and pulled him close, signaling to the shop assistant to give them a minute, as she started to walk over.

"What's up?"

"Nobody will be there for me," he tried to slow his breathing, "people always have somebody. Parents, siblings, grandparents, friends..."

George squeezed him tight and grabbed Harvey's face in both of his hands.

"You have me."

Harvey felt his heart twitch, and he immediately felt guilty. He knew George would be there, but for Harvey, it wasn't the same.

"I want to see Leo," Harvey whispered, looking down at his feet.

George dropped his hands and took a step back. The last time they'd seen Leo, George had given him a bag full of rolled up cash and he'd disappeared into the night.

"Are you sure you want to do that?"

"I just want to see him," he whispered

He couldn't even explain his sudden desire to see his brother. Harvey didn't really want him at his graduation, because he was unpredictable at the best of times, but Leo was the only connection he had to his parents. With his graduation only days away, he just wanted to see his face.

"I'm coming with you."

"That's fine," Harvey said, already taking it for granted that George would be there.

With Harvey's new gown in the trunk of the car, they

headed in the direction of Leo's filthy apartment. The nice clean streets were suddenly filled with litter and potholes, and the shoppers were replaced with questionable looking people loitering on street corners.

They pulled up slowly outside of the small liquor store, and he instantly noticed that the crusty curtains had disappeared out of the window, leaving it empty.

"Just give me a minute," he jumped out of the car.

He ran around the side of the store and up the outdoor steps, but his heart sank when he noticed the huge *'APARTMENT TO LET'* sign jutting out of the wall.

Harvey banged on the door and screamed Leo's name, but the knocks echoed around the empty apartment. Harvey tried his best to see into the apartment, through the tiny window. He didn't care if Leo wasn't there, he just wanted a sign that he hadn't completely left him.

When he saw the empty shell, he felt sick. The sofa was gone, the dirty carpet had been ripped up and the walls were bare and white. Harvey couldn't believe how big the place looked.

"Where's Leo?" Harvey demanded over the counter of the liquor store to the landlord.

"Are you over 21?" the large man replied.

"What?" Harvey recoiled, "Where's the guy who lived in the apartment above?"

The man licked his fingers and tossed the chicken wing he was eating into the cardboard bucket on the counter. The store was dark, and the only light came from the silent flickering TV in the corner. Harvey could almost forget it was the middle of the afternoon.

"I kicked him out," he said, still licking his fingers, "he owes me six months' rent. Do you know him?"

He gave Harvey a skeptical look. He'd lived above the store for nearly five years and he couldn't believe the landlord had no idea who he was.

"Do you know where he's gone?"

"Sorry, he didn't give me a forwarding address when I

dumped his stuff on the sidewalk and changed the locks," he eyed up the bucket of chicken in front of him, "do you want to buy any liquor?"

"Forget it," Harvey stormed out of the store, slamming the door hard in its frame.

The daylight felt harsh on his eyes. Before he jumped back into the car, he stared up at the tiny window, where he'd spent so many unhappy years of his life. Seeing it so empty cemented the feeling that part of his life was over.

"Where is he?"

"I don't know," he sighed, his voice cracking slightly, "he could be anywhere."

They were in silence for a moment as Harvey tried to remember any friends Leo had, but he had no idea where they lived. He didn't even have a phone number for Leo. It was as if he'd dropped off the face of the planet.

"Is that a bad thing?" George said, "Maybe he's gone for good."

Harvey turned to George, his mouth open and eyes wide.

"He's my brother!" Harvey shouted, "I know what he's done, but he's the last family I have."

"You wanted to be free from him for so long, and now you are," George whispered, putting his hand on Harvey's knee, "let him go, Harvey."

"What if he's dead?"

George's sudden coldness shocked Harvey. He knew that George was only being like this because Leo was less likely to turn up on his doorstep demanding money, now that he was completely out of the picture.

"He won't be dead," he said, "he'll be somewhere."

"I want to find him," Harvey whispered, "with or without your help."

They drove back in frosty silence. The empty driveway told Harvey that Paula was still at work. Usually, they'd use the time she spent at work to their advantage, but Harvey had a plan that didn't involve George.

When George unlocked the door, he ran straight up to his

room and ripped open his laptop. He searched for hours trying to find any trace of Leo. He searched the obituaries and was relieved when his name didn't show up anywhere. He searched every social network he could think of but knew Leo probably didn't have an internet connection wherever he was. He searched phone records but knew that Leo wouldn't have it registered in his name because he changed his number so many times.

Harvey was pouring through the 56th page of the search results for '*Leo Jasper*' when something caught his eye, just as he was about to slam the laptop shut. He clicked on the link, which took him to an article on the local newspaper website. It was a feature called '*Before The Judge*' and it listed all of the people who had appeared in court. Harvey quickly scanned the page, when his eyes landed on Leo's name.

'*Leo Jasper, 27, appeared before the judge on charges of shoplifting. He was given a postponed sentence and a $300 fine.*'

Harvey quickly scrolled to the top of the page and breathed a sigh of relief when he saw that it had been written a week ago. He wasn't bothered about the crime, he was just relieved at finding a small trace of his brother. They never had much money, so Harvey was always suspicious when food turned up in their apartment, but he was often too hungry to question it.

Harvey was ripped from reading the small passage for the 7th time when he heard a soft knock on the door.

"Come in."

George slipped through the door and walked over to Harvey. The room was starting to get dark and Harvey knew that Paula must be home because of the look on George's face.

"I've found him," he said, "he's still around."

"I'm sorry about what I said before," he gently placed his hand on Harvey's shoulder.

"It's okay," Harvey brushed his cheek against George's hand, "I shouldn't have snapped like that. I just freaked out."

"What happens now?" George perched on the edge of Harvey's bed.

Harvey left the desk and collapsed on the bed, next to

where George was sat.

"I don't know."

The truth was, he didn't have any idea if he wanted to see Leo anymore. The last time they'd spoken, Leo told Harvey that he didn't have a brother. Knowing that he was alive felt like the closure he'd been craving.

"I'll help you find him if you want?" George stroked Harvey's hair tenderly.

"It's okay," Harvey whispered, snuggling into George's side, "he has a habit of turning up when you least expect it."

FOURTEEN

I t was the day before Harvey's graduation, and to try and take his mind away from his brother, George organized a surprise barbecue party for Harvey.

"George you shouldn't have!" Harvey laughed as he walked out into the garden.

Harvey didn't know any of George and Paula's friends, but he was grateful for being included in the group. He felt as if George was trying to integrate him, before he revealed the truth about their relationship.

"That's Emma and Jack, I met them in college," George said as he waved to a couple across the pool, "and that's Marlon and Chase, they're gay."

Harvey eyed up the gay couple and they were a similar age to George, and they were both very good looking. He didn't know why, but he felt surprised that George had gay friends.

"Where did you meet them?" Harvey whispered quietly as they walked around the pool.

"I've been friends with Marlon since I worked at the

newspaper. We started at the same time and we were really good friends," George whispered as they walked up towards them.

"Oh, is this who we're here to celebrate?" the man who Harvey suspected was Chase said, as he put his hand out to shake Harvey's.

Chase had a shock of bleached blonde hair, slicked back from his tanned face. Marlon looked a lot like George in build, but Harvey didn't think he was as handsome. He knew he must be a similar age to George, but he looked a lot older.

Out of all of the problems surrounding George, his age had never been an issue for Harvey.

"George has told us a lot about you," Marlon smiled as he firmly shook Harvey's hand, "I hear you're a writer!"

Harvey blushed and smiled nervously. The thought of George telling his friends about him made his skin tingle. He looked up and caught Chase's eye, who was smiling peculiarly at Harvey, as he sipped from a pink straw.

Harvey glanced quickly around the pool and he could see Paula muttering in a low, furious whisper to Emma. Every few seconds, she glanced up and shot Harvey a sharp look. He could feel his ears burning.

"George!" Greg said, as he walked out into the garden holding a crate of beer, "Thanks for the invite!"

Harvey knew the minute he saw Greg, that George had invited him for his sake. George grabbed the crate from Greg and took it through to the kitchen.

Greg walked over in a salmon shirt, open slightly at the top, his grey hair swept off his face. He smiled at Harvey and there was a little twinkle in his eye. The suspicion and curiosity that had been there when Harvey first met him at the last barbecue, was long gone.

"Harvey, I must say I was surprised to learn you hadn't graduated high school!" Greg shook Harvey's hand.

"I'm 19," Harvey said, almost defensively.

Greg seemed to sense the defensiveness in his voice and slapped him playfully on the back.

"Don't worry, I still want an amazing writer like you on my books. I'm just glad I've snatched you up so young before anybody else could," Greg waved to Paula across the pool, "I must remind accounting to get finished with that contract so we can get the ball rolling."

With that, he wandered across to Paula, who was still whispering with Emma. Jack was sipping his beer awkwardly, in silence, as he stared into the blue water of the pool. Harvey guessed mindless gossip wasn't one of his favorite things to do.

"Marlon, come help me get these burgers out of the trunk," George shouted from the kitchen, "I think I've gone a bit overboard."

Harvey desperately tried to catch George's eye to tell him not to leave him alone with Chase, but he'd already disappeared back into the kitchen.

Smiling politely at Chase, Harvey half wished that he wouldn't start talking to him, and they could stand in silence.

"So, how long have you known George?" Chase asked, flicking a strand of his bleached blonde hair out of his eyes.

"A couple of months," Harvey smiled awkwardly, "I was his intern."

"He seems very fond of you," he said, winking at Harvey.

Harvey shifted uncomfortably on the spot. Was George's affection towards Harvey that obvious, or was he just teasing? Glancing back to the kitchen, he could see the shadows of George and Marlon. He willed them to hurry up.

"How long have you and Marlon been together?"

"Nearly a year," Chase said, without a hint of affection, "but between you and me, it's coming to a natural end."

Harvey was shocked at how comfortable Chase was to admit the imminent ending of his relationship. He couldn't help but wonder if that is what people in the real world were like. Would George drop him when he was bored of him? Is that what he was doing with Paula?

"The bathroom calls," he excused himself.

He walked quickly across the patio, sensing Paula's hateful gaze still fixed on him. He didn't care, he just wanted to get away from Chase.

In the downstairs bathroom, Harvey stared at his reflection in the mirror. He fiddled with his black hair, making sure it was neatly to the side, glad that George had taken him to get it cut in time for his graduation.

A soft knock on the door made Harvey jump. He wasn't sure if he'd locked it because he didn't actually need to use the bathroom. He called that he'd be a second, but the door opened and Chase slipped inside, still holding his drink.

"I said I'd be a minute," Harvey said drying his hands on a fluffy cream towel.

"Oh drop the act Harv," Chase winked seductively, "we all know what '*going to the bathroom*' means."

He tossed back the rest of his drink and slammed the empty glass on the counter next to the sink, causing the pink straw to bounce out. He lunged at Harvey and grabbed his face, forcing a kiss on his unassuming lips. In the confusion of the moment, Harvey stood there as Chase messily kissed him, trying to force his tongue into his mouth.

"What are you doing?" Harvey shouted.

"C'mon, I know you want me," Chase lunged at Harvey again.

He locked lips with Harvey, grabbing his face even tighter this time. Harvey tried to pull away from Chase, but his grip was strong.

Still locked in a kiss, Harvey fell forwards, sending Chase into the marble counter. He let go of Harvey and stumbled back into the empty glass, which shot into the sink, smashing into a million tiny shards.

"What's your problem?" Chase cried, straightening up his shirt collar.

As if nothing happened, he turned to look in the mirror and readjusted his hair.

"Get out!"

"I didn't realize you were so frigid," he sneered, before leaving the bathroom.

Harvey stared blankly at his reflection in the mirror as he

tried to comprehend what had happened. The tiny pieces of glass in the sink were the only evidence of what had just happened. He couldn't bear the thought of going back to the party, where Chase would no doubt be trying to hide his rejection.

The door slowly opened again, making Harvey back off. He started to shake as he expected to see a scorned Chase coming back to finish what he'd started, but the clenched fist around his stomach loosened when George appeared in front of him. Without a second thought he jumped on George, latching his arms around his neck. He never wanted to let go. Any feeling of fear melted away, in George's arms.

"Hey, what's up?" George said as he held Harvey's trembling body

He thought about keeping quiet. Telling George would only cause trouble, but he didn't want to think that he'd keep something like this from the man he loved.

"Chase," Harvey started, pulling away from George, "I came to the bathroom and he followed me in and he kissed me. I tried to stop him George, but he was so strong."

George's eyes opened wide, and without another word he ripped the bathroom door open and disappeared. Harvey quickly ran out into the kitchen to see George marching across the patio towards Chase, who was now laughing with Paula.

"I'm gonna kill you" he boomed as he grabbed the front of Chase's shirt.

"George! Have you lost your mind?" Paula screamed.

He let go of Chase's collar and turned away from him, and for a moment Harvey thought he was going to drop it, but he spun around and landed a heavy fist on Chase's nose.

Gasps echoed around the patio, as Chase fell off the small ledge down on to the lawn. Harvey stood frozen to the spot as he watched George jump down towards Chase. He kicked him in the stomach, causing Chase to fold in two and cover his face. Before George could plant another solid boot in Chase's stomach, Marlon ran over and stood in between them.

On the grass, quivering in Marlon's arms, Chase looked so

helpless and tiny.

"What are you playing at?" Jack shouted as he dragged George into the kitchen.

"He tried to kiss Harvey!" George spat through clenched teeth.

"What?" cried Paula as they all ate at the breakfast bar.

Harvey was still frozen to the spot next to the pool staring at Chase. He caught his eye for a second, and the guilt started. Had he really given him the impression that he wanted him to follow him?

"He threw himself on Harvey and when Harvey said no, he tried to force him," George said through heavy breaths as Jack handed him a glass of water.

"What a sleaze ball!" Emma cried, "I preferred Marlon's last one."

Harvey walked into the kitchen, followed by Marlon. Paula's eyes were fixed on him, like they had been all day, but the hatred had been replaced with bitter confusion.

"Why would he try to kiss you?" Paula shot at Harvey.

Harvey didn't know how to answer it. He didn't know himself why Chase had tried to kiss him. His best guess was that Chase had sensed he was gay and thought he'd be an easy target for a bit of fun.

"I don't know," he mumbled.

"It's not his fault!" George cried.

"Wait, is this true?" Marlon shouted.

"Why would he try to kiss you?" Paula asked again.

"I can't believe he'd do that to Marlon!" Emma sighed.

Harvey felt dizzy. All of the voices suffocated him. His lungs tightened as he struggled to catch his breath.

"Are you gay?" Paula spat, taking a daring step towards Harvey.

"Does it matter?" George stood up behind Paula, putting his hand on her shoulder.

Harvey didn't know how to answer the question. He had completely forgotten that Paula had no idea about his sexuality. Was that the only thing stopping her figuring out about their seedy affair?

"Answer me!" Paula screamed, taking another step towards Harvey.

Harvey suddenly felt scared of the blonde woman with rage in her. He wanted to speak, but his tongue felt like it was swelling painfully in his mouth.

"Paula, just leave him alone," George tried to pull her back.

She shrugged his hand off as she advanced even closer to Harvey.

"I knew it," she whispered, "are you trying to seduce my husband?"

George laughed nervously.

"Don't be so stupid!" George laughed again.

Harvey eyed George, trying to tell him silently that this was the perfect time to tell Paula everything. She was so close to guessing it, why stop her now?

It was the terrified look in George's eyes which made Harvey speak.

"I'm not gay," Harvey muttered, breaking away from Paula's intense stare, "Chase must have got it wrong."

FIFTEEN

A s a furious wind rattled the windows in their frames, Harvey tossed and turned, replaying the events from the night in his head. It was his graduation in the morning, but his mind couldn't have been further from receiving his diploma.

After Marlon had dragged Chase from the party, Emma and Jack swiftly followed and Paula hid in her bedroom. He tried to figure out if she was embarrassed at her actions, or if she was trying to piece things together. Harvey hoped it was the latter. When they were alone, George frantically told Harvey that he didn't want to expose their affair in front of their friends. He convinced him that he was still sticking to their plan to tell her after the graduation, he just wanted to do it alone and in private.

As Harvey buried his head under the pillows, he wanted to feel happy about what was going to be the biggest day of his life, but he couldn't summon the emotion. Instead he felt nervous and anxious.

He tried to cling onto the hope that George would finally tell his wife the truth so they could start their new life together, but as he drifted off to sleep, weeks of disappointment weighed heavily on his shoulders.

Bright light poured into the bedroom as Harvey woke up to a pale blue sky. Rubbing his eyes, he saw the black gown hung on the outside of his closet and his nerves started to bubble. He didn't care about his graduation anymore. For him, it was the day that he was about to start a brand new life with the man he loved.

By the time he made it downstairs, Paula had already left for work, leaving George and Harvey to eat breakfast alone.

"Today's the day, kid," George smiled as he slopped the eggs onto Harvey's plate.

He didn't know if he was talking about the graduation or the plan.

"Is the plan still on?" he asked cautiously.

There was a moment of silence as George chewed his eggs nervously.

"There's a plan now?"

Harvey could sense the fear in his voice. It was so clear and loud, even if he was trying to hide it.

"You know what I mean. You're not having second thoughts, are you?"

"You know it's you that I love," was all George said.

As Harvey slipped into his graduation gown and cap, he tried to shake the nerves away. Graduating high school was a big moment for any teenager, but he had much bigger things on his mind. Just as Paula wandered angrily into his thoughts, George appeared behind him to clear them away. His eyes glazed over as he walked slowly over to Harvey. When he was inches from Harvey, he ripped the cap off his head, exposing his jet black hair.

"We're going to be late!" Harvey whispered.

"I don't care," he said as he pushed him down on to the bed.

As Harvey felt the growing bulge in George's pants, he

wanted to think that it was George's way of telling him that the plan was still on, but part of him thought it was George trying to distract Harvey from the real problem.

He let George's kisses wash over him as he pulled up the long black gown and undid the buttons on his black jeans, he let the distraction work.

When they were finished, redressed and in the car, Harvey started to realize that he was actually about to graduate High School, something all his other classmates would be more excited for.

"Nervous?"

Harvey glanced at George. His hair was still ruffled, but he thought he looked cute, so he didn't tell him to flatten it.

"Like you wouldn't believe," he mumbled under his breath.

As they pulled into the parking lot, Harvey could see all of his classmates with their families, smiling happily as they took pictures and hugged. It only reminded him how alone he felt in the world.

"I'm here for you," George said, squeezing his hand firmly when he noticed the air of sadness spreading over Harvey.

He knew that George was the only person there for him on the day of his graduation, but he wondered if George would still be there at the end of the day.

Staring down at the gold watch on his wrist, he remembered the tiny letters carved into the back and told himself that George was going to stick to his 4 day promise.

After posing for a picture with his class for the local paper, they headed out onto the track field where the ceremony was being held. Harvey didn't mind skipping it, but there was something symbolic about receiving a diploma in his hand that he needed at that moment. He wanted to feel a wave of something ending and something new beginning.

The crowd gathered and Harvey waited with his class. They were all chattering and laughing as they talked about graduation parties. Standing there, Harvey felt invisible to them. He was the weird kid who'd sit on his own in the cafeteria. Most of them had never heard him speak, but it still hurt him not to be involved.

What hurt him most was not being part of something, something, which in another life, he would have had, if things hadn't gone so horribly sour for him.

One by one his class walked up to accept their diplomas from the principal as their fan clubs cheered for them from the seats. When it came to Harvey's turn, his legs transformed to jelly as he staggered awkwardly up the steps.

He squinted out in to the crowd and he saw George in the front row, cheering proudly. A smile spread across his lips as he accepted the diploma with a firm handshake. Turning back to the crowd, he imagined his mother and father at the back cheering for him.

Squinting into the sun, he could see his family cheering for him, Leo too. As he basked in his moment, he knew they were there in spirit. He headed off the stage, he looked back into the crowd. His mother and father had vanished, but Leo was still there.

George was still clapping loudly for him as terror racked Harvey's mind. He looked again, and Leo was standing there, clapping his hands with his eyes fixed strongly on Harvey. Pushing through the crowd of his classmates, he ran and dragged Leo off to the school, suddenly thankful for his invisibility. He found an empty classroom and locked the door.

"Where the fuck have you been?" Harvey screamed, ripping his cap off and throwing it down on a desk with his diploma.

Harvey examined Leo and was surprised to see that his clothes looked clean. He was freshly shaven, exposing his sharp cheekbones, and his hair was actually styled for once instead of sticking up dirtily in every direction.

"I've been staying with a friend," Leo said, not slurring.

"I tried looking for you," Harvey cried.

An uncomfortable look spread across Leo's pale face. Harvey looked him dead in the eyes, and for once they weren't red or glassy.

"I needed some time to clear my head," Leo said as he twisted his hands together, "I read about the graduation in the local paper and I wanted to be here for you."

For a moment, Harvey was sure that he'd suffered a head injury and he was actually unconscious on the stage hallucinating. He couldn't believe the brother he thought he'd never see again was standing in front of him, looking more like the brother he remembered from a long lost time.

"I thought you never wanted to see me again," Harvey whispered, staring out of the window at the celebrating crowd.

"I was a mess. I was a dickhead to you, I know that now," Leo said, reaching his hand out to put it on Harvey's shoulder, but Harvey stepped away, "I'm sober, bro. I haven't touched a drop in weeks."

"And drugs?"

"I haven't touched anything, I'm clean. I swear," Leo said looking deep into Harvey's eyes wanting desperately for him to believe him.

"What about all that money? Did you drink it away?"

"I didn't see a penny," Leo laughed, "I owed a lot of money to a lot of dangerous people."

Harvey wanted to believe him, but Leo had done this so many times over the years. He'd say he was clean, but that usually meant that he was just waiting to score or waiting for the next drink to be put in his hand.

"Why are you here Leo?" Harvey sighed, taking a seat in one of the chairs.

He played with his diploma scroll waiting for Leo to answer. The last time he'd seen Leo, his entire world had crashed down around him. He'd grown used to his brother ruining things whenever he was around.

"I couldn't miss my kid brother's graduation," Leo said, trying to smile at Harvey.

"Seriously? After all these years, you suddenly take an interest in me?"

"I know I've been useless," he sighed, rubbing his brow, "but it's not been easy for me."

"And it was easy for me?" Harvey shouted, standing up and knocking the chair back into the desk behind him, "They were my parents too, Leo. Why did you really come here?"

He wanted to believe that Leo would come just to see him, but he found it very unlikely.

"I wanted to make you an offer," he spoke slowly, "I've been given a job."

"A job?" Harvey laughed, "Why do you want me? I don't have any money, so don't ask."

Leo laughed softly.

"Just let me explain," he started, leaning against a desk, "the guy I'm crashing with, Lucas, he is part of this band. He's a great guy. They've been offered this amazing gig touring America as a support act for this huge band."

Harvey was failing to see how this involved him.

"They've asked me to go with them to be a roadie. I help with the equipment and stuff, and they pay me and I get to travel the country."

"Where do I come into this?" Harvey interrupted impatiently.

"I want you to come with us," he said, darting his eyes nervously from his feet to Harvey, "I want you to come with me."

Leo's proposition forced him back into the chair.

"You can't be serious?"

"Think about it, bro," Leo said, getting down on his knees to Harvey's level, "we'd travel America together. It'd be our chance to get away from this town, a fresh start!"

Planting his head in his hands, Harvey couldn't believe what his brother was asking of him. Part of him wished that he'd asked for money, because a least he'd have been able to say no.

"I can't Leo."

"Why not? What's keeping you here?"

Harvey wanted to say *'George'*, but he didn't know if that was the truth any more.

"I just can't," he repeated.

"Think about it bro," Leo sighed, "we're leaving tomorrow."

"Tomorrow?" Harvey cried.

Before they could discuss it any further, George's voice called out for Harvey.

"Get into that store room, now," Harvey whispered, pushing Leo across the classroom, "unless you want another fist in the face."

"Here's the address of the place I'm crashing," Leo shoved a screwed up piece of paper into Harvey's hand, "come and see me tonight."

As soon as Leo was hidden in the tiny supplies room, George appeared outside of the locked door.

"Here you are kid. I've been looking everywhere for you!"

"I just wanted to say goodbye to this place," Harvey lied, "this was my English classroom. I loved it in here."

That part wasn't a lie. He really did love his English lessons. He loved sinking his teeth into a good book and dissecting it into pieces. It was one of the only classes he got straight As in and truly enjoyed.

"I was worried about you," George whispered, putting his hand on Harvey's face.

He leaned in and softly kissed Harvey's lips.

"Y'know, we're all alone here," George whispered into Harvey's ear as his hand softly ran down his back through the baggy black gown.

For a second he let George's lips explore his neck, but when he heard a shuffle from Leo's hiding place, he pushed George off.

"Not here. Let's go home, we'll have the house to ourselves."

A seductive smile spread across George's face before grabbing him in for one last kiss.

"C'mon, let's get out of here," he whispered, "before I rip that gown off you and push you up against the chalkboard."

George pulled Harvey out of the classroom by the hand. He glanced back to the storeroom where his brother was hiding. He could hear George talking, but all he could think about was Leo's offer.

If he'd asked him a month ago he would have laughed in

his face, but he found himself thinking of nothing else.

As they sped back to George's house, he told himself that he could never leave, but the more he stared at George's handsome face, the more he didn't know what to do.

SIXTEEN

A s the sun started to set unusually early, Harvey pulled his clothes back on. George was still in bed naked, smiling up at him, but Harvey couldn't return the smile. The day was nearly over and Paula was late getting home from work.

They hadn't spoken about it since the morning, but Harvey felt like he needed to break the silence, which was eating away inside of him.

"I want you to tell her when she gets back," he said as he stuffed his foot into his socks.

George shot up in bed and pulled the covers up to his lap.

"I think she's doing overtime tonight. Can't it wait until tomorrow?"

Harvey spun around to stare at George in disbelief. Part of his heart melted when he saw his amazing body leaned up casually in bed, but the rest of it squeezed tight and felt like it was going to pop.

He couldn't stand any more delays.

"The minute she walks through that door. You tell her."

"Fine," he sighed as he pulled his clothes on, "If that's what you want."

"Isn't that what you want?"

"Of course it is," he pulled Harvey close to his chest, "it's just a big thing to do."

Harvey was sure that he was trying to make him feel guilty for putting pressure on him to do it, but Harvey knew it was now or never.

He had 24 hours to make up his mind about where he wanted his life to go next. He was standing at a crossroads and George wasn't making his decision any easier. His heart was screaming for his lover, but his head was telling him it would only lead to more heartache.

"Listen, kid," he checked his phone, "You know I love you and I want to be with you. Nothing is going to change that."

"I sense another *'but'*," he sighed, turning away from George.

"But, this is a big deal for me," George perched on the end of the bed.

As if on time, a car purred softly into the drive and the slam of a car door echoed around the silent bedroom, signaling for what was to come.

"It's now or never."

The front door closed and footsteps echoed around the hallway. Harvey could hear his heart beating loudly in his chest, and it was almost deafening.

"I'll go out and leave you to do it, alone," he whispered, "it's probably for the best."

George didn't say anything, instead he stared out of the window and looked down at Paula's blue car.

"Let's just go to the cabin for a few days," George said hastily, before Harvey left the room, "to celebrate your graduation. You said you really wanted to go there, remember?"

"Now or never."

"Where will you go?" he asked quietly.

Harvey didn't want to tell him that he was going to see his brother. The offer was all he could think about, but he didn't want to let George know he had a backup plan. Part of him thought George would only chicken out even more if he knew Harvey had another option.

"I'll just go for a walk," Harvey pulled on his sneakers and picked up his gown and cap, "I need to clear my head anyway."

He rushed into his bedroom and dumped his gown in the bottom of the closet, knowing that he'd never need it again. Pulling the small piece of paper out of his pocket, he read the address and knew it was only a couple of blocks away from Leo's apartment above the liquor store.

Heading out into the night, he felt the weight of the situation on his frail shoulders. He glanced back at George's house in the distance and hoped that the next time he stepped through those doors, George would be a free man and he'd be ready to finally live the dream they'd talk about for so long. Until then, he had to know all of his options.

Gray clouds started to fill the sky and the air was thick and humid as Harvey knocked heavily on the door.

He could sense a storm brewing.

"Who is it?" an unknown voice called from the other side of the door.

"It's Harvey," he called back, "Leo's brother."

The door quickly opened and a tall, skinny guy with sandy blonde hair swept over his eyes greeted him. He was wearing a band T-shirt, which Harvey assumed was the band Leo had spoken about.

"Harvey, come in," Lucas smiled, "Leo's just through here."

Stepping nervously into the apartment, Harvey felt a lump rise painfully in his throat. He didn't know if it was the best idea, and he didn't know what he was going to tell Leo. Part of him hoped that Leo would be drunk, to make up his mind for him.

"Bro, glad you made the right decision," Leo called.

He was sitting casually on a sofa watching TV. The apartment was small, but it was clean and nicely furnished. Scanning the sides, he couldn't see any trace of alcohol or drugs, which made him feel guilty for expecting his brother to have relapsed so quickly.

For years, he'd wanted his brother to get sober.

"I haven't decided anything yet," Harvey said in a low voice.

Lucas followed Harvey into the living room and he sat next to Leo on the sofa.

"Sit down, dude," Lucas smiled at Harvey.

As Harvey sat, he couldn't believe his brother would be friends with someone who wasn't an alcoholic like the rest of his friends he had forced upon him over the years. He wanted to know what situation they'd met in, but he hadn't gone to make small talk.

"I need to ask some stuff," Harvey said, his palms starting to sweat.

Leo flicked off the TV and leaned forwards, resting his elbows on his knees before saying, "I'm listening."

"If I say yes, and that's a big *if*, how will I know you'll stay clean?"

There was a moment's silence as Lucas and Leo glanced at each other.

"I've changed," he shrugged.

Harvey wanted desperately to believe it could be possible.

"You'll miss out on the trip of a lifetime if you don't come," Lucas said, "It's going to be dope!"

Harvey felt like they really wanted him to go. He didn't even know if he wanted to go himself, but he knew that Leo was the only family he had, and he seemed to have done the one thing that Harvey thought was impossible.

"Just say yes," Leo laughed nervously, running his hands through his hair, "It can be a fresh start for both of us."

Harvey knew what he was referring to. He knew he was talking about George and how if he left, he could leave that part of his life behind him. He didn't want to think that Leo would deny his sexuality, but he felt like a fresh start wouldn't be such a bad thing.

His heart twitched when he thought about George. He'd tried so hard to detach himself from that situation because he didn't want his heart to be broken again, but he couldn't help but feel the love swell up inside him.

The love was replaced with guilt when he thought about George back at the house getting ready to tell Paula. He wondered if he'd told her yet. Doubt raced through Harvey's mind.

"I don't know what to do," Harvey admitted.

His head was screaming '*yes*', but his heart was telling him to leave and go back to George as quickly as he could. He never thought that Leo would be the safe bet out of the two.

"Whatever you say now, we'll wait for you," Leo said, "we're leaving tomorrow morning at 10am. I'll be here waiting for you. If you don't turn up, I'll know what your answer is."

"And will you hate me if I don't turn up?" Harvey asked.

Another pause.

"No," Leo said, "but I don't know when I'll be back. I might never come back. I might settle somewhere new."

Sickness suddenly swept over Harvey's entire body as he realized that if he didn't go with him, he'd probably never see the only family he had, ever again. Would George be enough for him, forever?

As Harvey headed back into the night, Leo's words weighed on his heart. He seemed like a changed man, but would he stay that way? Could he really ditch the bottle for good? Thunder crashed around the street as he turned onto George's road, quickly followed by blue flashes, which artfully lit up the sky.

Heavy raindrops bounced off Harvey's face as he ran quickly towards the big green front door. Ever since Paula had returned, it didn't feel like his home any more. Instead, it felt like the walls were a prison for his emotions.

As his hand squeezed down on the door handle, he stood there letting the rain soak through his clothes. He wanted to go in and see Paula distraught and George apologetic.

He wanted to care about Paula, but he was blinded by love. All he could see was George. He opened the door softly not wanting them to hear him. As he walked across the hall towards the kitchen, he felt rain dripping from his clothes onto the perfect white marble tiles.

As he pushed the door open, his heart sank to the pit of his stomach and cracked into a thousand bloody shards.

Harvey stared as he watched George's hands exploring Paula's body. He listened to Paula's gentle moans as George pushed his body up against hers. Her blue nurses' uniform was open at the front, exposing her round breasts, which George was gently fondling as he kissed his wife with a passion Harvey had seen all too often.

A painful cry escaped Harvey's throat as he slammed the door shut. He had no words or thoughts, he just followed his instincts. He felt his feet taking him heavily up the stairs and straight to his bedroom. Tears rolled down his cheeks, blinding him, but he didn't need to see. His hands were already stuffing clothes into a bag.

"Harvey," George shouted from the doorframe.

"*How could you?*" he screeched, his voice already broken.

"I-I-..."

"I should have known you didn't have the balls," Harvey sobbed.

Out of the corner of his eye, he saw the photo of him and George at the cabin and instantly wanted it destroyed. He snatched it up angrily and launched it at the closet door, sending glass shards flying across the room.

"Please, let me explain," George cried, tears in his own eyes now.

"No," Harvey spat, "there's nothing you have to say that I want to hear. Not anymore."

Harvey rummaged through his drawers, roughly pulling out his underwear and stuffing them into a bag. Paula's confused voice made Harvey stop and turn around. Wiping away the tears, he saw her buttoning up her uniform and brushing the hair from her face.

"What's going on?"

"Harvey's just having some family trouble again. Isn't that right, kid?"

Harvey couldn't believe even now, George was trying to cover everything up.

"I'm not going to lie for you anymore," Harvey spat as he

zipped up the bag.

The white laptop caught his attention and for a moment he wanted to take it with him, but he doubted he'd have much use for it where he was going.

"Lie about what?" Paula shouted, her voice shaking.

"Nothing!" George said, trying to catch Harvey's eye, but Harvey was staring dead into Paula's eyes.

"Tell her George," Harvey said coldly, not breaking away from Paula's gaze.

"Tell me what?"

"Tell her!"

Tears filled George's eyes, as Harvey gave him one last chance.

"*Tell me what?*" Paula screamed at the top of her lungs, turning to George.

"It's nothing. Harvey is just being stupid," he tried to smile at Paula, but it seemed the tears in his eyes told Paula exactly what was going on without any words.

"We've been having an affair," Harvey said confidently, not wanting her to see how much he wanted to crumble to the ground, "we've been having sex."

Paula shot back to Harvey. She had her tears in her own eyes. He could see her mind quickly piecing everything together.

"Is this true?" she choked at George

"No. Tell her you're lying Harvey."

"I can't believe you," Harvey whispered as fresh tears fell from his eyes, "you said you loved me."

That was enough to make Paula crack. She thrashed, kicked and slapped George over and over. Harvey stood there and watched a marriage shatter right before his eyes.

"How could you do this to me?" she screamed as she beat George's chest.

George had his arms up to his face. She pushed him against the wall, and he slid down it, into a pile on the floor, sobbing.

"I'm sorry," he croaked.

Harvey didn't know who he was directing that at and he

didn't care anymore.

"You!" she sneered through gritted teeth, turning to Harvey.

Claws out, she launched at Harvey and turned her aggression to him. She grabbed his hair in her fist and started to scratch and slap his face as she wailed at the top of her lungs. He wanted to try and make her stop, but he knew he deserved it. George's spell was broken, and he felt he could see what was truly happening. Harvey had been selfish, and he'd forced his way into their marriage.

George probably did fall for him, but Harvey didn't exactly help the situation. Every slap, punch and kick from Paula felt like well-deserved punishment.

The barrage of pain stopped when George pulled Paula off Harvey and threw her on to the bed. His face stung as hot blood trickled down his pale skin.

"Get out!" Paula screamed.

Harvey grabbed his bag, pushed past George without looking him in the eye and headed for the door.

"Both of you!" she screamed even louder.

Harvey paused in the hall as he heard a fresh round of aggression come from Paula, but this time she was taking it out on the bedroom. He heard lamps smashing and chairs crashing to the ground. A huge, electronic crunch told him that even his laptop wouldn't come out alive. He regretted not making a backup copy of his book.

"Harvey, just wait there," George called from the bedroom.

Harvey wanted to run back out into the rain and straight to his brother, but he wanted to hear George's feeble excuse as to why he couldn't tell Paula.

"Where did you do it?" Paula screamed as she pulled the curtains from the rail, causing the fabric to tear in two, "In here? In our bedroom? In your study? I should have known. All those little looks and giggles you two had."

She stormed out of the bedroom and barged past Harvey. She launched an attack on her own bedroom as she slid all of her cosmetics and perfumes from the dresser and sent them crashing onto the ground.

Harvey winced as the ghosts of their sexual encounters laughed around the house. He was sure Paula could hear them as they echoed down the halls, the bedroom and the kitchen.

"I was going to tell her," George croaked to Harvey, his eyes still full of tears.

"When? After you fucked her?" Harvey shouted, "Or tomorrow? Next week? Next month? Next year?"

"Please, I was, I just didn't know how to start it," George cried as he tried to grab Harvey's arms.

Harvey took a step back towards the stairs as he felt George's touch, burn through his damp clothes.

"It's too late, '*kid*'," Harvey scoffed, "if you don't want me the first time around, then I don't want you."

"I do want you!"

"You've got a funny way of showing it. Even at the end, you denied me," Harvey cried, "*I'm done.*"

As he ran down the stairs and out into the night, he let the tears flow from his eyes freely, not even caring who saw him in the rain. He wailed as he ran, as quickly as his tired legs would take him. Paula's screams still echoed through his ears, as he felt the rain stinging the cuts on his face.

Part of him knew it would never end the way he craved. He knew all along that George was only going to break his heart. He never wanted to admit it to himself, but George didn't want to leave his wife. As he ran through dark streets, he knew that George didn't love Paula, but he knew that George was terrified of not being with her.

When Leo answered the door, Harvey wrapped his arms around his brother and cried his heart out on his shoulder.

Leo had won.

SEVENTEEN

"You aren't going to regret this kid," Lucas called to Harvey as he packed up his things from his bedroom.

Being called '*kid*' made his stomach churn. A sharp pain started to form in Harvey's neck, from sleeping on the lumpy sofa. He'd had restless dreams of being lost in a maze and not being able to find his way out, because George was blocking every exit, laughing cruelly at him.

He wished he could take a pill and forget every moment of the last two months. He wanted to erase the bookstore, the gardening, the cabin, the parties, the book signing and every other time they'd been happy because the memories only served to cause him more pain. When he'd finally stopped thinking about George, the wound would reopen when he'd remember something they'd done together or something George had said.

Sitting on the sofa next to his bag full of clothes, he felt the watch burning a hot ring around his wrist. He wanted to rip it off and throw it away, but he couldn't even bring himself to look at it. For him, the watch represented everything that was wrong with George.

Thinking about what was wrong with George made Harvey think about what was right with George and fresh pain swept over his fragile body.

Leo didn't ask what had happened, but he seemed to know without Harvey even telling him. He seemed to have known all along that George would do this. He'd tried to get Harvey back, but the hold that George had over him had stopped him from seeing sense. Leo had told himself that George was the problem, choosing to forget the years of alcohol and drug abuse, which had led to years of neglect and mistreatment for the brother he was responsible for.

"Cheer up, bro," Leo said as he handed Harvey a cup of coffee.

The coffee only reminded him of George. George would always hand him a coffee first thing in the morning. Forcing the tears back, he smiled weakly at his brother, not wanting him to see the real pain he was in.

"I'll be fine," Harvey said, wanting to believe his own words.

"It was just a silly phase," Leo said before heading off to help Lucas pack.

It was a phase.

Harvey tried to tell himself this, but it only made things worse. He didn't want to put his love for George down to a phase. He wanted to own it, and move on.

He knew he was gay, but he wasn't sure if Leo was ever going to be ready to accept that.

As they loaded the car, the future beamed brightly for Harvey. He was terrified, but the thought of getting as far away from George was a comfort. He'd soon be across the country in a place George could never find him. He told himself it was what he wanted, but when Leo slammed the trunk shut, his stomach knotted.

His mind wandered to Paula and George. He wondered if they were together in their house trying to get back to normal, or if Paula had kicked him out and he was sleeping in a hotel.

Shaking his head, he forced them both out of his mind, for what he hoped was the last time.

"This is going to be so much fun," Leo said as he slapped Harvey's back.

He heard Lucas lock the door of the house and knew there was no going back. They were about to set off into the unknown. The next chapter of Harvey's life was about to start, and he'd never felt so terrified.

They bundled into the car ready to pick up the other band members. Harvey heard the key slot in roughly and when it turned in the ignition and the engine roared into life, he felt physically sick. He prayed to a god that he didn't believe in, for a sign he was doing the right thing.

He glanced out of the window and looked for the sign. The gray clouds from the night before had completely cleared to show the bright blue sky. Looking up and down the street, the sign he'd hoped for came shooting down the road towards him in the form of George's huge car.

It stopped in the middle of the road and when George jumped out, Harvey felt like he was about the throw up, for real this time.

"Drive," Leo muttered to Lucas from the front seat.

The car started to slowly reverse down the street and as Harvey watched George frantically bang on the door where Harvey had been only a few minutes ago, part of him wanted to drive away unseen. He stole a glance and saw that George had the small piece of paper in his hand. Harvey patted his jeans pockets and suddenly realized that he must have dropped it during the struggle with Paula.

As the car edged around George's badly parked vehicle, an overwhelming desire spread through Harvey's body. It was coming from his heart, not his head.

"Stop the car!" he screamed.

"Don't," Leo shot back.

Lucas looked from Leo in the front seat, to Harvey in the back seat.

"I said stop the car!" Harvey screamed again.

Lucas slammed his foot on the brake, sending the car screeching down the road. Harvey jumped out of the tiny scratched up car and headed back up the road towards George.

He was frantically looking up and down the street, staring at the address on the piece of paper when he spotted Harvey walking slowly towards him. His heart pounded and relief spread through his body as he ran towards him with open arms. When he reached him, his hug was resisted and Harvey just stared at him.

"Harvey," George said, a smile spreading across his face, "I thought I'd lost you forever."

Harvey took a deep breath.

"I'm leaving, George."

"What? Where to?"

"I'm going travelling with my brother," Harvey whispered, not breaking eye contact, "I'm leaving and I don't think I'll be coming back."

"No," George muttered, shaking his head forcing the tears to fall from his eyes, "I won't let you."

"I've made up my mind."

They stood in silence, crying at each other. All of the love they felt, despite what had happened, was pouring out into the street and it completely surrounded them. Harvey wanted nothing more than to get back into George's car and go back with him. Part of him would go back to being his secret in a heartbeat, but the cat was out of the bag.

"Please -" he started.

"Don't George. Don't do this," Harvey smiled at him through the tears.

Harvey grabbed a sobbing George and pulled him close, trying to be the strong one for a change.

"You can't leave me," George sobbed as he wrapped his arms around Harvey's shoulders.

Harvey felt an overwhelming desire to explain himself. He knew this was the same desire that had made him get out of the car. It wasn't to go back with George, it was to explain to him why they wouldn't work. For the first time since he'd fallen in love, he was ready to admit to himself that it was doomed from the start.

"I can't do this anymore," Harvey cried, "I can't keep letting myself get hurt. I felt worthless for so many years, but then I found you and you showed me what it was like to love and be loved."

"So stay," George pulled away from Harvey, "we'll move away. We can have a fresh start anywhere you want. We can move to New York like you wanted. We can get married and have white roses and get that apartment we planned and get some dogs. We can be happy."

Harvey wanted to believe the words he was telling him. He wanted to have that life, but something told him there'd always be something in the way.

"You know as well as I do that it wouldn't work."

George smiled back with trembling lips as the tears cascaded down his cheeks.

"We could have been amazing," Harvey laughed, trying to blink the tears away.

George grabbed him and kissed him passionately for what Harvey knew would be the last time. He closed his eyes and let the tears fall to his mouth as George made him forget everything, if for only a few moments.

They pulled reluctantly away from each other and they wiped their tears.

"We were amazing, kid," George whispered.

"I know," Harvey sighed, "now go back to your wife."

With that, Harvey gave him one last smile and turned to head back to the car, where Leo was standing. He could hear George sobbing loudly in the street, and it broke his heart anew over and over, but he didn't turn around.

"C'mon, let's go."

Harvey wiped the last of the tears from his eyes and ducked into the car. They were soon speeding down the road, leaving George alone. As they turned the street, he wanted so badly to take one last glance at George, but he stopped himself.

"This is going to be awesome," Lucas said.

"I know," Harvey said, resting his head on the window as tears silently rolled down his face, "I'm really excited."

GEORGE & HARVEY
- PART THREE -

THE FIGHT

Ashley John

DEDICATION

This book is dedicated to my Nan, Adrienne, for being one of the strongest women I'll ever know.

ABOUT THIS BOOK

George & Harvey: Part Three
The Fight

Published: July 2014 (2nd Edition and print edition April 2015)
Words: 27,000

The Fight is the third novella from Ashley John (**first published July 2014**), and the third and final part of **The George & Harvey Series**. This brand new edition has been completely refined and re-edited, with brand new content!

5 months have passed since Harvey left George behind and he is touring the country with his brother Leo, but things aren't quite how he expected. After struggling to stay sober, Leo slips back into his old ways and Harvey's world quickly becomes hell on earth. Terrible and heart-breaking things happen to Harvey, forcing him to go back and fight for the only person who he truly loves, George Lewis.

Will George accept him with open arms once again? Will Paula step-aside and let Harvey take her husband? Will Leo ever let his brother go? Are Harvey's actions going to have deadly consequences?

Will George & Harvey ever get their happy ending?

ONE

A tear slowly fell from Harvey's eye and landed in the dark whiskey. Embarrassed, he quickly wiped the lone tear away, not wanting any of the people in the bar to see. Middle-aged men in flannel shirts surrounded him, and he didn't want to attract any unwanted attention.

He sighed heavily and pushed back the ocean of tears that were waiting to be shed. He focused his eyes on the whiskey, as the one man he didn't want to think about forced his way through.

George Lewis.

He couldn't do anything without being reminded of George. It had been 5 months since Harvey left George behind to travel with his brother, but so much had changed since that dark day. Every time he thought back, gray, heavy clouds filled his mind. He didn't care that it had been the middle of summer.

It was the last day he'd felt the heat.

Darting his eyes around the dive bar, he tried to remember

what city he was in. They moved around so often, he'd fall asleep in one place and wake up in another. The décor of the bar told him that he was somewhere in Texas, but that was all he knew.

He hadn't exactly picked the bar for the décor, more for the fact he was sure they wouldn't ask him for ID. He was still only 19, but the last 5 months had aged him more than anything else in his life. Every time he got changed, he tried not to notice his ribs and hips poking their way painfully through his pale skin. Every morning he tried to ignore the thick, purple bags that had formed under his sunken eyes.

As he ordered another whiskey with the little money he had, he hoped it would be the one to wash away the dull ache in the pit of his stomach.

"You're not from 'round these parts, are you?" the gruff bartender asked Harvey as he snatched the money from his hand.

Harvey quickly shook his head. The last thing he wanted to do was seem rude, but he didn't want to engage in any conversation with the locals. Brick by brick, he'd slowly built a wall around himself and he was reluctant to let anybody in.

As he tossed the whiskey back, his thoughts turned to his brother, and his heart ached even more. It ached more for Leo than it did for George. When he'd set off into the unknown with a broken heart, the thought of his brother turning his life around was the only thing holding him together. He'd been naive to believe that a few weeks of sobriety was enough to change the habits of a lifetime.

Things didn't start out so bad. In the early days of the tour, Harvey actually enjoyed himself. He was kept busy enough to keep his mind from hearing his broken heart and even though the work was tiring, he got to spend quality time with Leo. The bond they'd once shared a long time ago, slowly started to regrow.

It felt like the fresh start Leo had promised.

One night after a particularly energetic gig, the band and crew went to a dive bar. When Leo accepted a drink and said he'd just have '*one*', Harvey knew it would be the beginning of the end.

He watched as his brother slowly started to depend on alcohol to function. Every time Harvey confronted him, he'd tell him that he was fine. Soon the alcohol wasn't enough, and with drugs being so easily available, Leo couldn't resist. He was like a kid in a candy store. Every addiction and vice he'd ever had, was suddenly in front of him, and he wasn't a strong enough man to save himself, not even for Harvey's sake.

Watching his brother fade back into the monster he despised, Harvey looked for any way out he could, but they were hundreds of miles away from home and it was too late.

Harvey patted his pocket and knew there wasn't enough money to buy another drink. As he gazed into the empty glass, he thought about heading back to the tour bus. He dreaded spending time there with Leo and the band. On the nights that they didn't have gigs, they'd spend their time with large amounts of alcohol, drugs and girls. After a couple drinks, they'd usually turn on Harvey and ridicule him, on everything from his sexuality, to his clothes and body.

Standing up, he felt the alcohol kick in. He'd grown fond of whiskey, and if he ever wanted to drown his sorrows, it was the drink he'd choose. Deep down, he knew the only reason he drank it was to feel some closeness to George, but he didn't want to admit that to himself.

The fresh air hit his face as he walked out into the dark Texas night. A bitter chill in the air told him that Fall was ending and Winter was just around the corner. The days had blurred into each other and there'd ceased to be a distinction between one week and another.

As he turned into the alley behind the venue where the tour bus was parked, he heard the cold and dry laughter that he'd grown to dread.

Out of the corner of his eye, he spotted a payphone under a street light. For a second, he pivoted between the payphone and the tour bus. He slapped his pocket and felt the change, and almost instinctively, he walked over and slotted his last few coins in.

His fingers went into autopilot and punched in the numbers. The dial tone sounded and he could feel his heart slowing down.

Nervously, he held his breath as he waited for the voice he needed to hear. The urge to call him had been so strong for so long, but the alcohol infecting his blood had pushed him into finally doing it.

"Hello?" a cold female voice snarled down the handset.

Harvey felt a dagger sink deep into his chest. Every part of him was screaming at him to hang up, but instead he stood in the cold, wide-eyed with the phone pressed firmly to his ear.

"Who is this?" she spat, "Do you know what time this is?"

Hearing Paula's voice made every emotion he'd felt for George feel even rawer. For months he'd thought about what had happened to George and Paula. He'd convinced himself that Paula had moved out, leaving George to live his days pining for Harvey.

"It's you, isn't it?" she said, whispering now, "I don't know what you want, but if you call here again, I'll have this number disconnected."

The dial tone returned as Paula slammed the handset down. He'd hoped so desperately that George had left Paula. He wanted the love they'd had for each other to mean something, but it seemed that George could easily slot back into his old life and Paula had let him.

Wiping away the last of his tears, Harvey jumped onto the tour bus trying to hide that his heart was breaking all over again.

TWO

"**J**ust do it!" Leo snarled, "Don't be a fucking queer!"

Harvey stared down at the white line in front of him, hoping the stained sofa would swallow him up. The whole band had stopped to watch. Each pair of eyes burned fiercely into his skin. They were all waiting for his response, on the edge of their seats, with eager smiles. Out of the corner of his eye, he could see Lucas eyeing him over his book, shaking his head.

"No," Harvey whispered.

"Just do it," Scott, the lead singer sneered, "stop being such a fag."

He stared at the cocaine in front of him. The thought of touching drugs was something he'd never even considered. He never thought he'd drink, but he'd grown to enjoy it, just not to the excess that Leo did. As his eyes focused on the tiny white grains, he thought about the acceptance it would bring him, if he caved him and joined in.

"Do it," Leo snarled, gripping the back of Harvey's head.

He forced Harvey forwards and smashed his face into the table, rubbing it in the white powder. Harvey quickly clamped his eyes shut and felt it coat his face. He wanted to cry and scream but he felt completely numb.

"Leave him alone!" Lucas cried.

Harvey felt Leo's tight grip loosen as Lucas pushed him off. His eyes slowly opened as he rested his cheek on the glass table. When the numbness started to fade he could hear the piercing laughter of the rest of the band.

He felt Lucas' arms lift him up from the ground and take him to the tiny bathroom. The feeling quickly returned to his legs after his moment of being paralyzed.

"Here, let me wash it off."

"Don't touch me!" Harvey screamed, pushing Lucas away.

It was an instinct, a natural reaction.

He'd built the wall so high, feeling someone's touch on his skin made him want to explode.

"Jesus Christ!" Lucas shouted back, "I was just trying to help you!"

The door slammed and Harvey was alone in the dirty tour bus bathroom. Locking the door, he stared at his reflection in the cloudy, cracked mirror. His eyes looked sunken, and sharp cheekbones poking out painfully under them. It had been so long since he'd eaten a proper meal, he'd learned to ignore the feeling of hunger.

His skin was covered in the white powder. As he stared at his warped face in the cracks, pain washed over him. It wasn't a physical pain, but an emotional pain. He didn't know how his life had become the black hole that it was. He'd been so close to finally being happy, but nothing ever seemed to work out for him.

The days leading up to him leaving had been replayed over and over in his mind and every time, he thought of something he could have done differently to change his fate.

Staring at the white powder, he wanted to forget everything. He wanted the pain to finally stop. He didn't recognize the person in the mirror. He wiped his finger across his cheek and stared at the fine powder. Without even thinking about it, he rubbed it on his gums, something he'd seen Leo do, so many times.

Like a mad man, he scraped every last bit of the cocaine from his cheek and let the chemical race through his blood. His heart clenched and pumped blood around his body at the speed of light, making his skin burn to the touch. He swayed on the spot dizzily for a second, before falling back into the wall.

A gentle smile spread across his face as he thought of George. He quickly thought back to the cabin trip they'd shared. That was a moment when Harvey had felt most happy. He kept trying to imagine George's face but his features blurred and melted around. He tried to focus his fuzzy brain, and every time he thought he could remember, he would slip away.

He could only remember a feeling.

A feeling that he hadn't felt in a long time.

Love.

Many hours later, a loud banging on the door brought Harvey back to reality. He quickly opened his eyes and tried to ignore the swirling loud mess taking over his brain. He heard another banging, but he wasn't sure if it was on the door or in his skull. Splashing water on his face, he stared at his bloodshot eyes in the mirror.

"I need a piss," Leo shouted from the other side.

Harvey unlocked the tiny door and Leo pushed past him and unzipped in front of the toilet.

"You've been in here for hours. What have you been doing? Wanking over that pervert writer?" Leo laughed as he stared down into the toilet.

A violent rage spread through Harvey. He roughly grabbed Leo's T-shirt from behind and slammed him against the wall. Piss ran down Leo's pale jeans. Pushing him into the wall, he resisted the urge to choke his brother. He didn't care that Leo was the only family he had. He'd stopped caring a long time ago.

"Finally grown a pair of balls, I see?" Leo said, zipping up the front of his jeans.

Harvey panted as he stared deep into his brother's eyes, pushing his arm further into Leo's throat. Leo didn't try to escape, instead, he stared back into Harvey's eyes, making his skin crawl.

"What you gonna do? Choke me to death?" Leo gasped through the arm ramming against his windpipe.

Harvey snarled and pushed harder. He wanted to see the light fade from Leo's eyes. As he stared into Leo's eyes, he could see his own face. It was angry and sharp and he realized he was becoming the monster he'd always vowed he wouldn't. He ran his tongue across his gums as he remembered what he'd done.

Releasing Leo, he took a step back and roughly ran his hands through his hair as he desperately tried to find the real Harvey Jasper.

Rubbing his throat, Leo glared bitterly at Harvey, before slipping back to the rest of the band. Harvey quickly followed him, not wanting to be stuck with his own thoughts. He was too scared of who he was becoming.

He squinted through the strong smelling smoky cloud, and he could see the band sprawled out, with semi-naked girls draped over them. Harvey looked for Leo. He was already in the corner with a girl in front of him, on her knees. Just from his face, Harvey could tell that Leo was too high to even notice what she was doing. Lucas was next to him kissing another girl, with his hand down her shirt, groping her chest. The exit was only a few steps away, but before Harvey could reach it, Scott roughly grabbed his arm.

Harvey spun around to see his painfully bloodshot eyes. His arm was full of tiny red prick-marks.

"Not so fast, gay boy," he slurred, a sinister smile spreading across his face.

He tried to pull his arm away, but Scott's grip was tight.

"What do you want?" Harvey mumbled.

The anger quickly flooded back.

The hand around his arm tightened and dragged him off to the tiny bedroom where the main members of the band slept. The rest of the band were either too high to notice or they didn't care what was about to happen. He threw Harvey down onto the hard bed and gently locked the door.

"You think you're better than me, you little fag?" Scott laughed at him.

A mop of greasy brown hair flopped lifelessly on his head, and his entire body was covered in messy tattoos.

"Don't fucking ignore me, queer," Scott growled grabbing Harvey's face hard in his fist, "I asked you if you thought you were better than me."

For a second, Harvey's stared in shock at his dirty skin. It was covered in acne scars and looked like it hadn't been washed in weeks. He'd never seen any of the band use the shower on the bus.

"No," Harvey whispered through gritted teeth as Scott's grip tightened.

"You're worthless," Scott spat in Harvey's face, making him close his eyes, "I don't know why your brother begged me to let you come. You're a waste of space. You're a dirty little cock sucker, aren't you?"

"Please Scott," Harvey cried quietly, "just let me go, yeah?"

"I said you're a dirty little cock sucker aren't you?" Scott growled even louder.

Harvey fought back the tears. He didn't know what was going to happen to him. Squeezing his heavy eyes tighter he prayed for somebody to walk in and save him.

"*Answer me!*" Scott screamed in his face.

"Yes," Harvey mumbled, a tear rolling down his cheek.

"Say it," Scott sneered, "say *'I'm a dirty little cock sucker'*."

"I'm a dirty little cock sucker," another tear rolled down his face as he blinked heavily.

With his free hand Scott ripped the belt from the waistband of his jeans and yanked them down to his knees, pulling his underwear with them.

"Suck it, fag," Scott stared down into Harvey's face, his

hand trying to rip open Harvey's mouth, "it's what you want."

"Please," Harvey croaked as another tear rolled down his face.

Scott let go of Harvey and for a second, he thought he was going to leave, but he pulled a pocket knife from the jeans around his knees. He flicked the blade up with a quiet click and placed it gently against Harvey's cheek.

"I won't ask you again, fag," his eyes opened wide, letting Harvey see how high he really was.

Time stood still as the cold metal burned into his cheek. His lips trembled as he fought back the tears. He blinked them away and stared at Scott's solid shaft in front of him. He closed his eyes again and hoped for a miracle.

With his free hand, he grabbed the back of Harvey's hair and pushed him roughly towards his groin, shoving it deep into Harvey's throat, choking him.

"What the fuck is going on?" Lucas' voice made Scott release his vice-like grip on Harvey's hair and scramble for his jeans.

Lucas stood in the doorway, with the girl he'd been groping, hanging from his neck.

"What the fuck, bro?" Lucas said, prying the girl off him.

"He's a fag!" Scott said, taking a step back from Lucas.

Harvey sunk to the floor and leaned against the bed, tears tumbling from his raw eyes. The girl stood in the doorway and started to button her shirt up as she stared with disgust at Harvey on the floor.

"Harvey, are you okay?" Lucas said, quickly turning to him.

"Why do you care about him? He likes that shit," Scott shot back.

Lucas turned back to Scott and pushed him roughly by the shoulders, sending him crashing to the ground under the dark window in the tiny room.

"You can't do shit like that," Harvey heard Lucas say as he gently closed his eyes.

Every sense in his body was telling him to run and never look back, but he seemed to be frozen to the ground.

"I'm gonna go," the girl said as she headed for the door, "this shit got weird.

The tour bus door slamming seemed to re-inject life into Harvey. He jumped up and ran for the door, bursting out into the cold night. He could still feel the metal blade sinking into his cheek, sending a chill down his spine as he leaned against the side of tour bus, letting the crisp air fill his lungs.

"Are you okay?" Lucas asked, as he jumped from the tour bus.

"I don't know," Harvey shook his head, his lips trembling and eyes burning from the fresh tears, "I don't know who I am anymore."

"He had no right to do that," Lucas said, leaning next to Harvey, "he's a fucking scum bag."

Lucas pulled a packet of cigarettes from his back pocket and offered Harvey one. He nearly refused, but instead, he took one of the cigarettes and let Lucas light it for him. He took a long deep drag and instantly started to cough on the smoke.

He'd never smoked before, but he didn't care anymore. He felt like he'd already gone over the edge.

"Calm down, bro!" Lucas said as he watched Harvey puff frantically on the white cigarette.

Letting the nicotine race through his body, it seemed to make him feel more at ease and he suddenly understood how people could get addicted to the stuff.

"This life isn't for you," Lucas sighed, "I feel bad for bringing you along. I thought your brother could change."

"Me too," Harvey coughed through the smoke.

"What happened to make him like that? He won't talk about it," Lucas asked, stamping on the butt of his cigarette.

Harvey wondered how close they really were.

"Our parents died," Harvey said casually, as if detached from the life he'd once known, "In a fire."

"Fuck," Lucas sighed, "I'm sorry."

"Thanks," Harvey said, throwing the dead butt into the darkness of the alley, "it was a long time ago."

As he watched the amber light quickly fade, he thought about how long ago it really was. It was only 5 years, but it felt like he'd lived decade's worth since. His life had taken so many twists and turns, he found it hard to believe that it was his parents that had died in a fire. His heart told him that they were, but his head told him that it happened to someone else.

"How did it start?" Lucas asked, "The fire?"

"We never found out," Harvey stared into the dark, "the police seemed to think it was arson, but they could never prove it."

Harvey thought about going back onto the tour bus to grab the scraps of money he'd saved up, but the thought of facing Scott or Leo made him feel ill.

Instead, he looked to the opening of the alley and thought about his future and where it would take him. For a moment, he saw a dark tunnel, like he had done so many times, but at the end of the tunnel, he was sure he could see a light.

In the light, he could see the figure of a man.

A man his heart yearned loudly for.

THREE

With no destination in mind, Harvey left Lucas and wandered off into town. It reminded him of when he left George and ended up on Ginger's doorstep. He desperately longed to see Ginger's face. She'd know how to help him.

As he slowly walked around the dark streets, he cursed himself under his breath for not knowing any phone numbers. The only number he could remember was George's home phone. With each payphone he passed, he had to stop himself from jumping on one and punching in the number. Back when he left George and ended up at Ginger's café, he knew deep down that George would find him somehow.

He looked out into the road and willed George's car to speed towards him, like it had done so many times. He wanted George to turn up to save him, but he knew he wouldn't.

He was alone.

A red light in the distance pulled Harvey in. He didn't realize how hungry he really was until he was outside of the fast food restaurant. The smell of fries and burgers made the hairs on his arms stand up.

Harvey ripped his left shoe and sock off and the creased $20 he'd stashed for emergencies dropped out. With the crinkled money he ordered a cheeseburger with small fries. He had no idea how the $16.89 change would make a difference to his situation.

He swallowed the food almost whole and his stomach quickly cried for more, but he knew it would only be a waste of money. It tasted so good, but he couldn't let himself indulge like he really wanted. When he lived with Leo, food was scarce and he'd got used to going days without eating, but when he lived with George, he'd taken the free access to full cupboards for granted. He'd even started to gain a little bit of weight thanks to George's cooking.

He stared down at the money. In his mind, he was already slotting the coins into a payphone, but the thought of Paula's voice stopped him. It was a little past 10, so maybe George would pick up, but he had a feeling that Paula would be jumping on all of the incoming calls just to catch him out.

Harvey was torn from his thoughts when a man joined him. He looked up and stared confused at the man who looked like he was in his mid-20s. He was rugged, in a blue flannel shirt, but past the stubble and messy hair Harvey could tell that he was naturally good looking. Harvey glanced around the restaurant and they were the only two customers, so he knew he wasn't sitting across from him for lack of space.

"You look like I feel," the man sighed heavily.

His voice had a deep southern twang, which Harvey quite liked. It was rich and smooth. Harvey smiled weakly, but his eyes quickly darted down to his finished burger wrapper.

"I thought you could do with some company," the man said softly.

The brick wall instantly sprang up around Harvey making him sit up straight and press his back hard against the chair.

"I'm fine."

The man didn't budge. A young girl brought over a tray of

food without a smile, and Harvey watched as he tucked into his burger. A small splash of sauce fell out and caught in the man's stubble. Harvey tried to ignore it, but he could feel it bugging him.

"You've got a little -" Harvey said, pointing at the ketchup.

The man laughed and quickly wiped it away.

"My bad" he said, with a mouth full of food.

Harvey glanced away from the chewed up food. He thought back to George and how he always held himself so gentlemanly. Maybe that was part of his problem.

"I'm Harvey," he said quietly, feeling a few rows of brick crumbling from the wall.

"They call me Chip," the man said, mouth still full of food, "but my real name is Charlie."

"Nice to meet you, Chip," Harvey forced a polite smile.

Chip reached out his ketchup covered hand and Harvey shook it, not wanting to seem anymore rude than he already did. He messily wiped his hand on his already dirty jeans. He'd already broken so many of his own rules tonight, so he didn't feel bad about resisting Chip's southern charm.

"What's up then fella?" Chip asked as he licked the ketchup from his fingers.

Harvey didn't know where to begin. He had so many problems, they'd all formed into a big screaming ball of confusion.

"I'll start," Chip smiled, as if sensing Harvey's fear, "the girlfriend just dumped me. She says she doesn't want anything serious, but we've been dating for 2 years. 2 whole years! How stupid is that? I tell you, gals are from a whole different planet.

Harvey shook his head trying to rid his mind of Scott's voice that had been rattling around since he'd left the alley.

"Your turn," Chip said, sliding his tray away from him.

He didn't want to, but he told Chip every detail of his story. He started right at the beginning in the bookstore, and told him everything up until what had happened on the tour bus before he left. Harvey completely tuned out and just let his mouth move. Chip might as well have not been sitting across from him, it just felt good to say everything out loud, after bottling it up for so long.

When he finished, he sighed, leaned back in his chair and stared at Chip.

"That's heavy, man," Chip said, also sitting back in his chair.

Harvey suddenly remembered that he was in Texas and it probably wasn't a good idea shouting off about being gay. Quickly, he examined Chip's face, but he looked more exhausted than anything else.

"So yeah," Harvey said, "I don't know what my next move is."

"I know what my next move is," Chip stood up, "I'm going to a bar, and you're coming with me."

FOUR

In any normal circumstances Harvey would have ran a mile in the other direction, but instead, he got into Chip's car. So many crazy things had happened already, he didn't think things could possibly get any worse. He drove them to a small nightclub around the corner, where Chip seemed to know the guy on the door. They were quickly ushered inside, bypassing the line of waiting party-goers and entry fee.

"What are you drinking?" Chip shouted over the music.

Harvey stared blankly at him. He felt completely overwhelmed as he gazed around the bar. The place was packed with people dancing and chatting, and heavy strobe lights almost blinded him.

"Beer," Harvey said.

He suddenly remembered he hated the taste of beer and cursed himself under his breath. With two beers in hand, Chip led them off to a booth near the dance floor. For a second they watched the girls grinding up against the boys.

"So you're fully gay?" Chip asked.

"Yeah," Harvey said.

He didn't see the point in lying after he'd already told Chip everything.

"That's cool, man," Chip said, "no judgment."

Chip winked at him through the darkness. He'd always been scared of opening up about his sexuality because of Leo, so he'd forgotten that there were people out there who didn't care.

The thought of Scott gripping his face suddenly raced around Harvey's mind, making him take a long gulp of beer.

"So she packed up my stuff and told me to leave! She's still living in my house. I've had to move into a trailer. How messed up is that?" Chip shouted into Harvey's ear after what felt like the 10th bottle of beer.

They were still in the booth, but every time their bottles emptied, Chip would run to the bar to replace them and he didn't once ask Harvey for any money. When he returned, Harvey felt him sitting closer and closer, until he finally had his arm lazily around Harvey as he told him more and more stories about his ex-girlfriend, Linda.

"She's such a whore. She sold my *Xbox*," Chip slurred, resting his head on Harvey's shoulder as he paused to laugh, "I loved that fucking *Xbox*."

They both laughed loudly, with Chip on Harvey's shoulder. It wasn't very funny, but the alcohol made it seem like it was the most hysterical thing Harvey had ever heard. As Harvey laughed, he felt months of grayness lift from his shoulders. He couldn't remember the last time he'd laughed.

"I need the bathroom, hold my beer," Chip slurred before running messily across the dance floor.

Harvey stayed in the booth, holding the two beers as he examined the bar. He'd never been in a place like it. George took him to restaurants and cabins and they drank whiskey in his study. He'd never taken him to a bar to drink cheap beer. Harvey started laughing again, on his own this time, at how snooty he thought George was. He couldn't believe how bad of a fit they were for each other, but as he did, the love suddenly swelled up in his heart like a balloon.

They spent the night tossing back beers until Harvey couldn't taste it anymore and they laughed at all of the dumb things Linda did, leading Chip to proclaiming that he didn't need her and he didn't need women. The more they drank, the more hands-on Chip seemed to get. It grew into the small hours of the morning, and after spending a lot of time on the dance floor, they stumbled out of the club as the sun started to rise.

Chip clumsily tried to ram his keys into his pickup truck, but Harvey grabbed his hand and pulled it away from the car.

"No. Can't drive," Harvey slurred, "cab."

Harvey stumbled and pointed in the direction of a row of cabs outside the club.

"Quick! Before they all go!" Harvey cried, waving his arms around for no good reason, staggering into Chip.

"You're drunk!" Chip slurred, catching Harvey.

Harvey felt Chip support his weight as they leaned against the car.

"No, you're drunk!" Harvey exclaimed, pressing his finger into Chip's face.

Chip went to playfully bite it, but he was way off. Harvey wriggled free of Chip and started to sway on the spot. He felt his knees buckle, and he quickly grabbed onto the edge of the pick-up truck. Chip stumbled over and put his arms under Harvey's to prop him up. Pulling him up to eye-level, they stared intensely at each other.

The alcohol was clouding Harvey's brain. He couldn't remember where he was or why he was there. He blinked heavily and when he opened them, Chip was panting deeply, staring deeply into his eyes. His eyes flickered around his face and he noticed a tiny scar above his eyebrow.

As Chip leaned slowly in, Harvey could strongly smell the alcohol on his breath, but he didn't care. He gently closed his eyes and waited for their lips to touch.

For a moment, they messily kissed with their tongues sloppily exploring each other. Chip pulled away and smiled down at Harvey.

"You're stopping with me tonight," Chip whispered.

Harvey heavily nodded as he let Chip lead him off to a cab. A small voice in the back of his head was screaming at him for being so stupid, but the pulsing in his underwear didn't care.

It had been so long since he'd been properly intimate with anyone, he couldn't ignore the feelings stirring deep inside him.

The yellow cab pulled into a trailer park and pulled up outside of a run-down looking trailer. After throwing a fist-full of dollar bills at the driver, they stumbled out of the cab and up the steps to Chips' portable home.

The sun had nearly risen completely, making Harvey guess it was already well into the morning. He tried to shake the sleepiness from his eyes as he watched Chip fumble with the keys in his hand. When he finally found the right key, he tore the door open and Harvey followed him inside.

It was a lot nicer inside than he'd expected. Through the dim haze of the rising sun, he thought it just looked like a normal tiny house. Chip slammed the door, locked it and stumbled over to the windows and ripped all of the curtains shut, casting darkness on their surroundings.

Harvey stood silent for a moment and listened to his trembling, nervous breaths as he tried to focus his mind. He could feel the alcohol swishing around in his stomach. He thought back to being in the bathroom and rubbed his head and thought back to George and Leo and then back to Chip.

When his mind flicked to Scott gripping the back of his head, the urge to quickly leave washed over him, but he felt Chip's lips land forcefully on his as he dragged him over to the tiny bed. As they fumbled, ripping each other's clothes off, George, Leo and Scott left Harvey's mind.

He let Chip's tongue drunkenly explore his body. He felt so carefree in the moment and didn't care about the consequences. Closing his eyes, he let the stranger's lips kiss his hips as the room started to spin. When he reached his underwear, he cautiously pulled them back to reveal Harvey's already hard shaft.

"I've never done this with a guy before," Chip whispered nervously.

FIVE

L ight poured in through the thin curtains, making Harvey's heavy eyes twitch. They sprung open and the harsh brightness burned them, causing sirens to echo around his blurry mind. It took him a moment before he realized where he was.

As he looked around the tiny trailer, vague memories of being in a nightclub filled his painful head. He turned and saw a naked guy next to him. Harvey appreciated his hairy chest for a moment while he tried to piece together what had happened.

He stared at the man's sleeping face and he remembered he was called Chip.

Holding his breath, he gently climbed over Chip, not wanting to wake him. Sneaking out before Chip woke up was the best plan he had, but that was ruined when he heard a loud groaning.

"Fuck, my head!" Chip sighed as he stirred from his sleep.

Nervously, Harvey edged towards the door. He'd never had a one night stand before, but he felt ashamed and dirty. The only other man he'd slept with was George. He felt even dirtier, especially after what Scott had tried to force him to do.

"What time is it?" Chip said, as he rubbed his eyes, sitting up naked on top of the sheets.

Harvey glanced around the room looking for a clock, trying not to notice Chip's growing erection.

"I don't know," Harvey mumbled averting his eyes.

The door was calling for him to leave.

"There's a clock on the stove,"

Harvey walked over to the stove and squinted at the small and greasy display.

3pm.

"Shit, I should go," Harvey said, turning back to Chip, who was pulling a pair of jeans over his morning glory, without bothering to put underwear on.

"Why?" Chip croaked.

The question took Harvey by surprise. He had no idea why. He didn't have anywhere to go, and Chip was now the only person he knew in town.

"I don't wanna intrude," Harvey smiled, trying to stay polite.

He had no idea about morning-after etiquette.

"Stay, man," Chip's deep southern twang warmed Harvey.

He didn't know if he meant stay for breakfast or stay forever. He walked over to Harvey and flicked on the coffee machine. Dark stubble covered his face and his dark brown eyes were red and still fighting to stay open.

"I don't know," Harvey said as Chip rummaged in a drawer for coffee filters.

Harvey could tell he didn't entertain often.

"Where else have you got to go? You can stay here with me," Chip said as he poured ground coffee into the machine, "I've got nothing else, and I enjoyed last night."

A vision of living happily with Chip for the rest of his days flashed before Harvey's eyes. He was a nice man, and he'd probably treat Harvey well, but as he fiddled with the gold watch around his skinny wrist, he knew that he needed to go back to the man who owned his heart.

"It's been really fun, and you're a really nice guy, but...there's somewhere I need to go," Harvey sighed as his hand closed down on the handle.

"George?" Chip asked.

Hearing his name out loud, sent tingles rushing all over his body.

"I've got to try," Harvey sighed turning back to Chip, "If I don't, it'll kill me not knowing."

A smile spread across Chip's stubbly face, he leaned in and kissed Harvey gently on the cheek.

"Go get him."

"Thank you," Harvey whispered back, "for everything."

"There's something special about you, kid. I'm no homo, but there's something about you that would have made me forget all about Linda."

For a second, Harvey felt like George was talking to him, and instead of hearing Linda, he heard Paula.

Harvey headed out into the harsh and cold daylight, with a concrete plan in his mind.

He was going back to George and he wasn't going to let anything get in his way. He didn't regret spending the night with Chip. It had only made him realize how much he really did love George.

"How much for this?" Harvey said as he slid the heavy gold watch across the counter.

It was the first time he'd taken it off since George put it around his wrist all those months ago.

The old man behind the counter of the pawn shop picked it up and put it up to his eye. He turned it over and read the tiny inscription etched into the back. The words echoed throughout Harvey's mind.

'Harvey, with each passing day, I love you more than the last. Yours forever, George.'

As the man weighed the watch and put it through his various tests, Harvey wondered if George still cared for him. He tried to tell himself that George would still feel the same about him, but a small nagging voice in the back of his head taunted him with the same question that had tortured him since he first told George that he loved him.

Will he leave Paula?

"I'll give you $900 for it," the man said casually.

Harvey knew it was worth so much more just from the look on the man's face, but he wasn't going to be greedy.

"Can I just have one last look at it?" Harvey said, reaching out for the watch.

The man hesitated before cautiously handing it back to Harvey. He wondered how much money the man would make on it as he cursed George for spending so much. As Harvey re-read the engraved words, he thought back to how ungrateful he'd been when he'd received it. He felt like he was looking at it in a whole new light as he stood in the tiny pawn shop.

He wanted to put it back on his wrist and find another way to get the money, but he knew it was his only choice. Over the past 5 months, the watch had acted like a connection to George, even though it was just a piece of gold. He'd told Leo and the band that it was a fake piece of costume jewelry. If they discovered its true value, it would have sent dollar signs ringing through their eyes and they would have hacked Harvey's wrist off to get to it.

Reluctantly, Harvey passed the watch back to the man, who quickly hid it behind the counter as he hastily counted out the money. He slotted it into a brown envelope and slid it over to Harvey. He'd never had so much money in his hand before. As he walked through the street with it in his pocket, he could hear it shouting out to be stolen and he was sure everyone in the street could hear it.

After asking a stranger for directions, he headed for the bus station. He knew it would take hours to get home, but he didn't care. He wanted to get out of Texas as fast as he could.

As he raced through town, he thought about Leo and the rest of the band. He wondered if they'd even noticed that he wasn't there. For a second, he fought with himself as his legs started to change direction towards the theatre, where the bus was parked up.

When he turned into the alley, part of him wanted the bus to have left for its next destination, but it was still there. The bus symbolized everything that was wrong with Harvey's life. He wanted to run away from it and never think about it, or Leo, or the band ever again, but he felt compelled to get closure.

Nervously, he jumped onto the bus. Leo was alone with Lucas. They were sitting on the sofa playing a video game on the tiny TV, which was built into the wall. Neither of them had noticed Harvey get onto the bus so he stood and watched them in silence.

He thought about the way Lucas had tried to help him, and how Leo has fed him to the lions.

He took a deep breath before making himself known.

"I'm leaving, Leo," he said, trying to stop his voice shaking, "I'm going back home."

Lucas threw the game pad onto the table full of empty beer cans and vodka bottles. Leo however, just stared at the screen.

"I said, I'm going," Harvey repeated.

He didn't know what he was expecting from Leo. He didn't know if he wanted him to seem bothered, or to try to stop him. He was going regardless, but he just wanted to see something of the brother he'd once loved.

"We're going to Vegas tonight," Leo said, "you're not going back home. There's nothing for you there."

"I think we both know there is," Harvey sighed, still hovering around the door, waiting for a quick escape.

"You're going back to him?" Leo laughed, throwing the game pad down, knocking over a few cans, "what has he ever done for you?"

"A darn sight more than you have," Harvey snarled.

He turned and left the tour bus and headed to the opening of the alley. He was nearly out in the street when he felt Leo's hands dragging him back.

"You're not leaving me," Leo cried.

"Get off!" Harvey cried.

"You need me," Leo screamed through gritted teeth, his voice deep and raspy.

Harvey ripped free from his grip and pushed Leo, causing him to fall back against the cobbled alley. Harvey stepped over him and looked down at the man in front of him. He didn't know him.

He had no idea who he was, he wasn't his brother.

"I haven't needed you for a long time," he whispered.

Leo's face screwed up and it was an emotion Harvey hadn't seen in a long time. He looked hurt.

"Bro," Leo started.

"Don't *'bro'* me," Harvey screamed, "I'm not your *'bro'*."

Harvey pulled the envelope from his back pocket and pulled out a handful of the bills and sprinkled them down on Leo.

"Here," Harvey said, spitting down at Leo, "don't keep in touch."

As Harvey headed towards the bus station, he felt a sense of relief and freedom. It all suddenly seemed clear to him. Leo needed him. Leo needed him to make himself feel better and to make himself feel wanted. It had always been that way. He only lashed out at Harvey and treated him like rubbish because he wanted to crush Harvey's spirit so he would feel worthless, like Leo did.

After all the years together, it was suddenly so clear for him, and for the first time, he was truly ready to let the memory of Leo go.

To Harvey, the Leo he'd loved died in the fire along with his parents.

SIX

"K *id, I've missed you!" George cried as Harvey stepped off the bus. He ran over and grabbed him in his arms and spun him around. He didn't know how George knew he'd be at the bus station but he was happy.*

"Sir?" a soft voice broke into Harvey's dream, forcing him to open in eyes and accept that he was still on the bus he'd been on for hours, "Your stop is coming up next."

The conductor smiled down at Harvey and headed back to the front of the bus. Day had turned to night, and after dozens of changes, he was finally home.

His heart ached as the dream lingered in his cloudy mind. He hoped and prayed that George would be there to greet him, but it was impossible.

As Harvey headed to the front of the bus, he noticed the clock on the dashboard.

4:13am.

He rubbed the sleep from his eyes and he knew it was too late to go straight to George's. Besides, he wanted to confront him when Paula wasn't there.

Harvey stepped off the bus with no bag or luggage into the icy night. He just had the clothes on his back and the left over money in his pocket. He looked around the dark bus station, but he couldn't see George's car anywhere. His house was only a few miles away, but that wasn't what he had planned.

Instead, he headed over to the station bathroom, shivering in his T-shirt. He locked himself in a cubicle and planted himself on the toilet. He wrapped his scrawny arms around his body to warm himself, but it was useless. Winter was around the corner, and the nights were already bitter.

As he drifted off into a light sleep, seeing George's face clearly warmed him through. George smiled down at him, and Harvey felt safe.

When dawn broke, Harvey's eyes instantly sprang open from his light sleep. As he headed into town to the nearest clothes shop, his entire body felt stiff from the awkward position he'd slept in.

He bought himself a new pair of jeans, a new T-shirt and a jacket. When he tried them on in the cubicle, the sight of his naked body shocked him. He'd never seen himself looking so thin. Bones poked out through his fragile and pale skin.

Next, he headed to the nearest florist and bought the biggest bunch of flowers he could afford. Flowers in hand, and new clothes on, he headed straight to Ginger's café to settle some unfinished business. Ginger's face lit up as Harvey stepped into the café with the flowers. She quickly left the customer she was serving and ran over and hugged him.

"I was so worried about you!" she sighed as she brushed Harvey's grown out black hair from his eyes, "I thought I'd never hear from you after you left!"

Harvey instantly felt guilty. Ginger was the one who'd encouraged him to get George to tell Paula, but he'd never let her know if it had worked. The thought of Ginger fretting for months made him feel uneasy.

"These are for you," Harvey smiled, handing the flowers to Ginger, "to say thank you."

"Child, you have nothing to be thankful for," she cooed gently, rushing to put the flowers in a jug of water.

She quickly finished serving the customer and rushed back to Harvey, forcing him into a chair. Her motherly nature noticed how thin he was, and she seemed to want to feed him.

"Breakfast! On me!" she cried.

"I'll pay this time," Harvey smiled.

He still had some money left from the watch, so he couldn't let the kindest woman he'd known since his mother, give him her food for free.

As he wolfed down the last of the eggs, he suspected she'd piled his plate even higher than last time. He'd dreamt about Ginger's breakfast many nights since he'd left, and it tasted even better than he'd remembered.

Just as he was about to tell Ginger everything that had happened, he remembered George and his plan and vowed to return to tell her everything.

"You better come back soon!" she said as she pulled Harvey into a tight hug.

"I will," Harvey said quietly, "I promise."

She pulled back and smiled comfortingly at him. As he stared at her lined face, he imagined that it was his mother, just older. Her warmth and love was identical to his mothers.

As he turned the corner onto George's street, it was as if time had stood still. So much had changed within Harvey, he was expecting to see a change in the house he'd experienced so much in, but it stood as it did when he'd left, for what he thought was the final time.

Squinting through the bare bushes, he could see George's car, and next to it, Paula's little blue car. Feeling safe from his distance, he lingered and watched for movement. He wanted nothing more than to run to George, but he knew he'd have to bide his time and wait for Paula to leave for work.

An hour passed and Harvey started to panic. He wrapped the large jacket tighter around his tiny frame as he shivered in the cold breeze. Just as he did, he heard the big green door slam in a way that only Paula seemed to know how to do.

He quickly put his hood up and turned away from the house and leaned against someone's garden wall, as casually as he could. Paula catching him would only ruin everything. Her little blue car sped down the street towards him, and he held his breath when he heard her engine slow down right beside him.

Pulling his hood tighter around his face, he clamped his eyes shut and listened as he heard the car turn the corner and head off towards the hospital.

Nervously, he slowly marched towards George's house. So much had changed and he'd come so far, but he couldn't suppress his emotions anymore. He'd craved and dreamed of embracing George and with each step forward, his heart pounded even faster.

When he reached the edge of the white picket garden he thought about walking up to the front door and knocking, but that didn't feel right. Instead, he crept around the side of the house into the back yard. Harvey's heart skipped a beat when he saw George's once perfect garden. He glanced at the browning trees and bushes and noticed that the grass had lost its bright green hue.

Most of the flowers they'd spent the spring planting, had shriveled up and died, but the roses were tough and seemed to be battling the frost and rain. He hoped that George's heart was like the roses. He prayed that their love had made it through.

Nervously, Harvey tiptoed across the garden towards the patio. For a moment, he thought the pool had vanished when he saw new tables and chairs sitting where the pool once was, but he quickly noticed the metal covering hiding the water. He walked over to the patio doors, and tried the handle. When it clicked open, he let it swing open as if it was inviting him into the large, bright kitchen.

Feeling cautious, his eyes scanned the room. It was just as he remembered it, but it felt so different. It felt so cold and empty. George wasn't there making eggs and bacon or sitting at the breakfast bar drinking coffee, reading a book. He suspected he'd be tucked away in his study.

Carefully, Harvey crept across the white tiles of the kitchen, across the marble hall and into the living room, where he instantly noticed changes. The last time he'd been there, there had been simple frames scattered around the room, but they had been breeding and multiplied. Dozens of pictures smiled down at him, from vacations he didn't recognize and trips he'd never seen before. Paula had even cut her long hair into a sharp, short blonde bob, which only made her look even angrier.

Harvey felt his heart quiver as he spun around the living room staring at the images. He felt like it was Paula mocking him. He knew it would be her that had put them up.

As he stared at the happy memories, the smiling walls closed in around Harvey. He felt like a rat in a cage and he suddenly regretted everything. Seeing George happy with Paula made him think that he'd got over Harvey as fast as he'd fallen in love with him. He could hear them laughing at him, shredding his heart into bloody tatters, as they lived the life he knew that he should be having with George.

When he couldn't take anymore of Paula's smug and bitter smile teasing him, he turned to leave and forget all about George, but a figure in the doorway made his heart stop beating all together.

"Harvey? Is that you?"

SEVEN

George blinked his eyes tightly.

"Harvey?" George whispered again.

In silence, they stood staring at each other. Harvey's eyes examined George's face and he looked older than the last time he'd seen him.

Without reason or logic, Harvey ran at George and jumped into his strong, open arms. Any thoughts of leaving vanished instantly as he let the arms of the man he loved wrap tightly around him.

"But how? Why?" George mumbled as he squeezed Harvey into his chest.

"I couldn't stand it anymore," Harvey choked on the tears, "I had to come back to see you."

"Oh, kid," George said as he rested his head on Harvey's messy hair, "I've missed you so much."

"I love you," Harvey sobbed into George's chest.

George put Harvey down on the sofa and forced every last detail from him. He told him all about how Leo changed and all the horrendous things he put Harvey through. He paused before telling him about Scott, but the thought of more secrets made his skin itch.

"You should have called," George sighed as he dropped his head heavily, "I would have come and got you instantly."

"I did," Harvey whispered, wiping the tears from his cheeks, "Paula answered and told me to never call again. I thought you didn't care anymore."

Harvey could see the anger grow in George's eyes. He wondered if the pictures of happiness were only select moments from the months he'd been away.

"I fucking knew it. We've pretty much been living separate lives. She tried to get us back to how we used to be when you left, but it only made me realize how I didn't love her anymore. She really tried too. We went on all these trips, and she changed her hair, but it couldn't take away from the fact I couldn't stop thinking about you."

Harvey didn't know what to say. Suddenly, he felt foolish for believing the smiling frames dotted around the room. They didn't seem so happy after all

"I tried looking for you," George continued, "I searched online for any trace of your band, but they're so low-key and I didn't have much to go with. Every time I got something, you seemed to move and I was back to square one."

"You tried looking for me?" Harvey whispered, fighting back more tears.

"I didn't stop," George's voice started to shake, "I didn't at first because I knew it was what you wanted to do. I know I put you through hell, and I'm sorry for that, but I realized that I couldn't live without you and I'd been a complete fool."

"So why didn't you leave Paula when you had the chance? You never explained why you kept stalling," Harvey sighed.

George paused and noticed Harvey's mouth twitching. He could see the pain he'd caused on his face, and he couldn't look him in the eye.

"I was an idiot. I was scared. I didn't understand what was going on. You're the first guy I've ever loved. I never thought I was gay or anything, until you walked into my life and then you became everything I ever needed, and I didn't even know it. Me and Paula met in college. We got married and tried to start a family, but things didn't work out. She was my first love. It was just so hard to accept it had ended."

Regret washed over Harvey. He wanted to go back and change how things had happened. He'd been selfish and not understood that George needed the time to process what was going on.

"So, you're not gay?" Harvey asked.

He couldn't believe he was asking it, but it was the first question that came to his mind. It was a question he'd asked himself so many times.

"I don't know," George sighed, "the label isn't important to me. If I feel it, then it's real. I mean, I fooled around with guys in college, but I never felt the way I do about you."

The revelation that George had done things with other men in college shocked Harvey. He'd always assumed he was his first.

"I missed you so much," Harvey smiled through the tears.

He closed his eyes expecting to wake up on the tour bus next to Leo, but when he opened them and saw George sitting in front of him, he knew he wasn't dreaming.

"I missed you more than you'll ever know," George stroked Harvey's face gently, "I thought I'd never see you again, and it was killing me a little bit more each day."

As they stared at each other, neither of them cared what had happened or what had been said. They knew all they wanted was each other, and nothing was going to get in their way.

"What now?" Harvey asked.

"I haven't thought that far ahead," George admitted, "I'm still getting over the shock of you turning up here."

"I had to sell your watch for money to get back," Harvey said as he rested his head on George's shoulder.

"I'll buy you a new watch. I don't care as long as I have you back," George said.

ASHLEY JOHN

"Paula?" Harvey asked nervously.

"We'll tell her the minute she gets home. No more secrets, no more hiding," George softly pulled Harvey's face towards his and tenderly kissed the lips he thought he'd never feel again.

"There's something else," Harvey said as he pulled away from the kiss, "if there's going to be no secrets, I want to get it out in the open. I slept with a guy. Chip, he was called. He was really nice and I liked him and he wanted me to stay with him. I thought about it."

A gentle smile spread across George's face.

"But you didn't. You came back to me," he planted another soft kiss on Harvey, "today is the start of our life. The past doesn't matter."

Waves of warmth swept across Harvey. The time they'd spent apart had changed George. He was more direct and more committed than he'd ever been before. He wondered if he'd have stayed and tried to work things out, would things be different?

"First things first though, kid," George smiled, "we need to get you some food!"

Harvey laughed as he let George lead him off to the kitchen. It almost felt like he'd never been away.

Instead of cooking up the usual bacon and eggs, George rustled up an amazing banquet of food for Harvey to devour. Plates of salad, pasta and fruit were placed before him and he ate every last scrap. He didn't care that he'd had a huge fried breakfast at Ginger's café only a few hours earlier because the months of under-eating had finally caught up with him and his stomach felt like a screaming animal who needed constant feeding.

"I still can't believe you're here," George smiled across to Harvey as he cleared away the plates from the breakfast bar.

"I wasn't sure if you'd want to see me," Harvey mumbled as he sipped the huge glass of orange juice.

Without words, George wrapped his arms around Harvey's bony shoulders and started to kiss his neck.

246

"I made a promise to you a long time ago," he whispered deeply into Harvey's ear, "I told you I would protect you, and I've already broken that promise once. I promise I'll never do it again."

As George's soft kisses swept from his neck to his cheek, he'd remembered how intoxicating George's touch could be.

"Please," Harvey smiled, "promise me you won't buy me any more expensive gifts."

"No," George laughed as he grabbed the front of Harvey's jacket and pulled him into a passionate kiss.

Carefully, George started to peel off Harvey's clothes, but he didn't want him to see how skinny he really was. Standing naked in the kitchen, their hands explored every part of each other's bodies. Harvey had missed the feeling of George's solid abs under his fingertips.

George spun Harvey around and pushed him up against the breakfast bar. As he felt George's throbbing shaft press up against the small of his back, Harvey shuddered and turned around to face George.

"No George," Harvey mumbled, "I'm not ready."

George took a step back.

"Is it because of what happened with Scott?

"Please, don't mention his name again," Harvey snapped.

He remembered Chip, but knew that if he hadn't have been drunk, he would never have gone through with it.

George gripped Harvey's shoulder and pulled him into a tight embrace.

"We'll take it slow," George whispered as he held Harvey's fragile frame close to his, "I'm sorry, I just couldn't help myself."

"I want to," Harvey said, "but I just need some time."

With George's soft skin against his, he knew that he'd made the right decision returning. Leo would be well on his way to Vegas and out of his life forever.

He wanted to feel safe in George's arms at the thought of never seeing Leo again, but something he'd said to George before his graduation sprung into his mind.

'Leo has a habit of turning up when you least expect it.'

EIGHT

D arkness fell over the house as George and Harvey waited nervously in the living room. George's eyes watched the hands tick on the tiny clock on the mantelpiece as 5pm drew closer. With each passing minute, his nerves grew and grew.

"If you need more time, I'm cool with that," Harvey said, not really believing it, but wanting to make up for his previous persistence.

"No," George smiled, "thank you, but now is the time. I've dragged this out too long and it cost me losing you."

As if on time, the soft purr of an engine pulling into the driveway told Harvey that the moment he'd been waiting so long for, had finally arrived, even if it was 5 months late.

"United front," George said, as he stood up and gripped Harvey's hand tightly.

Harvey tried to smile, but his lips quivered. He felt skittish and anxious. Last time he'd been face to face with Paula, she'd trashed half the house in a fit of rage and drawn blood from his skin.

The key clicked in the lock and the door slammed, echoing

around the house. He could feel her frosty presence the second she stepped over the threshold. She had a way of turning the atmosphere sour.

The sound of his own heartbeat filled his ears as he clenched George's hand, in the center of the living room, staring at the door. Tiny beads of sweat started to appear on his forehead under his over-grown, shaggy, black hair. It reminded him of being a child and waiting for his mother to catch him stealing from the candy cupboard. George squeezed his hand tightly, reassuring him that everything was going to be okay, trying to ignore his own nerves.

He didn't want to think about the grenade he was about to pull the pin on.

The door slowly opened, causing George to take a long deep breath and puff his chest out. He gripped Harvey's hand even tighter. As Paula walked into the room, Harvey could see her eyes widen as she realized what was going on. They landed bitterly on Harvey first, sending her lips into a snarl.

"What is this?" she shot, switching her gaze to George.

"It's over, Paula," George said, trying to sound strong, but Harvey could hear the nerves in his voice.

"Over? We've been through this once," Paula laughed bitterly, "It was just a silly fling."

In an alternative universe, Harvey was sure that Paula and Leo would be the ones who were married. They seemed like the perfect fit for each other.

"I love him," George said as he let go of Harvey's hand and took a step towards Paula.

"Love? What about marriage? What about our marriage?" she cried, "Does that mean nothing to you? I found out about your seedy affair but I put it behind me, for the sake of us."

"Oh come on, Paula," George sighed, "do you actually believe your own bullshit?"

Paula reminded Harvey of a rat trying to scramble around for the last scraps of food in an empty bin.

"So, your little whore turns up and you suddenly want to leave me? What about these last few months?"

"I've been sleeping in the guest bedroom for weeks. Did you think a few vacations and a haircut were going to fix the gaping wound in our marriage? It was like putting a band aid over a gunshot."

Harvey braced himself for another attack, but she didn't move. She just stood there and stared coldly at her husband.

"The love died a long time ago," George said, trying to calm his voice, "I'm sorry, but it did. Why can't we just be honest with each other and admit that? For the sake of what our marriage was when it was good. It was over long before Harvey turned up, and you know it."

Paula's eyes flickered from Harvey to George as tears started to well up in her eyes. Harvey couldn't believe what he was seeing. He wanted to drag George out of the house before she exploded for real.

"Fuck you, George," she screeched, "just fuck you!"

"Please, Paula," George pleaded, taking another step towards her, "let's stop lying to ourselves."

"Lying to ourselves? This whole marriage has been one long lie. You think I didn't know about your little flings with those guys in college? Everyone was talking about them, laughing at me behind my back. They called me your *'beard'*, but I loved you so much, I was willing to look past it because I thought you loved me. Why do you think I was so quick to get married, eh? Because I knew if we did, you'd settle down and we could start a family."

George stared in disbelief. He'd always assumed that what happened in college was his secret, not hers.

A light bulb lit up in Harvey's head and he realized why Paula was so freaked out when she thought he was gay at the barbecue after Chase tried to kiss him.

"And then there was all that with your mother. I stood by you through all those court hearings, and the trial. But you changed after it. We grew apart. You'd lock yourself in your study for hours on end and I started taking longer shifts at the hospital so I didn't have to be around you. It was like living with a zombie. I tried so hard."

George stared wide-eyed and open-mouthed at Paula as she spilled her heart out to him. He'd never even considered he was the one that had pushed Paula away.

"Why did you never tell me any of this?" George sighed.

"Because I had hope," Paula's voice cracked, "hope that the man I loved would come back to me."

Harvey wanted the ground to swallow him up. He'd never realized how deep the problems in George's marriage ran. He'd always put the blame on Paula from the few scraps of information George had given him. He surprised himself by actually feeling pity for her.

"I'm sorry," George said, "I really am."

George grabbed Paula and pulled her into a hug. Harvey's gut twisted. He couldn't believe what he was seeing, after everything George had said. He wanted to rip him off her.

"But it's over," he whispered into her ear before letting go and rejoining Harvey.

"Just get out George," Paula sighed in defeat, "the sight of you actually makes me feel sick."

Her eyes flicked to Harvey and stared deeply at him for what seemed like a lifetime.

"Harvey," she said, in a deep raspy voice, "good luck."

George's hand quickly wrapped around Harvey's as he pulled him across the living room and into the hall. George grabbed his keys from the kitchen and headed towards the front door. Harvey could hear Paula's heals clicking softly across the hall behind them.

"There's something you should know before you go," Paula muttered bitterly, "you're going to be a dad. I'm pregnant."

NINE

"**G**eorge, slow down!" Harvey cried as they sped down the freeway.

Harvey clung to his seat looking nervously at George as he weaved in and out of the traffic.

"Please George! You're scaring me!" Harvey cried.

"I'm sorry, kid. I can't think straight," George mumbled, clenching his fists tightly around the wheel.

"Where are we going?"

"The cabin," he said, "I need time to think."

"How the fuck is she pregnant?" George screamed, honking his horn as he cut in front of a car at speed.

"When did you last have sex?" Harvey asked, not really wanting to know.

"It was ages ago. We only did it a couple of few times after you left, but she told me she was taking contraceptive pills."

Harvey instantly knew what was going on, and it felt like a huge trap at his expense.

"You don't think she-"

"No, she wouldn't do that," George cut Harvey off before he got a chance to say anything, "would she?"

George frantically ran his hand through his hair, the last remaining color draining from his face. Harvey knew the thought of a baby only complicated everything.

"Maybe she's making it up?" Harvey said quietly, "To mess with you?"

Harvey could tell he was an unwanted distraction to George's thoughts.

"Or maybe it's not yours?" Harvey said, even quieter.

"Just shut up, please?" he snapped, "I'm trying to think!"

The car sped up again as it turned off in the direction of the forest, where the cabin was. As he stared out of the window into the frosty night, Harvey longed for the fairytale return he'd dreamed of.

He hadn't been relying on Paula having a trump card.

Twigs and gravel crunched under the car tires as the tires screeched to a halt outside of the cabin. The sight of it should have made Harvey fill with joy, but it only filled him with dread. It had once been a place of happiness for him, and it was a place he'd visited many times on lonely nights in his memories, but seeing it in the dark, with a tense silence between him and George, it was suddenly tainted.

"I didn't mean to shout," George said, trying to calm his panting breath.

"It's fine," Harvey said quietly, "let's go and get a fire started. It's freezing."

As George unloaded firewood from the cellar, Harvey cleared away the dustsheets and geared up the generator, sending a soft glow out into the woods.

"We haven't even eaten," George said as they collapsed onto the sofa in front of a roaring fire.

"I'm not hungry," Harvey lied, "and I don't think a pizza will deliver out here."

George laughed softly as he rested his head on Harvey's lap, staring into the fire. He felt safe, but not at ease.

"I could drive to that little store," George suggested as

Harvey gently stroked his hair.

"Let's just stay here," Harvey said, "we can eat tomorrow."

His stomach had got so used to not eating for days, he could quite easily survive without food, even if his body was crying out for it.

"What are you going to do?"

"I don't know," George sighed, "I really don't know."

"You're going to be a dad," he whispered, "you said you always wanted kids."

There was a moment's silence as George considered what Harvey was saying.

"I guess. I just didn't want it to happen like this."

"It was never going to be easy was it?" Harvey laughed softly.

George turned his head to look up at Harvey.

"I've spent months thinking about how I was going to end it with Paula. I knew I'd have to do it one day. I just always imagined she'd try to rinse me of my money. I never expected this," he sighed, "and I can't exactly kick her out of my house. She's carrying my baby."

"We don't know for certain," Harvey said as he stroked George's face, "we don't know if she's really pregnant yet."

George smiled.

"You're so optimistic," George chuckled softly.

"Do you want her to be?"

He knew that George would make a brilliant dad, but it was going to complicate their already complex life.

"I don't know," he admitted, "part of me felt happy when she told me. When the shock of it finally sank in, it's what I've always wanted. It just never seemed like the right time."

Hearing George talk about time made him remember what Paula said about how George had changed, and it made him think about the last time they were at the log cabin together.

"Last time we were at the cabin, you never told me anything about your mother and father," Harvey said, "why not?"

George's brow furrowed.

"Really?" he said, sitting up and facing the fire, "That's what you want to talk about?"

Pausing, Harvey thought for a second, but he remembered what he'd said about secrets.

"I told you all about my parents, but you didn't tell me about yours. I had to find out from Leo."

"I don't like talking about it," George mumbled, "I feel responsible. I should never have driven her home after those drinks. As far as I'm concerned, I killed her and I have to live with that. It's part of the reason I'm so protective of you. I felt like you were sent to me to save."

"What about your father?" Harvey asked.

There was another silence.

"The last time he spoke to me was at the funeral when he kicked me out and told everyone that I killed her. Then he re-married and moved to New York and I've never seen him since," George stared deeply into the flickering flames, "I've never told anyone this but it really affected me. Paula was right, I did change."

Harvey snuggled up into George's side.

"It wasn't your fault," Harvey whispered.

"Wasn't it?" George said, "My mother loved Paula y'know. She adored her."

Harvey couldn't understand why. He tried to imagine a different Paula who was nice and warm, but he couldn't muster the images.

"Is that part of the reason you didn't want to break up with her?" Harvey asked.

"Maybe. Maybe it was my conscience," George mumbled, "I don't know anymore. My head's cloudy."

Harvey ran to the freezing bedroom and grabbed a huge itchy blanket. Realizing why cabins were reserved for summer vacations, he wrapped the blanket around them and they cuddled up on the huge sofa in front of the roaring fire.

When he heard George's soft purring and snoring, he looked down at the man he loved. After everything he had told him, he felt like he finally knew the real George, and his vulnerability only made him love him more.

TEN

"Y**ou're** insane!" Harvey cried, "It's the middle of November. I'm not going canoeing!"

Harvey shivered as he watched George drag the old wooden canoe from the cabin basement.

"Oh c'mon," George mumbled as he dragged it across the twigs and gravel, towards the flat icy lake.

Heavy gray clouds loomed on the horizon of the early morning sky. Over breakfast, Harvey wanted to bring everything up so they could talk about it properly in the cold light of day, but he could plainly see in George's eyes that he didn't want to talk about any of it.

It was too soon.

"Me and my dad always used to canoe when we came out here," George smiled, "of course, it was usually summer."

Goosebumps spread across Harvey's skin as he listened to the fire inside beckoning him back, but there was something calling him to the water.

"This is crazy," he stepped into the canoe on the edge of

the flat water.

He could feel his legs shivering and wobbling as he gently perched in the small boat. Harvey's stomach dropped when George jumped in and quickly slid the canoe down the ice bank and calmly into the water. They set off across the cloudy lake, which stretched out as far as the eye could see.

"Here, kid," George said as he passed Harvey an oar.

Paddle in hand, Harvey felt regretful for not adding more layers from the old hunting clothes in the bedroom closet. The wool sweater irritated his skin as he shivered, and the coarse material grazed against his frozen nipples.

The further into the lake they rowed, the more alone it seemed they were. The dense trees around the edge of the lake were as still as they always were. As far as Harvey was concerned, they were the only people left on the planet.

"Have you thought anymore about Paula?" Harvey said quietly, not wanting George to get upset.

"I keep trying," George sighed, "but it's hard. I'm just going to have to be there for her and the baby."

"I'm too young to be a step-dad," Harvey laughed.

George chuckled softly as they paddled across the water, sending soft ripples across the still surface. Something about the water and the fresh air seemed to calm George, even if it was cold.

"When are we going back?" Harvey asked.

Last time he'd been at the cabin, he never wanted to leave, but the winter had brought out another side to the romantic retreat, which Harvey didn't love as much. It felt cold and hostile and he was dying to hear an explanation from Paula. He knew George trusted what she said, but Harvey had a sneaky feeling that Paula was up to something.

"This afternoon," George said, "I just needed some space and this is where my car ended up. It was almost automatic. I really need to stop running away from my problems."

A heavy drop of rain fell from the dark clouds, sending a shiver running through Harvey.

"Did you-?"

"I felt it," George was already turning the canoe back in the direction of the cabin.

Thunder and lightning lit up the dull sky, sending light dancing across the surface of the water. There was a moment of eerie silence before the clouds unleashed their heavy load, instantly soaking Harvey and George through to the skin.

Through the dancing rain and darkness, the bank quickly appeared and the small canoe, which had filled up with water, was gliding gracefully up the icy grass.

"Here, kid," George cried through the rain as he tried to help Harvey out from the tiny boat.

As he stood up, his borrowed boot slipped on the wet wood, and he fell backwards, tumbling over the edge of the canoe and into the icy shallow water. The breath quickly escaped from Harvey's lungs, his body in the water, frozen from the shock.

George quickly yanked the canoe and scooped Harvey from the shallow water.

"Let's get you in the shower," George whispered as he carried him back to the cabin like a child.

When George put Harvey in front of the fire, the roaring flames didn't take the chill away. He felt as if he'd never be warm again, cross legged on the floor in his thick, wet clothes.

The sound of rushing water echoed throughout the cabin and hot steam spilled over the edge of the old bathtub and into the living room, calling to Harvey.

"Get your clothes off," George whispered as he started to pull his own clothes off, "it's only going to make you colder."

Harvey's numb fingers uselessly fumbled with the many zips and buttons, but with each attempt, they stung even more.

"I c-can't," his voice trembled uncontrollably.

George started to peal Harvey's wet clothes off, revealing his almost blue body.

Once in the shower, George ripped the curtain around the tub and he let the hot water rush over them. Holding Harvey close, he could feel his skin slowly heating up and the shivers stop, and when it did, he felt the throbbing pressing against his leg.

Harvey glanced up and smiled at George.

"That was fun," Harvey whispered, regaining his breath.

"I should listen to you," George smiled back before leaning down to gently kiss Harvey.

Harvey's hands softly caressed George's firm chest, before disappearing below his waist.

"Are you sure you're ready?" George panted through the kissing.

Harvey didn't say anything. Instead, he turned around and pressed his front up against the wet tiles, guiding George towards him with his hands.

"I love you so much," George whispered into his ear as he slowly pushed himself up against his back.

After they dried off, they killed the fire and headed back down the freeway to Paula. With each road sign counting down the miles, the tension grew inside Harvey. He didn't want another showdown with her, but he was sure that's what they were going to get.

ELEVEN

I t was dinnertime, and the winter sun was already starting to set.

Taking a deep breath, George stepped slowly into the dark house. Squinting across the hallway, he could see the kitchen was empty.

"Maybe she's out," Harvey suggested as they searched the living room.

"Her car's outside," George said as he checked the empty, dark dining room.

Just as they were about to check upstairs, Paula appeared at the top of the staircase in a loose, white silk robe. Her hair was scraped back under a headband, and Harvey couldn't see an ounce of make-up on her cold, sharp face.

Her puffy eyes reminded Harvey of all of the tears he'd shed over George.

"Oh, it's you," she sighed before heading back to the bedroom.

"Paula, wait!" George cried as he ran up the stairs after her, "we need to talk."

He didn't care if he was wanted or not, but Harvey quickly followed. He wasn't chancing leaving Paula alone with him so she could work her black magic.

"I don't want to talk to you," she mumbled back.

"You said you were pregnant," George sighed as he followed her into the dark bedroom, quickly followed by Harvey.

Harvey flicked on the light to see the shredded remains of George's clothes scattered across the floor. He spotted a huge pair of fabric scissors sitting in the wreckage.

"What the fuck, Paula!" George cried as he picked up one leg from his favorite pair of jeans, "did you really need to do this?"

"Did you really need to cheat on me?" she climbed heavily back into bed.

Harvey didn't want to admit it, but her cutting up George's clothes felt light compared to what he'd done.

"We want to see a pregnancy test," Harvey mumbled quietly, stepping out from George's shadow.

Paula quickly shot Harvey a dark look. Her eyes burnt Harvey into a smoldering pile of ash for daring to speak to her. She jumped out of bed and stormed to the bathroom, returning with a small trashcan. She threw the contents over the bed, scattering used toilet rolls and razors across the mattress. Scrambling amongst the trash, she pulled out a white stick and thrust it in George's hands.

"Believe me now?" she said as George examined the tiny pink positive symbol on the pregnancy test.

Harvey stared at George, and he watched as his eyes widened. He could see that he was imagining seeing the baby in his arms for the first time.

Harvey on the other hand, felt sick. He felt sick for convincing himself that Paula was lying and he felt sick for the fresh problems that the baby was going to bring. He thought back to leaving George to travel with Leo, and knew that if he'd given George the chance to prove himself all those months ago, things would have turned out differently.

The baby was his punishment.

He could see the pride and happiness on George's face, and even though he tried not to, he felt guilty for wishing the baby never happened.

"I'm actually going to be a dad," a shaky smile spread across his face as he turned to Harvey.

Harvey tried to smile back, but he could feel Paula watching them both. He didn't know if he was imagining it, but he was sure he could see a flicker of a smirk on her face.

"Happy now?" she shot at Harvey.

Harvey retreated back behind George, intent on not letting Paula get to him. Even standing there with no make-up and her hair messy, she still looked like a powerful and manipulative woman.

"What now?" Harvey whispered to George.

He wished they'd spent their time at the cabin formulating an actual plan. Harvey had to live somewhere and he could feel what the answer was going to be, and he already knew he didn't like it.

"Yes, George," Paula smirked fully this time, "please do tell us what now."

The dark circles around her eyes made her slender face look hallow and terrifying.

"We're staying here," George said firmly, "this is my house."

Harvey suppressed a smile. He slyly raised an eyebrow to Paula, but she raised one right back.

"If you think I'm going anywhere you can think again," Paula brushed the trash from the bed and pulled back the covers, "or are you going to throw your pregnant wife out on to the streets?"

The smile vanished from Harvey's face and his eyes quickly narrowed. She had played her trump card again, and he knew she was going to use it to get exactly what she wanted from George.

"We'll stay in the guest bedroom," George said, "you can

ASHLEY JOHN

stay in here."

Paula's lips quickly curled from a smirk to a snarl.

"Me and Harvey are together now," his arm wrapped firmly around Harvey as he pulled him close, "I love him, Paula, and you're just going to have to deal with that."

Harvey quickly remembered what it was like last time they all lived together. Just from the look on Paula's face, he could tell she was going to make things difficult.

"Can't we just stay in a hotel?" Harvey whispered into George's ear.

"Listen, kid," he said, staring deeply into Harvey's eyes, "nothing is going to change between us, but she's carrying my child and I need to keep my eye on her."

Reluctantly, Harvey accepted that George was right and backed down. Having Paula under their noses would mean that any scheming or plotting she was going to do, they'd surely see it. He just didn't know if he wanted to do that until the end of her pregnancy.

"Home sweet home," Harvey sighed as they walked into the very familiar guest bedroom.

It had been so long since he'd been there, it all looked so different to what he'd remembered. As he walked around the room, examining the bed, the desk and the curtains, he realized that it was different.

"It's all changed," Harvey sighed as he ran his finger along the new desk.

He thought back to Greg and his book deal, but it felt so long ago he was sure it wouldn't still be on the cards.

"She had the place redone pretty much straight after," George sighed as he flopped down on the new bed, "she wanted to re-do the whole house, but I put my foot down."

Harvey fell down onto the bed next to George and snuggled into his side.

"It's just for a few weeks, I promise," George whispered, "just until we get things sorted out. She'll calm down eventually and we can all start planning a proper future."

A sense of deja vu filled Harvey at hearing another '*just a few weeks'* promise.

TWELVE

The weeks quickly passed and as Christmas drew closer, George's perfect garden was buried under a thick blanket of snow.

The pink and white marshmallows bobbed around in Harvey's hot chocolate as he thought about how easy it had been to live with Paula again. He glanced over his book at George as they lay in front of the roaring fire in the study and smiled secretly to himself as he watched George typing away.

Paula was rarely seen, and when she did appear, their communication was limited to a few brief conversations. Most of the time she pretended Harvey wasn't even there, and that's how he liked it.

Instead of slotting back into their old routine, George and Harvey openly spent precious hours together. Missing out on each other for so long had only made them appreciate their love. Harvey had lost count of the number of hours they'd spent together, just enjoying each other's company as they read and wrote in George's study. They didn't have to be doing anything interesting, it was enough to be together.

The study had quickly become their little hideaway, and for

Harvey, it was perfect.

"Did the divorce lawyer get back to you?" Harvey asked over the top of *A Christmas Carol*.

"Yeah," George sighed rubbing his temples at his desk in the dim light of the flickering fire, "we need to sit Paula down tonight and have a serious talk with her, because we're getting nowhere as we are."

For Harvey, it almost felt as if they were happily living together in their own home. The closet in their bedroom was full of new clothes, Harvey had a new journal to write in and he was happy pretending Paula wasn't there, carrying George's baby.

Deep down, however, he knew they couldn't carry on burying their heads in the sand, playing happy families. Very soon, there would be a baby in the picture, and he had no idea how things were going to work.

He knew the three-month scan picture of the baby was on George's desk and he'd catch him looking at it multiple times a day. The smile that filled his face warmed Harvey, but it also scared him

"Remember what I told you, kid," George laughed as he watched Harvey clumsily try to knead the dough.

"I can't do it!" Harvey cried, wiping his floury hand across his forehead.

He slammed the dough on the counter, which sent a white dust cloud shooting around the perfect kitchen. George smiled and grabbed the dough.

"Use the palms of your hands," George laughed as he expertly kneaded, "see!"

Harvey watched as his strong hands handled the messy blob.

"You're such a show-off!" Harvey smiled as he slapped George on the back, "I don't know why we couldn't just order pizza in."

"Because this is more fun!" George cried.

Harvey left George to it, grabbing a glass from the sink and heaving over to the ice dispenser.

"Hey," George said, "I've got something for you."

Harvey turned around sipping his water, just in time for George to blow a cloud of flour into the middle of his face. Laughing, he quickly wiped it out of his eyes before jumping on the bag himself. For a second, he thought about throwing a small handful at George, but instead he grabbed the entire bag and emptied it over him.

They both erupted into hysteric fits of laughter as they watched the flour cover every part of the kitchen.

"Oh you're a dead man!" George cried as Harvey jumped over the counter and hid behind the safety of the breakfast bar.

Cautiously, Harvey slowly raised his flour-covered hair over the edge of the counter, only to be hit in the face with a raw egg.

"Gotcha!" George cried proudly.

"Truce!" he waved a flour covered hand in the air.

As Harvey slowly crept from around the counter, Paula appeared in the kitchen doorway and he could instantly see the anger in her eyes, but instead of reacting, she walked coldly towards the fridge, leaving a trail in the flour.

"Paula," George smiled nervously, dusting the flour from his hair, "sorry about the mess."

Harvey suppressed the laughter as he watched George acting like a naughty school child after being caught out.

"It's fine. Just clean it up," she sighed as she grabbed a bottle of water, "I'm going for dinner with Emma from work."

"I thought we could all eat in tonight," George said, "there's some things we need to talk about. We were trying to make pizza."

Paula stared at her flour soaked husband for a second before putting the water back in the fridge. She looked mildly curious, but it didn't falter her icy features.

"Fine," she said quietly.

"Here, kid," George said as he threw his cell phone to Harvey, "order the pizza."

Sitting around the dinner table eating pizza from the boxes, Harvey could have cut the tense atmosphere with a knife. They all chewed in silence, but he could tell Paula was just as curious as he was, to find out what George had to say.

"I've been talking to the divorce lawyer," George said, setting down the slice of pizza he was about to eat, "I think it's time we discuss terms."

Paula joined him and set her pizza down, but Harvey stayed at the end of the table and carried on eating as if he was watching television. His stomach wasn't going to let him waste good pizza, and he'd only just started to re-gain some of the weight he'd lost on tour.

"Talk," Paula said, folding her arms and sitting back in her chair.

Harvey noticed she wasn't pressing down too hard on the floating blouse, which hung from her breasts, hiding her stomach.

"I was hoping for a clean divorce. You keep what's yours and I keep what's mine."

"No, George," Paula smirked as she leaned her elbows against the table cloth, "I want the house."

Harvey almost choked on the pizza. His eyes quickly darted to George, but he wasn't giving anything away. Instead he watched and chewed his lip as he thought over what Paula had just said. They'd always known she was going to make it as hard as possible.

"You know I can't do that," George sighed.

"All I want is this house," Paula said, "or are you going to throw your pregnant wife onto the streets?"

"You know most of my money is tied up in this place!" George cried, slamming his fist down on the table, "I bought it with my life savings."

"I know," she smirked slyly, "and I want it."

Harvey couldn't believe what he was hearing. Even pregnancy hadn't softened her hard edge. He couldn't believe she was letting herself be so driven by money, but part of him knew it was just to punish George.

"Fine," George sighed, "but I want this divorce to be quick."

"Fine," Paula agreed as she stood up and grabbed a final slice of pizza before heading for the door, "I'll have my lawyer draw up the paperwork to sign the deeds over before the end of the week and then we'll go ahead with the divorce."

With that, she left a stunned Harvey and exhausted George to finish their pizza in silence.

"Where are we going to go?" Harvey asked quietly.

"We'll have to rent somewhere," George smiled, "don't worry. It'll be okay."

Harvey could see right through George's shaky smile, and as they headed up to their bedroom, he knew that it wasn't as easy for George as he was trying to make out. He knew how much the house meant to George. It symbolized all of his success as a writer because his books had paid for it.

That night, George fell straight into a deep sleep, but for Harvey it wasn't as easy. The sudden urge to update his journal filled him, but he knew he'd left it on one of the tiny tables in George's study. Carefully, he pulled back the covers, not wanting to disturb George. Even in the dull winter moonlight, he was still the most beautiful person Harvey had ever seen.

Carefully, he crept slowly down the stairs, trying his best to avoid the creaky ones. As he headed across the hall to the dining room to retrieve his journal from the study, a low whisper coming from behind the closed kitchen door stopped him in his tracks. At first, he nearly ignored it and he took another step towards the study, but curiosity got the better of him and forced him to listen against the closed door.

"I told you this would work," he could hear Paula's muffled voice talking to someone, "he's going to sign the house over to me at the end of the week. Of course I know what I'm doing! I'm going to rinse him. When I'm finished, the great George Lewis won't have a penny to his name. Not even that little slut Harvey will want to stick around. You know how I think he's only sniffing around for the money. The baby thing was just genius."

Harvey gasped and clamped his hand tightly over his mouth as he stepped slowly away from the door. Knowing that he'd heard enough, he gently bolted back to the bedroom and jumped back into bed with George.

As he closed his eyes, a light bulb lit up in his head as something Paula had said began to make sense in his mind.

'The baby thing was just genius.'

As George slept, Harvey rested quietly on the window ledge, watching soft snow flakes fall on the already covered ground. He glanced back to his semi-naked lover in the bed as the sun started to rise and he thought about the best way he was going to break the news to him.

Sleep had escaped him, so instead he stayed up all night and tried to analyze what he'd heard Paula say. His mind batted around different scenarios, and he'd even told himself that he'd misheard her, but in the end he had to accept what it could be.

As he gazed at George's face, his heart ached for the heartbreak he was about to feel. For Harvey, the baby was only a wrench in the works, but he was growing to accept the idea. For George, it was something he'd always wanted, and even though the situation wasn't perfect, he already loved the baby with all of his heart.

Glancing back down onto the street below, he watched as the daylight claimed the night. A thick white sheet covered every house and car, freezing everything in its tracks.

"What are you doing up?" George croaked as he rubbed the sleep from his eyes, "come back to bed."

George pulled the covers back and firmly patted Harvey's side of the bed, but he couldn't face telling him so close. Instead, he glanced back out of the frosty window and stared deeply at the frozen world outside.

"There's something I need to tell you."

THIRTEEN

"Wake up you bitch!" George screamed, ripping back Paula's covers.

She quickly scrambled up against the headboard, the shock and confusion at being suddenly woken, all over her face. Her short blonde hair was matted and sticking up at one side.

"What the fuck, George?" she flicked her nightstand light on.

"George, just calm down," Harvey ran after him, into the bedroom.

It was as if George couldn't hear any of them, instead letting his rage take over his mind. Running around the side of the bed, he clutched Paula's arm, yanking her out of bed.

"Get your hands off me!" she screamed as George dragged her across the bedroom, "What are you doing?"

With Paula still gripped firmly in his hand, he kicked open the bathroom door and ripped open the medicine cabinet above the sink. With one hand, he rummaged through the shelves, sending pill bottles and boxes crashing into the bowl below. Harvey knew what he was looking for, and when George found the long box, he pulled out the white stick, thrusting it in Paula's face.

"God help me. You're going to do another test," George growled, "and it better be positive."

Yanking her arm free, she laughed nervously as she backed into the corner of the bathroom. As she rubbed her arm, which was quickly bruising, she could see from the manic look in her husband's eyes that he was being very serious, he was even scaring Harvey.

"I've done a test," she said nervously, "you've seen it."

"Don't bullshit me. What was it you said on the phone last night? The baby idea was genius and you were getting just what you wanted?"

Paula glared at Harvey before slamming the bathroom door shut so that he couldn't see anything, but the silence spoke more than any words.

"I don't have to do this."

"I was going to be a dad," George's voice trembled, "was it all a lie?"

Harvey pressed his ear against the door. He heard the sound of running water.

"It takes 15 minutes."

It felt like the longest 15 minutes of Harvey's life, as he waited on the other side of the bathroom door, wishing he was with George. He could hear Paula begging for release, but it seemed like George couldn't hear her.

As the seconds ticked by, Harvey thought about the baby. Even though it was going to cause them problems, he was hoping it was real. He knew how much George wanted the baby, because it was the one thing he'd always wanted, but never thought he'd get. He tried to imagine the tiny pink lines on the test, and he hoped they were forming into a tiny pink cross.

"You're not pregnant!" the sound of plastic crunched against tiles, "how could you do this to me?"

"I must have lost it," Paula's voice was shaking out of control, "it's normal in the first 3 months."

"*No!*" George screamed, "*You lied! You made this whole thing up to get at me!*"

Harvey didn't need to see George to know that the tears would be rolling down his face. He could hear them in his voice.

"George..." he heard her plead.

"I want the truth."

There was a long and dark silence, the only sound coming from George's muffled cries.

"I wanted to hurt you," she sneered, "I wanted to burn you like you burned me. I wanted your heart to bleed. I didn't plan to fake a pregnancy, it just slipped out, but when it did, I knew it was the perfect way to get exactly what I wanted."

"The positive test?" he mumbled, "the scan picture?"

"Oh c'mon George. Keep up," she laughed, "I work in a hospital. Do you think it was really that hard to get hold of a pregnant woman's piss and a scan picture? It really was too easy."

Harvey's stomach knotted. He'd been right all along, but it didn't feel as good as he'd hoped.

"You're sick," George screamed.

"Maybe," she sighed, "I guess we're equal now, right?"

Was she right? Were they equal? What Harvey and George had done was bad, but did it really compare to destroying a man's hope, just for fun? He saw now that she was truly a sick woman. Harvey had no idea how he'd stayed married to her for so many years.

"Get out of my house," he said, "you're getting nothing, god dammit. I will fight you until the day I die."

***

George stormed out of the bedroom, past Harvey, down the stairs and out into the freezing cold snow. He stared out into the street and let the snow fall gently and melt into his hair. He could feel his bare feet and bare chest turning blue, but he didn't care. When Harvey wrapped a blanket around him and dragged him inside, he didn't care.

He felt completely numb.

He felt like he was grieving for a scan picture that belonged to a stranger.

"It's going to be okay," Harvey whispered into his ear as they snuggled on the sofa, "we'll have our own kids one day. You and me."

George turned to Harvey and a faint smile spread across his face. Just being next to Harvey, he could feel a bandage being wrapped firmly around his cracked heart, but he knew he needed time to heal properly.

The sound of clicking heels down the stairs signaled Paula's arrival. She dumped her huge bag outside of the living room door and hesitated for a moment. They should have had the baby and the perfect marriage. They'd been together since college, and even though it was over, she'd just destroyed any chance of them even ending it on any civil ground.

"I'm going to my father's house," she said in a monotonous, emotionless voice, "you'll be hearing from my lawyer."

Harvey watched Paula's small blue car creep slowly along the snow, until she was just a dot at the end of the road. Harvey gripped George close and breathed a huge sigh of relief into George's ear.

"This is the beginning," Harvey whispered, "nothing else matters."

Snuggling closer to his love, George let their future flow over him and he smiled gently as he closed his eyes and leaned his head on Harvey's bare, boney shoulder.

FOURTEEN

I t was the last days leading up to Christmas when George's old friend Marlon visited to help decorate the huge tree George had insisted on buying.

"I can't believe you never told me!" Marlon laughed as he hung a silver bauble on the tree, "I've known you for years and I had no idea you were gay."

George blushed. He still didn't seem comfortable with the label. He buried his head in untangling the messy ball of Christmas lights. Harvey smiled when he saw George squirming under Marlon's interrogation.

"If I'd have known, I would have tried to bag you years back," Marlon winked at Harvey, but George wasn't catching the bait.

Harvey liked Marlon. He was the first person he'd met who could challenge George on his own level and he liked it. He liked him even more since he dumped Chase. Marlon kept the explanation brief, but Harvey suspected his pass at him at the barbecue had something to do with it.

"I didn't think I was your type Marlon," George smirked as he finally untangled the lights, "I thought you liked the skinny boys. Harvey's more up your alley."

It was Harvey's turn to blush. He glanced at Marlon, but he could see he was laughing. Something told him he wasn't the type of person to try and take someone else's partner, unlike Chase.

"Not today," Marlon laughed, "I'm happy for you two. I really am. I was sure I sensed something at the barbecue. You couldn't keep your eyes off each other."

"He is gorgeous," George leaned in to kiss Harvey softly on the cheek.

When he slowly pulled away, he winked at him and reached into the box to grab a gold bauble to hang on the huge Christmas tree that was sitting in the bay window of the living room. Harvey bit his lip as he felt his skin burn crimson. He'd never been used to public displays of affection, but he knew that Marlon didn't mind.

"You two are so adorable," Marlon sighed, "I wish I could find something like it. Mine either cheat on me, or they get bored."

"You'll find your prince one day," George laughed as he smacked Marlon on the back, "I found mine."

"I never wanted to tell you this," Marlon smirked, "but I never liked Paula. I always thought she was a sour faced bitch."

Harvey laughed, but George backed off, looking uncomfortable he disappeared behind the television to plug in the lights. Harvey knew it wasn't the mention of Paula which was making him act strange, it was the baby. Every time her name was mentioned, he could see the hurt in his eyes.

"Do you want to stay for dinner?" Harvey asked, sensing that the conversation needed steering in a different direction.

"I'd love to, but I have a date with a hot Spanish guy, and my balls are turning blue."

A nervous smile spread across Harvey's face. For a moment he thought he was joking, but the look on his face as they wrapped the lights around the tree told him that he wasn't.

When the lights flickered into life, the trio stood back and admired their handy work. The baubles were unevenly spaced and the lights were wonky, but to Harvey, it was the most beautiful tree he'd ever seen. Christmas was something he hadn't celebrated for a long time. When his parents died, Christmas died too.

The first year they were alone, Leo really tried to make it special. They ate ham and pumpkin pie and he'd even managed to put a few gifts under the tree, but as the years passed, Harvey started to spend the day alone pretending it was just any other day. Christmas tree shopping with George had re-awakened his inner child and he was suddenly more excited for Christmas than he'd been in his entire life.

It was also his first Christmas with George, which only made things more magical for him. He hoped it was the first of many.

"Can you squeeze in coffee before you head off?" George asked.

"I guess so," Marlon smiled, "I've always liked the expensive coffee you buy."

They crowded around the breakfast bar and Marlon told stories about when they both worked at the newspaper together.

"George here was the most eager journalist you have ever seen!" he laughed, "Do you remember when you were given the obituary page to write and you went overboard with the adjectives?"

"I remember," George smiled, "what was it that I wrote? *'Mrs. Jones was a boisterous and vivacious woman who enjoyed long walks with her younger companions'*?"

"I was the one who had to calm the family down when they rang up screaming about suing!"

"It's safe to say I wasn't asked to write any more obituaries after that," George laughed as he sipped his coffee.

Marlon was staring into his mug, when suddenly, his eyes lit up.

"Harvey!" he cried, "Have you thought about working at

the newspaper? I'm good friends with the editor and I could give him a nudge for you!"

Setting his coffee down, Harvey looked to George who was as surprised as Harvey. His book deal had completely fallen through thanks to his absence and when George tried to call Greg, he told him that they'd decided to go in a new direction. Harvey wasn't bitter about it, because he'd abandoned the idea of ever writing the book the day he left.

Seeing Marlon's serious expression, something whirled in his stomach. He knew he'd have to get a job eventually, but he hadn't even considered it would be in writing.

Ginger had told him she'd have a job at the café for him, in the New Year, when he'd visited to give her a Christmas card. The thought of working with Ginger was appealing to him, but his heart was in writing.

"Do you think they'd want me?" Harvey mumbled.

"If you're as good as George says, I can't see why not. It's only a small team, so you could work your way up quickly and it's amazing experience!" Marlon pulled his cellphone from his jeans and started to tap on the screen, "Let me call the editor now."

As Marlon talked on the phone, Harvey zoned out and looked at George. George was smiling reassuringly at him letting him know it was a good idea. Money wasn't important to George and he didn't seem to care that he'd been supporting Harvey, but Harvey was itching to write again.

"George?" Harvey started.

"I think it's a brilliant idea," he smiled softly at Harvey, sensing the nerves, "it's the first job I got after college and I loved it."

The thought of following in George's footprints felt appealing. He'd be working in the place where his favorite author started, which made the old Harvey deep inside scream with excitement.

"It's done," Marlon smiled, throwing his phone on the counter pleased with himself, "You start at the beginning of next month."

"That quick?" said George.

"When I mentioned that he was your prodigy, he practically bit my hand off! You know how they hated losing you when your writing career took off."

"So, I have a job?"

Marlon smiled and nodded.

"Thanks man," George said as he hugged Marlon at the front door, "we really appreciate it."

"Don't worry about it. I just want you guys to be happy," he hugged Harvey and headed out into the icy snow.

As soon as he closed the door, George pulled Harvey close and embraced him, holding him tight.

"You're gonna do amazing," George whispered into his ear.

"I hope so," Harvey said flatly.

The nerves were already starting, but he tried to drown them out with the feeling of excitement. When he started to feel George's hands slowly sneak down his back and his lips softly kiss his neck, a different feeling started to spread through his body.

He pulled his T-shirt off and firmly gripped Harvey's face, pulling him into a deep and fuelled kiss. Everything had finally fallen into place and he felt at peace for the first time in a long time. Every morning when he woke up, he wanted to pinch himself because everything felt so perfect, he was sure he was dreaming.

The grainy ringing of the house phone on the kitchen wall sounded through the hallway.

"I'll get it," Harvey said through the kisses, "wait for me upstairs."

George growled and with one last kiss, he ran up the stairs as Harvey headed to the kitchen, not taking their eyes off each other until they both vanished.

"Hello?" Harvey said as he ripped the phone off the wall, "hello?"

Harvey listened into the handset but all he could hear was silence.

"Is anyone there?" he said, raising his voice.

Silence.

"I'm going to hang up,"

He heard the sound of a man breathing. It sounded hoarse and messy but Harvey instantly knew who it was. It made every muscle in his body tighten. He heard a click and then the dial tone. He stood frozen to the spot as he listened to the dead buzz, but he couldn't seem to hang up.

"Come on," he heard George shout down the stairs, "tell whoever it is that I'm horny as fuck and I need my sexy boyfriend here naked, now!"

Harvey slammed the handset against the wall and slowly wandered up the stairs. He could feel his legs starting to turn to jelly with each step, and any feeling of lust quickly left him and was replaced with fear.

"Who was it?" George asked, pulling the covers over his naked body.

"They didn't say anything," Harvey croaked, his voice shaking uncontrollably, "but I think it was Leo."

FIFTEEN

George and Harvey were in front of the roaring fireplace, shivering in each other's arms under a blanket. Their first perfect Christmas together seemed to be going from bad to worse.

"Who's going to come out and fix the power on Christmas Eve?" Harvey's teeth chattered out of control, "I think we're doomed."

He didn't want to believe it, but every time things seemed to be going good, something would happen to dampen the sparkle. When George pulled him in closer to the fire, he thought back to the phone call he'd received. He'd been so sure it had been Leo, but George had managed to convince him it was just a wrong number.

After all, how would Leo even get George's house number?

"The ham is going to be ruined," George sighed, resting his head gently on Harvey's, "not that I'd be able to cook it. We're completely dead."

"It's only going to get colder," Harvey shivered.

George glanced out of the window at the heavy snow falling in the dark, covering the street in another layer of trouble. He hadn't seen a snowstorm so bad in a long time.

"We'll sleep in here tonight," George kissed the top of Harvey's head, "I'll get the covers and pillows and we'll make a nice comfy bed in front of the fire."

Harvey tried to smile, but his lips wouldn't move. He'd been looking forward to his first real Christmas in a long time, but as he looked at the lifeless Christmas tree in the dark, he couldn't help but feel deflated. There were presents under the tree, but none of them were from him. They were all from George to Harvey, which made him feel even worse for having no money.

"What are we going to eat tomorrow?"

"There'll be somewhere open in town doing something," George suggested, "but they will probably have been booked up months ago."

Harvey sighed heavily. He knew none of it mattered, and as long as he was with George everything would be okay, but he couldn't help feeling disappointed.

A faint thud in the hallway made his ears prick up.

"Did you hear that?" Harvey was already starting to stand up.

They both wandered into the ice-cold hall. Harvey's feet stung against the frozen marble tiles. He'd always thought of the house as a warm place, but maybe that was because of the ridiculous amount of heaters, which were now non-functioning.

"It's a Christmas card," George bent down and picked up the white envelope from the ground.

"It's probably from one of your neighbors."

"It's for you," George said, raising an eyebrow as he handed the slightly damp card out to Harvey.

Harvey recognized the handwriting in an instant, causing his hands to shake, and not from the cold. He snatched the card from George's trembling hands and ripped it open. His stomach twisted and he dropped the card on the cold ground and ran over to the front door.

He stared out into the thick snow, but he couldn't see a thing. It was so dense and dark. Harvey grabbed the card from the ground and read the messy handwriting inside, which reminded him of a child's.

'*Merry Christmas Bro*'.

"He's back George," Harvey whispered as he slammed the door, "he's never going to leave me alone."

They resumed their place in front of the fireplace and Harvey read the words over and over again. He could hear Leo's voice reading it to him, but there was nothing '*merry*' about it.

The thought of Leo being back in town trying to contact him made Harvey want to get as far away as possible.

"It was him who called the other day," Harvey sighed, ripping the card straight down the middle.

"Maybe he just wants to talk," George said.

"I don't think he wants a social visit," Harvey tossed the pieces of the card onto the open fire and watched them burn and curl up into ash, "remember what he put me through. Remember what Scott did to me. It was his entire fault. He could have stopped it. I think the only reason he took me on tour was because he wanted to win one over on you."

George pulled Harvey tightly, but he wriggled free and let the blanket fall off him.

"We're not safe," Harvey muttered, "he could be outside watching."

They both glanced to the window and tried to focus their eyes on the dark snow, but they couldn't see a thing.

"He's just trying to mess with you," George sighed, "he can't stand you being happy. He'd rather you be miserable and alone with him, than happy without him. It's like he needs you to survive."

"Well he's not having me," Harvey snapped, "I told you I was done with him."

"You know I'm going to protect you."

Harvey stood up and walked over to the window. He

scanned every direction but he couldn't see a thing. He knew George would try his best to protect him, but he didn't know how much of a chance he'd stand against Leo.

"He changed," Harvey's voice started to quiver, "I had my brother back. It's like he died all those years ago in the fire and he came back from the dead."

"People don't change," George sighed.

"You did," Harvey shot back, "you finally grew a pair of fucking balls and left Paula."

"That's not fair!"

Harvey knew he wasn't being fair, but he didn't care. He could feel the rage and hatred flowing through him, and all of the mean and hurtful things he'd ever thought were bubbling to the surface.

"You put me through hell, George. You're the reason I went with Leo in the first place. If you'd just done the right thing, I would have stayed and none of those horrible things would have happened to me."

"Harvey, please," George tried to pull Harvey away from the window.

"No George!" Harvey batted his hands away, "I've been holding this in since I got back here. You really hurt me. You treated me like shit for weeks, and I still came crawling back to you. Doesn't that make me such an idiot?"

Harvey stared at George's face, which was half cast in the shadow. Even in the dark he could tell that he'd upset him, and it hurt him to know that, but he kept his face stern because he needed to get it off his chest.

"You know I'm sorry. I've said sorry over and over. I did the right thing in the end," George snapped back, "I'm not the one who is your enemy here."

Harvey knew he was right, but he needed somebody to take his frustration out on.

"I'm sorry," Harvey muttered, staring back out into the snowstorm.

"Don't apologize," he said, "you never have to apologize to me. I'll never be finished apologizing to you for what I put you through. My head was a mess, but I just kept it all inside and I tried to do what was right for everyone, and I fucked up. I don't need you to tell me that. Every time I look at you, my heart breaks for what I did to you. Every time I look at you, I see you crying, and it hurts me too. But I promise, and I'll promise you every day for the rest of our lives, I'll never do anything to hurt you, and I'll spend the rest of our lives together treating you like you deserve, because you're special, it just took me a long time to realize it."

Harvey's heart broke and healed a hundred times as he listened to George's outpour of emotion. He'd never heard him speak so raw before and he felt like a fool for dragging up the very past he'd promised to bury and move on from.

It was the effect Leo had on him. He turned him into a horrible version of himself who he didn't recognize.

Eyes planted firmly on the ground, Harvey ran over to George and grabbed him firmly around the waist. He didn't know he was crying until he could feel George's wet shirt against his cheek.

"I'm never letting you go, kid," George whispered, "Leo can't hurt you if I'm here."

SIXTEEN

hristmas came and went and Harvey didn't hear from Leo again. When he started his new job, and January was well under way, he accepted that Leo was just trying to play games with him, and he probably got bored and moved on.

"Harvey, can I see you in my office?"

Instantly, Harvey wondered what he'd done wrong. He'd been at the newspaper for a month, and even though he was only writing small entertainment pieces on local events, he was having the time of his life. He had made friends for the first time since he was a small child, and he was enjoying getting back into the swing of writing.

"Yes, sir?" Harvey said, as he closed the office door behind him.

"How many times. Call me Theo," the editor said, "take a seat."

Harvey smiled, not wanting to admit that he didn't like calling him Theo because it reminded him too much of Leo.

"Am I in trouble?" he nervously lowered himself into the chair opposite Theo's desk.

"Not at all! The opposite, in fact," he beamed at Harvey, "I just wanted to thank you for the effort you've put in. You've only been here a month, but we're all really impressed with your enthusiasm and your work."

Theo looked like the typical grandfather type. Even George said he looked like an old man when he worked under him.

"Thank you sir - I mean - Thank you Theo," Harvey smiled, "I'm really enjoying it here."

He didn't want to tell Theo how he looked forward to coming to work every morning for fear of embarrassment.

"That's good to hear. We're a small local paper, but we're a family, and you're fitting in really good. Everyone loves you," Harvey blushed at hearing that, "I just wanted to give you your first paycheck."

He handed a thick brown envelope over the desk to Harvey. His heart nearly stopped when he saw the green bills sleeping peacefully inside.

"I think I've been overpaid," Harvey raised his eyebrows as he stared down at the money.

"There's a little bonus in there for doing so well in your first month," he smiled, "don't expect that every month, but we do reward hard work around here and you're one of the hardest workers since – well - since George Lewis himself, dare I say it."

Harvey blushed at the comparison. Theo didn't know his official relationship status with George, but he knew they were close. Ever since his first day, when George dropped him off, he could tell Theo was so proud of George. Theo clearly liked to think he played a part in his success, and George liked to let him think that.

"Thank you so much!" Harvey gushed, "This is so kind of you."

"Just keep up the good work," he smiled at Harvey one last time before turning to his laptop, letting Harvey know he was allowed to leave.

When he returned to his desk to finish a piece about a local theatre production of *Cats*, he stuffed the money into his canvas bag, and let the satisfaction spread over him. It was the first money he'd ever earned himself and it felt good. He thought back to all of the money George had given to him to keep him going until his first paycheck. He wanted to pay him back somehow, but he knew he wouldn't accept cash.

He looked down at this bag, and when he saw the envelope poking out of the zipper, he could hear it whispering to him, telling him what it wanted to be spent on and he smiled satisfied as he let the plan formulate in his head.

"Are you coming for a drink?" Eve asked as the workforce headed out into the frosty January air, "A couple of us are going for one at *The Spoons*."

It was the first time he'd been asked to go with *'the gang'* for a drink. He wondered if it was because they all had their money for the month and they wanted to splash some cash. Part of him was tempted, but he knew what he needed to do.

"I can't tonight, Eve," Harvey walked in the opposite direction, "another time?"

"Sure thing!" she waved back.

Harvey knew it wouldn't be until the end of next month, but he could wait. He quickly rushed into town, wanting to beat the shops before they closed, and as he did, he noticed the eerie darkness drop over the buildings as twilight set in.

When he reached the shop he was looking for, he took a deep breath before stepping inside. He'd never been inside before, but he knew it as the place where George had bought the watch, which he'd eventually pawned.

"I was just about to close," the young brunette woman behind the counter sighed.

"It won't take long," Harvey pulled out a handful of bills, "I'm looking for an engagement ring."

The woman's eyes lit up when she saw the money and she quickly forgot all about closing, thanking her lucky stars for a nice little commission before the end of the month.

With the box safely in his bag, Harvey hailed a taxi and headed back home. There was something about going home in a taxi, which made him feel grown up. He could never afford taxis usually, so he normally walked home in the cold, but today, he wanted to get home as fast as possible.

His heart was driving him, and it was screaming out for the man he loved.

As the taxi pulled onto George's street, Harvey imagined George inside cooking dinner. Every day since Harvey had started his job, he'd come home to find George putting dinner on the table. He didn't ask for it, but he secretly loved it.

"Keep the change," Harvey said, passing a $10 bill through the window.

"Thanks dude!" the driver said, before speeding off into the night.

As Harvey walked up to the front door in the dark, the porch light's sensor activated and the tiny bulb flickered in to life. The light cast a soft glow on the green front door, but it wasn't what Harvey was expecting to see. The glass in the middle of the door was missing and the door was wide open, leaving the dark hallway open to the world.

Harvey's heart stopped beating as he ran inside. He instantly knew something was wrong. He tried to push the horrible images to the back of his head, as he remembered who had smashed the glass in the door last time.

"*George*?" Harvey called out in the kitchen, "*George*?"

Thick black smoke was pouring out of the stove and the air smelled strongly of burnt chicken. Harvey twisted the dial and turned it off, but he didn't have time to sort out the burnt food. He ran through the dining room and into the study. He was hoping to see George in the study asleep, not knowing about the food or the front door. He wanted to see him peacefully behind his desk, in the faint laptop light.

He felt his heart drop further when he saw the room in complete darkness.

"*George*?" he called out again, his voice breaking from desperation.

His legs took him quickly up the grand staircase, taking the steps three at a time. The door to their bedroom was shut, and as he walked slowly towards the door, he could feel the vein in the side of his head throbbing loudly.

What he saw made tears instantly pour uncontrollably from his face. His heart broke and broke again as he knelt down next to George's limp body as he lay on the ground lifeless. A dark pool of blood had soaked through into the cream carpet.

"George?" Harvey screamed, shaking his shoulders, "Wake up George! It's me! It's Harvey."

George's head wobbled as Harvey frantically shook him, tears falling heavily on his pale and cold skin. His eyelids were firmly shut and his lips had turned a frosty shade of purple. Hands shaking, he tried to find his cellphone in his bag, but when he couldn't, he ripped it open and emptied the contents onto the floor. Tears obscured his vision as he felt around for the tiny metal device.

"I need an ambulance."

His eyes flicked to George's bloody hands, which were clutching his stomach. Out of the corner of his eye, he could see the engagement ring box in the pile of money and paperwork.

"It's my boyfriend. He's been stabbed," Harvey screeched painfully, *"I think he's dead."*

SEVENTEEN

"He's in critical condition, Mr. Jasper," the doctor whispered to Harvey as they gazed at George through the window, "the next 24 hours are going to be crucial for him, but I suggest you call his loved ones now."

Harvey stared blankly at George in the hospital bed. His eyes were dry from the hours of crying and screaming. They had nothing left to give, but inside, he was still crying. Plastic tubes were coming from every part of George's body. He watched as the machine forced George's lungs to breathe.

When the ambulance finally arrived, they managed to find a faint pulse and immediately rushed him to the hospital. From what they could tell, he'd been stabbed in the stomach with a sharp instrument and he'd lost a lot of blood.

Harvey blamed himself. He knew if he'd have gone straight home from work, he might have been able to stop it happening. He might have been able to stop Leo stabbing George.

He didn't need any more evidence or convincing, he knew exactly what had happened. As he watched George's chest rise slowly up and down, he promised himself that if George didn't make it, he wouldn't rest until he saw Leo lying in his own hospital bed.

"Paula," Harvey croaked down his cellphone, as he slotted coins into the coffee vending machine, "I know you don't want to hear from me, but there's something you need to know. I think you need to come back."

The stale coffee burnt his tongue, but he didn't care. He carelessly sipped it, letting the burning sensation wash over him. His entire body felt completely numb. He'd been by George's side for hours, watching him and willing him to do something.

"Harvey!" Paula cried from the end of the corridor.

She ran towards Harvey in her robe and slippers. He noticed that her hair had started to grow out from the extreme short bob she'd had cut in.

"He's in here," Harvey whispered dryly.

He'd cried and wailed so much, it hurt to speak.

Paula joined Harvey at the window and her shaky hand rose slowly to her mouth when she saw her estranged husband lying lifelessly in the hospital bed.

"Who would do this to him?"

"I don't know," he lied.

"Will he make it?" she turned to Harvey.

"They don't know."

He watched as Paula's eyes realized what was going on. In a split second he saw regret and heartbreak. He knew the first thought that had come to her mind was the pregnancy, because that was the last thing she'd done to him.

Harvey watched Paula break down, similar to how he had hours earlier. Deep down, he knew there was still some kind of love there, and she was always going to be an important person in George's life. He grabbed her and pulled her into a tight hug.

"He's tough," Harvey tried to smile, "he'll pull through."

As Paula sobbed on his shoulder, he felt like for the first time since he'd met her, they truly understood each other. They weren't enemies or foes. They both loved the same man, and that made them closer than they'd ever realized.

"I'm sorry for everything I did," Paula sighed as she watched the machine pour her a black coffee, "I think I was possessed."

"I'm sorry too," Harvey said as he sipped a fresh coffee, "for stealing your husband."

A weak smile trembled across her lips as she tried to laugh. Harvey had never seen her laugh properly before. As they waited next to each other, outside of the hospital room, he leaned his head against the wall, wanting to feel closer to George somehow.

"You didn't steal him," she said, "he hadn't been mine for a long time. I just didn't want to admit it. I hate losing."

"I'm still sorry," he turned to her, "really, I am."

She smiled and kindness filled her eyes, replacing the usual bitterness. It was bizarre how crisis could bring the most unlikely people together.

"I was going to propose to him," Harvey whispered, feeling a fresh wave of tears bubble to the surface as he pulled the ring box from his jacket pocket, "I bought this on the way home from work. I shouldn't have gone. If I'd have gone straight home I could have stopped it."

"You can't think like that," she put her hand awkwardly on Harvey's knee, "It could be both of you in that room if you had gone home."

Harvey knew she was wrong. All along George had told Harvey that he'd protect him, but he knew Leo would never physically hurt him. It was George he had the vendetta against. It was George who needed protecting, he just didn't think Leo would go to such extreme lengths to get his revenge.

A beeping sound suddenly echoed through George's room, followed by a flashing red light.

"Doctor!" Harvey screamed, "What's going on?"

A team of doctors and nurses ran down the corridor and pushed past Harvey and Paula. Once inside, they flicked the blinds shut.

"He's going to die Paula," Harvey sobbed, "I can feel it."

It was Paula's turn to embrace Harvey.

"Look at me Harvey," she said sternly, "he's a fighter."

The door to the room burst open, and the doctors and nurses wheeled George's bed out of the room, surrounding him so Harvey couldn't get a glimpse.

"What's going on?" he cried.

Nobody answered.

Instead, they sped down the hallway, wheeling George away.

"Paula, where are they taking him?" he cried, turning frantically to Paula for answers.

She watched as they wheeled her husband down the corridor, she held her breath and she watched which direction they were going to turn. Harvey knew she'd worked in the hospital they were standing in.

"Emergency surgery," she sobbed, "something has gone wrong."

Darkness washed over Harvey, and he felt his knees buckle as his eyes closed and he crashed to the cold ground.

***

He could see George smiling at him and calling for him, but he was too far away to reach. Every time he tried to reach out to him, he seemed to be further and further in the distance.

"Harvey!" George cried.

"George?" Harvey mumbled, shaking his head as his eyes flickered open.

"Harvey, it's Paula."

Harvey bolted up and looked around. He was in the hospital waiting room, across four chairs with a thin, green blanket draped messily over him.

"I thought it was all a bad dream for a moment," he said, looking at Paula's fluffy pink slippers.

"He's out of surgery," she said calmly.

Surgery. How could Harvey forget?

"What's happened?

"They managed to fix the rupture in his stomach, but he hasn't awoken yet. They're not sure if he will."

Harvey pushed past her and headed straight to the room where George was.

"He's been moved," Paula called after him, "follow me."

Paula led him through the hospital, and as they got closer to George's new destination, the hospital seemed to get quieter and more clinical.

She took him through a door that read, '*Critical Unit*'.

"Hi Jack," Paula waved to the guy behind reception.

He winked at her and waved his hand letting her know it was okay to come in.

"Are we not allowed to be here?"

"They prefer it if they don't have visitors here."

They paused outside of the room. Inside, the lights were turned off, except for one dim light over George's face, casting an eerie glow over him, making him look old and frail.

"Harvey," Paula said, but Harvey's eyes were fixed on the unrecognizable body strapped into the bed covered in hundreds of plastic tubes, "Harvey look at me. Anything you want to say to him. Now is the time to say it."

Harvey stepped away from her and shook his head.

"I'm not saying goodbye!" Harvey cried, fighting back more tears.

"Keep your voice down!" she whispered angrily, "I've spoken to some of my friends and I told them to cut the bullshit. They don't think he's going to pull through. He's not in a good place."

"No!" Harvey mumbled, ripping away from Paula and slipping into the room.

He closed the door behind him and paused for a second before approaching. He looked terrifying, hooked up to the machines. He listened as they beeped, as they kept George's body functioning. He slowly lowered himself into the chair next to George.

"Why now?" Harvey groaned, "Things were going so

perfectly. We were so happy."

The tears rolled softly down his face.

"You can't leave me George. I won't let you. You're not going without me because without you I'm nothing. I tried to exist without you, but it nearly killed me, so I won't let you go. I'm selfish like that. You told me that you'd be here to look after me for the rest of my life so you can't go. You promised me bastard!"

His voice broke more with every word and the heavy tears landed in his lap. He slowly pulled the ring box from his pocket and snapped it open. He'd chosen a beautiful silver band with three diamonds set in the middle. It had cost him most of his wage but he didn't care.

It all seemed so pointless.

"I was going to ask you to marry me today. We were going to be so happy."

Harvey couldn't control himself anymore. He couldn't cry the tears fast enough. Heavily, he threw his head and arms on George's chest and sobbed loudly as he felt the machine raising him up and down. When he felt a vibrating in his chest, he thought something was going wrong.

Quickly, he shot his head up ready to call for help, when he noticed George's eyelids twitching heavily under the dim light.

"George? Are you there?" Harvey cried, jumping up and grabbing his hand tightly, "It's me, can you hear me?"

Slowly and painfully, his lids peeled open to reveal watery and pale, bloodshot eyes. He stared at Harvey and groaned.

Harvey stared down at the eyes he'd stared into so many times. Behind the pain, they were still the same eyes he loved so much.

George grunted again, like he was trying to say something, but the tubes in his throat were stopping him.

"Don't try to speak," Harvey whispered softly, squeezing his hand tightly, "I'm here for you."

The door opened and Paula appeared at the entrance.

"He's awake," Harvey laughed, tears still flowing freely, "he's fucking awake."

EIGHTEEN

"It's just remarkable. I've never seen a recovery like it," the doctor said to Harvey and Paula outside the room as nurses attended to him.

It was the same doctor who told Harvey that he should call his loved ones. It was the same doctor who had written George off.

"What happens now?" Harvey asked quietly, not taking his eyes off George through the glass.

"We let him breath for himself, and then we monitor him. He's by no means out of the woods yet, but he seems to be strong. There must be something making him cling on," he said, leaving Harvey and Paula to watch the nurses pull the long breathing tube from George's throat.

"That's you," Paula said with a smile on her face.

"What is?"

"He's come back for you. He's fought his way back to get back to you," she smiled softly, "he must really love you. I'm going to give you the divorce."

Harvey was lost for words. He never thought he'd be

looking at Paula like he was, but a new light had been shed on her. The resentment towards her was completely gone.

The nurses emerged from the room and smiled at Harvey and Paula.

"He's asking for you," she said kindly to Harvey.

Paula let him go into the room alone. Harvey ran over to the bed and wrapped his arms tightly around George's neck. There was no need for words because they could both feel the love radiating from their bodies. Harvey looked up when he felt a tear drop on his cheek that wasn't his own.

He wiped the tears from George's eyes, trying to hold back his own.

"No more tears," Harvey smiled, "we've had enough of those to last a lifetime."

"Yes," George croaked.

His voice sounded raw and faint.

"Yes?" Harvey asked.

"Yes," George repeated, "I'll marry you."

Harvey planted his lips on George's mouth and gently kissed him. He vowed to himself that from that moment on, he was going to protect George.

"He wants to see you now," Harvey said quietly to Paula, "I'm going to go outside and get some fresh air."

Harvey stood outside of the hospital and craved a cigarette. He'd only ever smoked once before, but as he watched all of the people in gowns puffing out clouds of smoke, he knew they were made for situations like this.

He looked up into the sky and it was light. He had no idea what time or day it was, or how long he'd been in the hospital. He laughed gently to himself, out of relief.

"Harvey?" Harvey's head shot down from the sky to the face of his brother walking slowly towards him.

Harvey couldn't believe his eyes. In front of him, stood a husk he barely recognized. He was twice as thin as the last time he'd seen him, and he looked on the verge of death.

He could feel his fists clenching up, but he forced them to his side as the crowd of smokers grew.

"I need to explain," Leo trembled, holding his hands out.

They were still covered in George's blood.

Harvey pulled his phone from his pocket and dialed 911.

"What are you doing?" Leo cried, "Let me explain. I'm sorry."

Reluctantly, Harvey hung up the phone and stared numbly at the man who used to be his brother.

"You have nothing to say to me," Harvey said coldly, "you nearly killed him, and I'm going to make sure you rot in prison for the rest of your life."

"I didn't mean to, I swear," he sobbed with no tears, "you know I couldn't kill anyone."

"No, I don't know you," Harvey snarled, "my brother died a long time ago. You're just a rodent. You don't deserve to breathe the same air as people like George."

"I went to see you. I'm in trouble. Remember Scott from the band? I owe him some money and he got violent. I tried to find you, but you weren't there. I didn't mean to stab him, he fell on my knife. I just needed some cash."

"Fell on your knife?" Harvey screamed, "Are you sick in the head Leo? Why did you even have a knife? It's always the same with you. You get into trouble with people and you think you can come running to George and me again for money? Wasn't that first bag enough for you?"

"I didn't even take any this time."

"That's because you don't know the combination for the safe," Harvey cried, "you would have if you could. You left him for dead."

"I didn't mean to -"

"Even if I wanted to believe you, I couldn't. You called his house before Christmas, and you sent me that card. You were clearly plotting something. You were trying to mess with me."

"It wasn't like that," Leo cried, "I wanted to talk to you, to sort things out. I thought the Christmas card would help, but I never heard from you."

"Oh come on," Harvey laughed, "do you really think I'm going to believe that? You don't have a sincere bone left in your body Leo."

"I tried to change for you," Leo cried.

"*No!*" Harvey shouted, noticing people were starting to stare and whisper, "You didn't change, you just paused the inevitable so you could get me as far away from him as you could, but it didn't work."

"Please, I -"

"You don't have the right to plead with me," Harvey spat at Leo's feet, "You made me do drugs and Scott nearly raped me. That's all on you '*brother*'. You don't care about anyone but yourself."

"I'm sorry," tears started to well up in Leo's bloodshot eyes.

"Save your breath," Harvey muttered, "I hate you. I hate you, Leo."

Harvey pulled the cell phone back from his pocket and dialed 911 again. This time, he put it up to his ear.

"Don't do this to me, bro."

"You did this to yourself," he sneered, "Police please."

Leo's eyes widened as he glanced around the hospital parking lot for a second. Without hesitation, he bolted across the parking lot and across the road, narrowly being missed by a car.

When Harvey finished talking to the police, he wanted to feel something for his brother. He wanted to feel some connection to the last family member he had, but he felt nothing but hate. He wished with all his heart the police would catch him and throw away the key.

He turned and headed back in the hospital, and he felt a weight lift from his shoulders as he slowly walked back to the only family he wanted.

George Lewis.

EPILOGUE

"**H**ow are you going to have a party with no ice?" Ginger laughed.

"I forgot the ice machine was broken!" George cried, "Blame Harvey for not reminding me."

He winked at Harvey across the counter. Harvey winked back as he watched Ginger and George prepare the food for their engagement party.

"I'll run to the store and get some," Harvey said, kissing George on the cheek.

"I'll go," George said, "I don't mind."

"No, you need to stay and help get the food sorted because you know I'll only mess it up."

"He's right," Ginger smiled wickedly, "I tried to teach him how to make bread last week and it tasted like my shoe."

"Rude!" Harvey laughed, "You said you liked it!"

"I did," she winked at George slyly over the cake they were both icing.

Harvey grabbed the car keys and their little black dog, Milo, jumped up at his knees.

"I'll walk you when I get back!" Harvey beamed down at the dog and stroked his ears roughly.

After making sure the dog was still in the house, he jumped into his very own small silver car, which was parked messily in the drive. He'd saved up for months to buy it after passing his test, and it made George's look like a monster truck, but he didn't care, it was all his.

George had offered to pay for it, but Harvey decided he wasn't going to take any more handouts. Instead, George just surprised Harvey with regular expensive gifts. As he reversed out of the drive, he looked down at the glittering engagement ring George had bought him when he finally got out of hospital. It had been a long and slow recovery, and George now had an ugly scar across his once perfect washboard abs, but Harvey didn't care.

When he passed the bookstore, he slowed down and the past year flashed before his eyes. It had been the most eventful year of his life, and despite everything, he wouldn't have changed it. As he sped up and headed for the store, he knew George planned it on purpose so that their engagement party would be exactly one year after he met Harvey on the bookstore floor.

He pulled up outside of the store and he knew he could have walked there, but he enjoyed his new found driving freedom, and he used any excuse to jump behind the wheel.

As he walked towards the store, he noticed a scruffy homeless man slumped outside the entrance. Remembering his night sleeping rough outside of Ginger's café, he dropped a $10 bill into the man's lap and went into the store.

He grabbed a couple of bags of ice and paid for them, telling the cashier to keep the change. He'd never had so much money before in his life, especially after his promotion to junior editor at the newspaper.

After putting the ice in his trunk, he was just about to jump back into the car, when an ever so familiar voice sent a bitter chill running down his spine.

"*Nice car, bro.*"

Harvey spun around and stared at the homeless man. He looked past the layers of dirty clothes and the scruffy long beard. If it wasn't for the eyes, he wouldn't have recognized him at all, but he would recognize those cold eyes anywhere. His hand slipped into his pocket ready to call 911. The police never managed to find Leo after everything. He just seemed to fall off the face of the planet.

He slipped the cell back into his pocket and crouched down and stared into the man's face.

"I don't have a brother," Harvey muttered quietly.

He snatched the $10 out of Leo's lap and ripped it into shreds, sprinkling it over his dirty hair.

"Get running Leo. I'm going to call the police."

Leo's eyes narrowed with fear as Harvey stared down at him. He had no intention of calling the police anymore. He knew that Leo's life was a lot worse than it would be in prison and living rough was more than punishment enough. Just seeing the fear in his eyes made it worth it.

"That was quick," George smiled as Harvey walked into the kitchen with two bags of ice stuffed under his arms.

"Milo get down!" Ginger cried as he tried to jump up on the breakfast bar to attack her perfect cake.

He was such a hungry dog.

"Hey Harvey," Paula walked from the dining room holding a file, "I've got an engagement present for you."

She handed the file over to Harvey and he pulled it open to see her neat signature next to George's at the bottom of the final divorce papers. A smile spread across his face.

"Thank you," he whispered, putting his hand on her shoulder.

"I like what you've done with the place," she smiled gazing around the newly decorated kitchen.

"It was all Harvey," George beamed, "he has quite the eye."

After everything that had happened, he was glad they had gained a friend in Paula. He didn't want to start his new life with any ghosts from his past looming over them.

He dumped the file and the ice on the counter next to

Ginger's cake, and wrapped his arms around George's neck, locking him in a kiss. Ginger quickly busied herself with putting the finishing touches on the engagement cake, pretending not to notice.

"What was that for?" George smiled.

"I think it's time for us to move," Harvey whispered softly, staring deeply into George's eyes.

"Where to?"

"Anywhere," Harvey smiled, "let's go and live that fantasy."

"Let's do it," George smiled back, locking Harvey in another kiss.

"I love you George Lewis."

The End

MORE BOOKS
BY ASHLEY JOHN

The Surf Bay Series
Lost & Found
Full Circle
Saving Michael
Love's Medicine

All available on Amazon in print and eBook format!

For more information about Ashley John books and releases,
sign up to his newsletter **ashleyjohn.co.uk/newsletter**

ABOUT ASHLEY JOHN

Ashley John lives in the North of England with his fiancé Reece, and his two cats, Jinx and Jeremy. Ashley is a lover of love and a lover of life, and that's why he writes Romance novels.

He's a sucker for a gripping love story. His characters are fighters, strong and complex, and they'll do anything to get the happy endings they deserve (and there is usually tears and heartache along the way!). Ashley is best known for his best selling Surf Bay series.

When Ashley isn't writing, he uses his creativity to paint and draw, and when he's not being creative, he's usually taking a nap.

To find out more about Ashley John, visit his official website and blog at **ashleyjohn.co.uk**

THANK YOU!

We made it into print! I would just like to say the biggest thank you to **every single person** who has supported me, and more importantly, my work. If you picked up this paperback or not, I appreciate every book sale, every comment, every email...**so much**!

Without you guys, I wouldn't be doing this. You give me the strength to share myself and my life, so thank you.

Don't forget to leave a review for **The Secret** on **Goodreads** and **Amazon**!

33370695R00180

Made in the USA
San Bernardino, CA
30 April 2016